omniphobia

omniphobia

stories by
R. H. W. Dillard

LOUISIANA STATE UNIVERSITY PRESS
BATON ROUGE AND LONDON

1995

Copyright © 1995 by R. H. W. Dillard
All rights reserved
Manufactured in the United States of America
First printing
04 03 02 01 00 99 98 97 96 95   5 4 3 2 1

Designer: Amanda McDonald Key
Typeface: Trump Mediaeval
Typesetter: Moran Printing
Printer and binder: Thomson–Shore, Inc.

Library of Congress Cataloging-in-Publication Data
Dillard, R. H. W. (Richard H. W.), 1937–
   Omniphobia : stories / by R. H. W. Dillard.
     p. cm.
   ISBN 0-8071-1839-7 (cl)
   I. Title.
PS3554.I4046 1995
813'.54—dc20   94-27047
                                                                   CIP

The stories in this volume first appeared in the following publications: "The Adventures of the Butterfat Boy," in John William Corrington and Miller Williams, eds., *Southern Writing in the Sixties: Fiction* (LSU Press, 1966); "The Death Eater," in Mary MacArthur, ed., *Carry Me Back: An Anthology of Virginia Fiction* (Gallimaufry, 1978); "The Bog," in *Iowa Review* (1981); "The Road," in *Quarterly West* (1985); "Omniphobia," in *New Virginia Review* (1989); "Their Wedding Journey," in Susan Stamberg and George Garrett, eds., *The Wedding Cake in the Middle of the Road* (Norton, 1992); "That's What I Like (About the South)," in George Garrett and Paul Ruffin, eds., *That's What I Like (About the South)* (University of South Carolina Press, 1992).

"The Road" was a winner of the *Quarterly West* Novella Competition in 1985.

The paper in this book meets the guidelines for permanence and durability of the Committee on Production Guidelines for Book Longevity of the Council on Library Resources. ∞

FOR
Nelson Bond

I guess I might as well warn
you . . . you won't believe this.
It's gospel truth, but you won't
believe a word of it.

Contents

1
OH LOVE LOVE LOVE

The Bog: A Naturalist's Notebook 3
Their Wedding Journey 52

2
WAY DOWN YONDER

The Adventures of the Butterfat Boy 63
The Road 72
That's What I Like (About the South) 114

3
WALKING ON SHALLOW WATER

The Death Eater 133
Omniphobia 144

1

OH LOVE LOVE LOVE

The Bog

A Naturalist's Notebook

.

The ideal scientific mind . . . should be capable of thinking out a point of abstract knowledge in the interval between its owner falling from a balloon and reaching the earth.

—George E. Challenger

This notebook is the property of C. Cotswaldo, Ph.D., and should be promptly returned if and when found to the Institute of Theoretical Studies, Room 18, Desk 5/9. I shall be happy to pay a suitable reward, and I should add that the contents of this notebook will be of no use or interest to you, although they are of extreme value to me.
   Thank you.

Sink or swim, here I am. The Institute of Theoretical Studies with its odd acronym ITS, a gathering of rectangular buildings, relatively windowless, almost medieval in its defensive stance toward the surrounding natural world, fully air-conditioned against the sultry summer which is encamped around it with the surrounding forest, the low stagnant bog, even the distant hazy blue mountains, an ice cube of ideas afloat in a soup of steaming reality. An appropriate place for me, or so I feel, in more ways than one. Have been here over a week, have overcome my initial awe and the usual sense of spatial/temporal displacement which I always feel in a new place. Have settled in at my desk in the yellow cube which is, for the time, mine (yellow a stimulant to thought according to the psychic designer who did the ITS buildings, although I remember that it often rouses schizophrenics to split and shatter like bits of fossilized shale). Have explored the woods, many paths, the edges of the large bog tracked by the lanes of egg-heavy female turtles heading for their destinies. Am, in other words, at home.

But, this notebook: I have realized that if I am to use my time, organize my thinking, aim it toward a new book, I'll need to follow the lead of my New England forebears, Emerson & Thoreau, and keep a journal of sorts, a grab bag of sensations and ideas from which, with some diligence and a little bit of luck, I can gather the data for the new book relatively whole and not have to start from raw scratch as I did with *Darwin's Bassoon*. Thus, here I'll put into the best prose I can the events that strike me as grist for my grinders, the day's events, memories, quotations, citations, et cetera cetera.

The drive to ITS winds through the low mountains, scruffy around the collar with edgy pine and alien kudzu, the road narrow and ridgy at the bends, coiling away from the interstate and the airport, the hum and buzz, the daily variety, into a nature lacking in the sublime but making up for it with a primitive urgency. A deer looks steadily at you from the side of the road, a black runner slides across the gravel and tar like a stream of spilled mercury, an eagle (buzzard?) soars, on an updraft up and away. The wild, mindless, energy without end (endless and purposeless), a ragged world running on its aimless way, a machine wound up so long ago that its Prime Winder has long since forgotten that He ever touched the stem and set it blindly ticking.

You look closer and you see death in this wilderness: a groundhog, yellow teeth, the bushy tail flat and rotten, sinking back into the soil, feet up, back first; trees broken and ruined, tent caterpillars settled in the sick branches like bedouin tribes (hippies?) riding the dead tree down; a rabbit torn open and mashed on the road by the tire of an ITS scholar doubtless, his mind focused on the stars as his wheel crushes the round inoffensive bunny head into the rock and stone; withered blackberries unpicked, uneaten on the dry stems, dry and hard and unfertile; a dogwood smothering in sweet honeysuckle, the pale small yellow blooms, the vines twining like a baby's fingers around the branches, the frail tree sinking in its odorous, female clutches, perfumed and soft and grasping. Even the stone is eaten away by air and water, the rootlets of wild flowers, the sledge hammers of man. It is dizzying, all this death, this mindless life and death.

And it is our fault, our fault. Bearers of the watch key, given the power to twist the very stem of life, we live instead in this mindless nightmare. Samuel Butler was right when he said that Darwin had banished "mind from the universe," and I have discussed the reasons for that banishment in *Darwin's Bassoon*. Mad reasons with mad results. And now my task: to restore mind to the universe!!!

I keep wanting to rush ahead: from the road to ITS to the cosmos, from the problem to the solution with no intermediate steps. I must settle back like a wise toad, tongue poised, wait for the fat foolish green flies. Describe plainly and simply. Lie in wait in my stalker's blind.

Myself:
My name is Cosmo Cotswaldo. I write under the name C. Cotswaldo, for the obvious reason. I have always hated my name. Usually I give my first name as Charles. I call myself Chuck, have since I was old enough to impose my wishes on the world around me.

Thirty-seven years old, I am a full professor of philosophy, albeit at Albert University, no Cambridge or Harvard, a school primarily renowned for its education department and its experimental use of candy as positive reinforcement, as an incentive to learning in higher as well as lower education—the Butterfingers System, as it came to be known around the land.

How many embarrassed hours have I spent offering senior majors Clark bars or Baby Ruths for a particularly apt discussion of the *Dasein* or the Dissimilarity of the Diverse? Albert professors are always easily identifiable by the sagging pockets of their tweed jackets, those pockets distorted not with pipe or shag tobacco, but candy kisses and Necco wafers. My teeth are riddled with the silvery residue of absent-minded munching; my belly is soft with eager cells permanently awaiting fresh infusions of sugary fat. I still find Zero bars and boxes of Boston Baked Beans in my pockets here at ITS; in fact, I feel almost inadequate without the familiar weight and fill my pockets every morning in some sort of ritualistic communion with my daily Albert life.

Why I should feel the need for this grounding in Albert is beyond me. The same reason flowers blossom better where cows have paused, I suspect. The rest of my department is composed of a collection of aging hacks or incompetent young ABDs inscribing syllogistic circles on chalkdusty blackboards of the old classrooms or engaging in eggy arguments with bright-eyed undergraduates on the nature of love in Plato in what they proudly, if inaccurately, call seminars. But I suppose they do no great harm, juggling ideas like red balls in a burlesque act, occasionally rousing some alert student to strive for greater things. Albert is blessed with tenure, and despite their reluctance to recognize my light (only partially hidden under the bushel of obscurity), they have offered me a home.

But, more of my background:

My undergraduate years were spent at a small college aptly named Wampum State (the Wampum Warriors bravely succumbing on the playing fields each weekend as were the Wampum maidens under every bush and shrub). I majored in philosophy despite my desire to become a biologist; the biology department seemed able only to metamorphose frightened cats into stiff packages of skin, fur, and skewered guts as they all the while mouthed the pages of the textbooks and looked out the windows of the labs toward the distant golf courses. I hated them and their aimless cruelty, their foetal pigs and vivisected turtles (a string signaling each sad heartbeat through a ragged vent cut in their belly plates), their frogs, their pain and death, pain and death, pain and death.

I was, then, a philosophy major, able to think about nature without being forced to torture it. I wanted to do a thesis on Thoreau's horror of the inanimate, but was steered into a prize-winning one titled "Moral Implications of Overcrowding as Exemplified by Desmond Morris' Homosexualization of Ten Spined Sticklebacks." The chairman of the department was an ethics man; I needed the Phil Club prize to help me get a fellowship for graduate school.

I went on to Pennsylvania Commonwealth University. There I lost my innocence in more ways than one: to a remarkably thin, greasy-haired waitress (who looked about thirty but was reputed to be sweet sixteen) who worked behind the counter at the College

Inn and who would duck down behind that counter and initiate the newcomers with such a deadly seriousness that the young men (mostly freshmen) seldom even blushed as they stood there in plain view from the waist up, slapping idly at the counter with a damp dishcloth which she always kept at hand; and to my adviser in the philosophy department, Thorless Turnbull, who gave an annual lecture to the graduate students called "On Being a Hunting Tiger in the Academic Jungle" and who advised me not to attempt to advance human knowledge ("Who needs or will pay for more human wisdom?") but rather to attach myself with parasitic intensity to some little-known or -read philosopher with some potential for discovery or rediscovery and, once hitched, wait for his star to rise.

Now that I look back on it, both waitress and old professor have much in common, both pale and unhealthy, both attended by long lines of yearning youths, both supplying an ugly release with little variety from day to day but with a great and unswerving steadiness, both of them rousing in me a deep and nearly despairing cynicism, a hatred of life so fierce as almost to drive me into the behavioristic clutches of the university psychology department's aberrant experimentation clinic.

Almost, but not quite. I adjusted. I survived. I did my master's thesis under Professor Luther Hagins, whose sole joy seemed to reside in his tidy shelves of collected copies of *The Popular Science Monthly*; so naturally and practically enough my thesis concerned certain aspects of secondness in Peirce. And I extended my experience into the usual neckings and gropings with the few female graduate students (always, therefore, in demand), who seemed always to be drunk at the time but nevertheless always wanting to discuss causality between kisses or belligerently insisting that I defend the doctrine of determining correspondence while striving the while to get my shirt unbuttoned or my scuffed sneakers off.

I produced a dissertation entitled "A Critical Analysis of the Loving Self in J. M. E. McTaggart." Yes, James McTaggart Ellis McTaggart, whose star, despite Broad's extensive (if negative) work, refuses to this day to climb too high in the philosophical sky. No excited university press scooped the dissertation up, although it traveled patiently from Cambridge U. to South Alabama, and it still sits (I assume) in its shiny black binder on a dusty back shelf in the university library in Gibbsville, Pa.

I took a position at Albert, climbed to assistant professor quickly enough, buoyed by the paperback edition of H. G. Wells's *Anticipations of the Reaction of Mechanical and Scientific Progress upon Human Life and Thought* for which I supplied an introduction for College Classics, a reprint house which hovered always on the edge of the fifty-six-year copyright expiration date, swooping down on those titles just venturing out into the public domain with the alertness and rapacity of a turkey vulture, paying the authors or their estates nothing and the introducers (all, it seems, assistant professors or stale desperate associates) in copies (10 free, 20 more at a 50 percent discount). And there I stagnated for seven years, candy melting in my clutched hand, my day built around my daily trip to my post office box to see whether some lightning had struck even in the cloudless sky of my professional horizon.

And then came *Darwin's Bassoon.* My thunderclap.

Talking with Cortapiedras today. Learned some important things. I suppose I should try to describe him, describe ITS. Now, while my thinking is focused on the place and the society here.

You enter ITS by way of a long curving drive which leads from the narrow mountain highway through two brick pillars appropriately inscribed, the road swinging in a slow even arc up a rounded hill (really a knoll), the grass clipped smooth and kept green by dint of watering and feeding, cedars and spruce scattered over the lawn, a pleasant, even-looking place, clearly a place designed to soothe rather than distract the mind. The buildings (six of them) are rectangular and brick with little glass.

Oh, this doesn't matter. Should try to describe them later, and the woods, the paths, the bog. Essential that a reader feel the place, the cool indirect lighting of ITS, the hum of the air conditioning, the quiet in the halls, the mathematicians sitting slumped before their blackboards (green, of course) for hours on end, not even looking at the problem they've chalked up, staring at the wall or floor or out the door (you pass like a wisp, a ghost, insubstantial in that unwavering gaze), and how occasionally with a burst and clatter they bound up, erase one number or slash with a sleeve and replace it with another, then settle back down and enter that abstract formal world of absolute meaning again.

Describe that and contrast it with the weedy paths, the unkempt woods, the rabbits flashing into brambles, the shuffling groundhogs, the bloated pale hairless floating (sinking?) thing in the bog, four swollen legs poked up at the sky, so repulsive and formless that I could never figure what it was, could not even try. The burgeoning life everywhere, the spider webs that cling to your face invisibly, the spider scurrying down your sleeve, that profusion of shivering, bulging, creeping, growing, growing, growing life, plant and animal, insect and humming air.

Describe them both, ITS and outside. Then the problem will come clear: how to join ITS to OUTS(ide), how to take that mathematical clarity, that meaning, and infuse it into that whirling confusion outside, how to restore mind to matter.

But, now, to Cortapiedras, to our conversation. I lack the strength or purity of mind to describe those things now. He has given me much else to think about.

Juan Cortapiedras, the geologist, the geode man, whose studies of stone have pressed mind deeper into the inanimate than almost anyone before him. I have always stood in awe of his work, was even afraid to speak to him when I was introduced my first day by Horace Dolgrum, the director of ITS, its stern administrator. But Cortapiedras, the man at ease, not the mind at work, is an easygoing fellow, small, olive skinned, black hair, brown eyes, always smiling, red shirts and yellow trousers (in his yellow study he must be a sight indeed—maybe it is all that gray stone he works with). He promised to put me in touch with Langdon-Davies, whose studies with peasant ESP would be of definite use to my work, and he has always been friendly. But only today has he become personal.

"Women," he began, grabbing my left elbow, squeezing it as he spoke, the electricity of his intense emotion actually causing my whole arm to shake (vibrate?) with its force, "what this place needs is women." And before I could reply, he continued, "God, some days, looking at all the beards and pipes and goddam corduroys around this dump, I could piss on the floor I want a woman so bad. You feel it, you know, you do, yes. Jesus, a woman, one hot woman, call her research assistant, research ass, yes, you see? One woman," his clutch got even tighter, "I can tell, you are a man, too, not just a ball-less mental think-think. Oh, for one good lay, yes? One hundred miles from the nearest woman, oh holy hell," here he clutched his crotch with his free hand, "how we supposed to make progress when all I can think of is women, huh? Yes, you see? You know?"

I almost felt raped, almost fell over when he let my arm go, but then he continued, "But that old bastard Dolgrum, he goes into town today to bring a new research fellow back from the airport. Sure, I'll bet, sure, he goes to get his ashes shifted, I tell you."

"New fellow?" I tried to change the subject.

"Biologist." His intensity waned; he slumped back in his chair (we were in the snack bar, drinking ice tea). "Ethologist." Then, his interest quickening again, he added, "Maybe it's a woman, eh? Hot piece, nature lover type, huh? Yes."

Then he got up, walked away, his stride a curious scrabbling gait, almost sideways like a brightly colored crab. No word of parting. I sat there stunned, a complex of emotions swirling in me that I had not felt since leaving Albert.

It is, I suppose, important to say that I am not married. I lived with a woman, a linguist, for two years. Ostensibly in adjoining apartments, but I slept in her bed every night. She satisfied me sexually, cut my hair, criticized my work, nagged at my clothes, demanded that I take her dancing, the usual. I assume I offered her about as much pleasure as she did me. We talked. We screwed. No, I have to find a way to say all this, to indicate that I am normally male, no male chauvinist or feminist. Prey to human needs. Not a loner. Must find a voice for this section.

She left, went on to another job. I kissed her on the cheek at the airport. I still find bits of her hair on my suits, scraps of underwear or hairpins in my drawers. I have come to realize that she meant little to me, that I satisfied certain nest-building needs of hers (sexual, social, even intellectual as she tidied up my prose), that she satisfied certain territorial needs of mine (dominance, sexual, social, so on).

I have never married. I have had few liaisons with students. Somehow it is no pleasure to me to seduce a young woman by praising her analysis of the infinite divisibility of particulars. Besides that, they have mothers and fathers (seldom still married to each other) and big brothers. So I live alone and look the other way when they cross their legs on the front row of class or lean across the desk with unbuttoned blouses, delivering their papers or accepting their candy bars.

So what, then, are these emotions that Cortapiedras has roused in me? They are not, I'm reasonably sure, mine. I seriously believe that they are his feelings, purely his, transmitted to me by the force of his utterance, the very grip of his fingers, cell to cell, his lust short-circuiting the normal electrical business of my own cellular structure, racing through me like a wild current through a line without proper resistance. I must talk to him when he is this way again. Or—and this way I gain something like an experimental control—when he is that excited, to impose my own thinking on him, to cool him down with a burst of sheer mental clarity, to focus my sense of meaning in such away as to force his sexual energy into a creative channel. The breakthrough in geological thought might be enormous. And I will be prepared. I won't allow the force of his lust to surprise me, to drive me to my bedroom, to shame me into that kind of behavior again.

Am writing this on a low bank by a sagging willow tree poised on the edge of the large bog which stretches over about three acres at the foot of the hill upon which ITS stands. You make your way down here by long narrow, weedy paths. Occasionally the institute sends a man and a power mower along all of the paths, but his trips are few. The woods are second growth but fairly old. The trees stand on the average some thirty feet or better, but there is undergrowth, kudzu mad and rapacious, mayapples, poison oak and ivy, jewel weeds with their seed ready to spring forth like tiny animals at the slightest touch, the thin green coils whirling in your palm, the small brown seed spinning out into the soil.

You see rabbits and groundhogs, at night opossums, lumbering and gray-whiskered. I have seen and heard (and felt) the slick departure of snakes, but I have not yet seen one, have no idea whether they are black snakes or runners, corn or hog, or maybe even the cottonmouth moccasins that Lew Dark, the institute herpetologist, warned me about, lurking in the bog waters, ready to sear your veins with their needle fangs.

Mainly here, by the bog, where I plan to come often to write these notes, closer to my problem than I can ever be in my yellow study, I see frogs, bulging along under the bog slime like green moles, urping and skittering into the water at my every move. I enjoy their awareness of me. We are in communion whether they like it or not, and I plan to focus myself into them soon, to attempt intercellular communication with their whole beings, to impose my mind into their random behavior, to (using Koestler's brilliant metaphor) fill their froggy machines with my own ghost, to add mind to their sleek scared matter.

Deeper out, beyond the frogs, the bog seems to thicken, its green scum cover giving way to a deeper brown. Dark tells me that is quicksand and warns me to stay out of it. He lost a dog, a valuable mastiff named Moe, to this bog, the big beast swimming out after a stick, then sinking, slowly, horribly while Dark raced frantically around, trying to get a pole, a fallen tree, something long enough to reach the animal. But the dog struggled furiously and sank, could not understand that it would sink infinitely more slowly if it remained still—another victim of mindlessness, of the absurd world we have allowed ourselves to inhabit for so long with so little real effort to educate it, to bring it to consciousness. Poor Moe, woofing down into the deadly quicksand, clawing only at death with his poor paws, running down into the smothering, filling bog. Perhaps I will avenge you, quicken that dead sand to bring forth something alive rather than swallow everything whole. I shall certainly try, my fellow Mo(e). I shall surely try.

Myself (cont'd.):

Four years ago, bored by my job, my life, almost literally to death (to actual tears too often to mention), sinking in survey histories of Western thought and lengthy essays at Boolean algebra, I took a year's leave at half pay and produced a small book, as much for my own amusement as anything else, a book venting my emotional overload by attacking Darwin's approach to evolution and assessing its impact on modern life.

Darwin's Bassoon, much to my surprise and certainly to that of my stunned colleagues at Albert, was immediately accepted by a small but very respectable New York publisher and became a best seller. It was an alternate selection of the Book-of-the-Month Club, a regular selection of the Occult Book Society, and a mass trade paperback special with a puzzling introduction by Erich von Däniken, all this within one year. It was distributed free to all associate members of the Natural History Museum, and it was nominated for a National Book Award (although it lost out to Matthew Hooper's personal narrative of shark attacks).

I became something of an overnight cult figure, acquired an unlisted phone number, a tax accountant, and a bright red Alfa Romeo. I was promoted in succeeding years to associate and then full professor (ending for good and all my tenure nerves), attracted the sudden romantic attention of at least six attractive and inventive co-eds from Albert and three other nearby universities and colleges, had the locks on my doors changed twice, and was invited to be a fellow at ITS (working on intercellular communication and its philosophical implications) for this summer.

I suppose I should include at least a brief account of the thesis of *Darwin's Bassoon* for those unacquainted with *Masterplots*.

I had always been concerned about Darwin and Darwinism, the blighted world he left us, allowing us to be victimized by Marx and Freud, left like corpses from the very second of our births to the clacking jaws of the vultures of materialism, reductionism, absurdity, and despair. Then I read Donald Fleming's penetrating essay "Charles Darwin, the Anaesthetic Man," in *Victorian Studies*, and realized for the first time that he was his own chief victim, that he turned away from all aesthetic experience in order to avoid the vision of beauty and harmony and meaning which he had, almost single-handedly, destroyed. His disavowal of the delights of art and music and all literature save those sickly sweet Victorian novels of family sentiment is clearly the act of a madman, a man so fearful of the power of his imagination that he attempts to stifle it utterly.

I began to study Darwin's life and writings with some thoroughness and arrived at the conclusion that, although he was undoubtedly brilliant and began on the right track, he veered away into madness and produced from his own psychoses that depressed and depressing world of chance, that world at once random and mechanistic (a machine gone wildly out of control) in which we all grew up and are only now growing out of.

I searched for the source of Darwin's madness, some moment

that threw the powerful engine of his mind onto its permanent sidetrack. The clue to the source of that madness came to me in a flash of intuition when I was reading of Darwin's attempt to stimulate movement in the pinnae of his *Mimosa pudica* by poising himself before it and playing to it on his bassoon.

As a former (mercifully with a brief career on the instrument) oboist, I knew the truth. The plant never quivered (though it may have suffered great agony), but the action of the double reed of the bassoon vibrated through Darwin's firm embouchure, through his clenched teeth, through the bones of his face and sinuses, through his forehead, the bone thrumming like a taut drumskin, and deeply into his brain. No double-reeded instrument player—oboist, English hornist, bassoonist—as all musicians know from painful and personal experience, ever maintains full sanity for more than eight years of play upon his instrument, and Darwin played the bassoon steadily for most of his life.

The key, I asserted in my book, to the darkness and despair of our lives for the last century was that bassoon, for it literally shook the fine mind of Charles Darwin into madness and produced the theory of random selection that continues to this day to deny the place of mind in the movement of nature. Think as you will, says Darwin (or rather, Darwin's bassoon speaking through Darwin), but for all your effort, all your subtle thoughts, you are of no more value or significance than the ringing of a buoy bell on a rising sea, ringing and ringing, random and mad, or a cattail reed nodding pointlessly in a winter wind, or one of those hideous little dogs with its head bobbing up and down and up and down in the rear window of a battered automobile.

We have been living in the empty, echoing world of a madman's brain for over a century, I said, and the time has come to break out, to impose mind on bare fact, to restore mind and purpose to blank nature by the active force of human will.

So here I am at ITS, a fellow among fellows, all of us fully funded to explore any path we choose, whether out from this hilltop into the vast swirl of cosmic reaches or down through the snarled woods into the enormous bog bubbling and peeping at the foot of the hill.

If Einstein had done nothing else, the awareness that relativity physics has given us of the inescapable participation of the so-called "objective" observer in the event he is observing would have been enough to make him worthy of our sung praises for generations to come. The eye and the mind's eye of the human observer and thinker are themselves as much a part of the scene observed as that scene itself. I think of James Thurber peering into a microscope and taking notes on his own eye peering back and realize that he is at that moment the type of us all, all scientists and thinkers, all human beings not wholly caught up in Darwin's thoughtless machine.

We see and our seeing changes what we see. That is the most exciting fact of our existence, for it reveals to us the method whereby we may restore mind to matter and fulfill what must surely be the purpose of our existence. Seeing, thinking, the mysterious power of ESP, the wonders of intercellular communication. We can think cancer into our bones as thoroughly as we can think health into the plant we are watering. The faith healer pounding health into the head of a cripple is the next extension of Thurber's eye: we see ourselves, we see ourselves in the world, we impose ourselves upon the world, we change the world to ourselves, we become the world.

Tomorrow I begin my experiments in earnest.

Today by dint of my careful study of him, eye to eyes, I caused a spider to back away from a moth caught in his web. A small, delicate six-eyed spider, an orb weaver; a pale, dull moth, scarcely worth the saving. But, alive—quick! I have, of course, no proper control of the sort necessary to allow me to state my success as scientifically verified fact. But, at this stage, I don't need that; I need merely to convince myself, and I am convinced. I have cancelled the first deadly event in my life as a naturalist; I have made right the original sin of my life as an active participant in the mindless natural world.

That needs, I suppose, some explanation. Somewhere I have stashed away my first naturalist's journal with my original account of the event. But can I find it?

This is the gist: I was about twelve, pimply I suppose, alert, intense, eager to discover everything. For some reason, I had suddenly discovered the existence of variegated nature, a world full of interesting things to observe and note down. It was a major discovery, for it turned daily existence into something as complex and exciting as a baseball game. I had been scoring games I heard on the radio, a complex and cryptic nexus of little lines, diamonds, *K*'s, *HR*'s, *BB*'s and *E*'s, carefully saving the sheets and clipping them into a three-ring binder, sure in the innocence and ignorance of youth that I would be consulting them time and again for a lifetime, an eternity to come. And now I had suddenly discovered that I could chart the entire natural world in the same manner, making of each day's observation an elaborate and exciting girandole of birds and insects and mammals and stones and trees and plants, lists and descriptions, a universe in a notebook.

I made the discovery simply because my uncle, a quiet and bearded bachelor, had pointed out to me in a tree in front of our house a female cardinal, a catbird, and a brown thrasher. Before that moment I had been aware of the concept *bird* and the existence of the particulars, *robin* (harbinger of spring) and *chickadee*. But I simply had never noticed the cast of hundreds of differing birds who filled the air, trees, bushes, and grass around me every day. I was stunned, overwhelmed.

My uncle promised me a Peterson field guide on his next visit, and I made my first naturalist's notebook that night. I could hardly wait for the dawn to come and woke up instantly with the unnatural vigor and enthusiasm of a Christmas morning. I rushed through breakfast, took my notebook and pen in hand (a practice that I follow to this day), and strode out to greet the wonders of the living world head on.

I paused by the back door and noticed out of the corner of my eye something moving on the windowsill beside me, a slim, almost transparent insect, its clear wings trembling and stretching open in the first warmth of the new day. I tugged a folding lawn chair over by the window and settled myself down on the stiff canvas to watch this tiny bit of life wake up in the early sunlight. I opened my notebook on my knees, uncapped my speckled brown Esterbrook school pen, and looked carefully and closely at the insect.

It stepped very slowly and carefully, once, twice, and then with no apparent transition, it fell over on its side, stiff, dry and dead. I almost threw up. Dead. I had settled down to watch it live, and all it had done was die. I wanted to smash it, to flatten it into the flaking white paint with one quick blow of my fist, to smash it out of nature, out of my consciousness, out of existence. But instead I picked it up by one frail, stiff wing and then replaced it carefully where it had fallen over.

It was a mayfly, I learned later. An insect whose major activity, it would seem, is to die. Birth and death almost in a single breath. This was the gift that nature gave me on my first day as a naturalist. Thanks a lot.

No wonder that I fell prey so easily to the Darwinian world of mad chance. No wonder that I fled from nature to philosophy even while I peered back from the ivory tower at that procreating, dying madhouse of nature that surrounded it.

But did nature supply me with that disillusioning surprise by chance? I rejected then and reject now the idea that it was some malignant fate or supernatural overlord who set me up and knocked me down. It was chance and chance alone. But was that chance of my own making, a chance closer to Jung and Pauli's synchronicity than to Darwin's randomness? Did some darkness within myself, some youthful cynicism I was not even aware of, flow out of me and into the world of chance, shaping it to my own dark desires? Did my peering eye stagger that small insect and literally stop it in its tracks? Did I, as Strindberg and Powys thought they did, have the power to destroy with a glance, a wave of living thought? Do we all share that blind and deadly power?

I have come to think that we do, that our very cells are in humming communion with the natural world, the universe, the cosmos. Foucault's pendulum, turning not with the movement of the planet, but with the actual rhythm of the cosmos, comes as no surprise to me. I feel and have felt it for some time in the marrow of my bones. We are *of* life; we give it mind and meaning, directly, purely, truly.

Thus, my excitement today when the six-eyed spider moving down his orbed web toward the struggling moth withdrew, not because he saw me (for he had seen me before, had seen me watching him long before the moth touched the web) but because I willed it so. He backed away, paused at the web's periphery, watched me free the moth with my fingertips (careful not to damage the web too seriously), watched the stunned moth waver on a nearby leaf and then gather courage and fly away. Watched and understood. Because I willed it so. I willed his behavior, and I willed his understanding of it. He is the Einstein of spiders now, possessed of an awareness so far beyond that of any other of his tribe (save perhaps that ancient ancestor of his who wove his web at Robert Bruce's unknowing behest) that he might as well be a different creature altogether.

I did this thing. Today. Mayfly, you are avenged!!

Watched a mantis mating today, actually saw it. Just this quick note. Tried to stop it. The drive to sex and death was too powerful, or perhaps I was too revulsed by the whole thing, the pulsing male I willed to leave the female, to stop, perhaps I should have tried tuning my will into hers, to make her stop, he was totally a puppet to his heaving loins, scarcely a real thing at all beyond the fact of orgasmic pressure itself, I could not reach him, maybe I could have reached her, but she sickened me, I was afraid of her, her triangular head, those enormous eyes like black buttons, chewing away at his head, eating him, chewing and eating him, devouring him as he pumped his seed into her, and she was watching me with those horrible black eyes while she calmly and steadily chewed off his head.

I failed. I willed him away and I failed. I threw up, right there, the vomit steaming on the ground by them. And I stomped them both into mud, screaming, cursing at them at the top of my lungs, the bottom of my foot wrenching into a terrible cramp, coiling away from them within my boot as I stomped and stomped.

I still feel sick. My foot aches. I feel blank and awful and empty. I can't go on.

I should go back down to the bog today. The principle of the thrown rider remounting the horse. Try the frogs. Maybe the insects were too simple, too deeply mindless to be reached until I have learned how to focus my will more fully.

But that won't explain it. I have urged plants into full and blooming health. I reached the spider, so infinitely smaller than a mantis; I reached him (her?). Him, I suspect.

It must have been the act and fact of sex itself. It was like

Cortapiedras. The sex drive is so explosively powerful that you cannot overcome it, only channel it. Perhaps sublimation is more central than anyone has supposed, or at least the only way to manage the unreleased power of sex.

I must find Cortapiedras and this time try to focus my self on him, not to overcome the fury of his sexual tensions but to channel them, to aim them at his geological interests.

Then perhaps I shall have laid the horror of those mantis lovers away for good.

I found Juan Cortapiedras in the snack bar finally, after winding through the blue labyrinth of the halls in the laboratory building (the blue halls are to calm you between yellow study and green lab). He was with Miller, the balding energetic cancer man, and Gilbert Austin, the English psychologist and philosopher, who was sipping something from a large beer stein and discussing the details of some gruesome British murder or the other with apparent relish. I was rather shy of both men, awed by their fame, put off by their casual manner (as though they didn't know their own greatness or refused to accept the consequences of it).

I finally caught Cortapiedras' eye and beckoned him over to my small table as the three were rising to leave. He waved a quick, friendly good-bye to Miller and Austin, who wandered on away, and then came over to me.

"Chuck, Chuck," he said, before I could say a word, his hands continuing to wave, this time at me, excitedly, "have you heard? Yes, you have. No?"

"What, Juan, what?"

"The new associate, the one Dolgrum has taken such a long time picking up, yes, she is a woman, is going to be a woman, a young woman, yes." His eyes were flashing (quite literally), and I was as overwhelmed by my good luck. You could feel the sexual force radiating from him, washing over you like an eighth wave at the beach, hot, wet, salty, overwhelming.

He continued to talk excitedly, his hands shaping the classic woman shape in the air, assuring me that she would be young, beautiful, loose, horny, long black hair, eyes, lips, "boobs like nothing you ever seen, yes," legs.

I let him talk on, looking steadily at his eyes (like looking into an old woodstove through the tiny isinglass window in the door), tuning my mind in to the force of his lust (mounting word by word).

"Who is she? What's her name?" I asked, to keep him talking, to keep the fire burning.

"Chuck," he shouted, "Chuck, who knows, who cares?"

He then began to repeat his imaginative description of who and what she must be, and as he spoke, I suddenly lashed a thought, a command, full force at him, my every conscious cell (all of my cells, I believe) sending the message to his every cell. Not cancelling his lust but redirecting it to geology, assenting with his passion and thinking geology, lusting for geology all the time.

He faltered, he stammered, he stopped.

"But Chuck," he said, the passion still in his face, in his voice, "but Chuck, I got to go. I just remembered. I got to get to a geode," he nudged me across the table as he got up to leave, "put the chisel in, crack her open, yes, get into a geode, yes, yes. See you, Chuck, got a heavy date with a geode, hot damn."

And that was it. I did it! I did it!

He practically ran out the snack bar, so eager was he to assault a geode. I was beside myself with joy. I am sure now, totally sure that I am right. I can win. I must plan a laboratory experiment to prove my theory for a doubting scientific world. I can do it. I gave myself a Fifth Avenue!

One problem: It is almost like some sort of electrical backlash. How can I control it? All I can think about is the new woman. I see her everywhere. Or I see Juan's image of her, the legs, the breasts, the face, the long black hair. The sexual tension is stronger than any I have felt since I was a teenager, I want her so bad.

They are all reacting to the news that she is coming. Cortapiedras is polishing himself up; everyone is straightening up their studies, tidying their bedrooms. But I want her, I want her with all the fury of Cortapiedras' lust. The power of it is literally shaking me all over, but I refuse the only release available to me. I will not stoop to that again.

I'll work on my experiment. I shall. I will.

Must determine the exact nature of my experiment. I know now that I can influence the direction of thought of another man, but lack the apparatus here to produce a controlled experiment which would convince anyone, especially with the air cluttered with ESP traditions, Zener cards, thrown dice, stars and bars, circles and pluses. Must remember von Frisch's theorem: "If we use excessively elaborate apparatus to examine simple natural phenomena Nature herself may escape us." Where exactly does he say that? Must look up *The Dancing Bees* in the library here. Maybe ask Collembola about it. In fact he may have the stuff in the lab that I need. Insects might well be the place to start formally, just as they have been all along in my own private studies.

Try as I may, I cannot get her out of my mind. My frequency of urination has increased; I find myself swallowing air and belching it back nervously; I start up from sleep at the slightest sound. How can Cortapiedras stand it if this is the way he is all the time?

She is due here tomorrow. In the morning.

Copies of an article by her were circulated to us all at dinner. From *Ms.* magazine. Her name is Sara Band. No picture. No author's biographical note. Many fellows seemed to be reading it over their meals. I could hear a good deal of talk, some very vigorous, a lot of laughter. I avoided it all, pled a migraine, rushed to my room. The title is interesting, if a bit puzzling: "Psyche—Myth and Moth: The Bagworm as a Type of Oppressed Sisterhood." I started to read it but could not keep my eyes or mind on the page. Cannot think of my work either. Must try to go to bed and get to sleep early. Maybe I will find relief in my sleep.

Sara.

Slept through and missed her arrival.

Nightmares of the mantis mating, my foot covered with mantises, then my head. Would wake up sweating and writhing. Drift back to sleep. Repeat. Repeat.

Must go by Dolgrum's office. Ask for an introduction. Make apologies.

Still haunted by the black eyes of the mantis. Almost feel them watching me now, black and huge and hungry.

So much has happened today. Some of it productive, I suppose. At least I have the von Frisch book and a lead on the experiment I must construct.

Before I forget it: the von Frisch quotation which I copied down years ago is, alas, on p. vii of *The Dancing Bees*. Collembola's copy is the English edition (British?)—Methuen, London, 1954. A shame. Now, if I note the pages properly, everyone will assume I only read the preface. What to do?

But I must put down the events of the day, my most social day, my meeting with Sara Band. My feelings are terribly mixed at the moment (anger, shame, regret, some lingering lust), but my memory is sharp.

I arose late, dressed casually in Levi's, my blue Lacoste knit shirt, blue seersucker jacket, sneakers, my usual working garb in summer, and went across from the dorm building to the administrative offices. It was nearly noon, and the brown gravel (pebbles?) of the walkways had already been raked smooth by the groundskeepers. Again ITS's desire to maintain the air of calm rationality even on the paths. I had seldom visited the ad building, and by the time I had located Dolgrum's office, he had gone to lunch. I dared not ask if Ms. Band were with him.

I went to lunch myself along another pebbled path, my eyes scanning the gravel for hints, his footprints, hers. But the rakes had been at work here, too. I began to hate their antlike efficiency. I had to stop in the men's room before going into the dining hall (the usual malady), and then all my tension remained unresolved when I discovered the room to be nearly empty and especially empty of Sara Band.

I did see Juan Cortapiedras, who waved me over to his table. I made my way to him, balancing the tray with some lunch or the other on it which I had failed to notice really.

"Ah, Chuck," he shouted, "you have seen her, yes?"

"No," I said and shook my head and started to explain, but he pressed on, his voice running over itself, tripping like a clumsy hound puppy.

"Oh, you will be so pleased, yes. She is exactly as I described her, exactly. What a piece! Yes, exactly. Oh, you will like her, yes."

Exactly. I belched nervously and tried to concentrate on getting my lunch chewed and swallowed, over with.

"But Chuck," Juan continued, his voice dropping a little, almost conspiratorial, "I hate to run, but I got work to do, you know, new stones, yes, but I promise you," this time with a wink and nudge, his elbow banging into my shoulder, "I tell you one thing, yes, I promise I'm going to get into that hot pants piece before this day is over, yes," he began to laugh as he spoke, "I'm going to flutter over to her house and do my thing, watch her stick her tail out the door and bang bang, eh, Chuck? She stick it out and bang bang, yes?"

I had no idea what he was talking about beyond the crude essentials, but I nodded as though I were in on the joke. He walked away, stowing his tray, piled high with dishes and forks and knives and crumpled napkins, in one of the large carts left about the room for that purpose (no waiters at ITS, only busboys), and winked at me as he passed through the main door.

Why would Sara Band make Juan think she would "stick her tail out the door"? It made no sense, and I felt none of his usual lust, that overpowering, shuddering force. Just his gaiety, his laughter.

I finished lunch without noticing and made my worried way to Hector Collembola's lab. Collembola, a tiny little man, taut, seemingly ready to spring at any second, is a friendly enough man, not boisterous and open like Cortapiedras, quieter, more abstracted, but filled with a kinetic energy which I could feel as strongly as Juan's sexual cravings. Just being near him inspires me to make a larger effort, to leap higher.

He found me the copy of von Frisch I asked for, told me to take it along with me. Then, in response to my asking what insects he might have that I could use in an experiment in intercellular communication, he forced a copy of Henri Fabre's *The Life of the Caterpillar* on me, saying that the only things he had in sufficient quantity were a colony of pine processionaries. I knew of Fabre's famous experiment with them, but Collembola insisted that I could find something new and interesting to do with them if I read through Fabre thoroughly. And, he added, I was welcome to all the little caterpillars I could use.

I started to ask him about Sara Band, but he was clearly impatient to get back to his worms and bugs, so I left, thanking him, promising to return the books tomorrow.

And then, totally by surprise, I met Sara Band. In the hall. Outside Collembola's lab door. With Dolgrum.

She was dressed in a green pants suit that matched her eyes, a cold green, edgy and deep. I got the feeling that those clear eyes, if they ever cried, would not cry salt tears, but clear, cold, green tears without a trace of warm salt.

You see, she is nothing like my dream (Juan's dream), nothing at all. She is young, in her twenties I'd say, medium height. Could tell nothing about her body in that suit except that she seems slim, she has a bosom though nothing like the vast overwhelming one of Juan's imagining, her face is pretty enough, freckled, she wears large glasses with thin rims that circle her eyes and much of her face like a delicate picture frame. Her skin is fair, her shingled hair is deep red. When I shook her hand, it seemed as cold to me as her eyes, icy, frosted. But enough of Juan's sexual fury remained in me that I stood there desiring her (no doubt obviously), staring into those green eyes while Dolgrum grumbled through an introduction.

"I'm sorry about your headache," she said.

"Headache?" I couldn't make it out.

"Professor Cortapiedras, your friend," she added with what seemed some irony, "told me all about it this morning."

"Oh, my headache," I said, finally remembering my clumsy ruse of the evening before. "Yes, of course, my headache." I think I may have rapped on my forehead with my knuckles.

She smiled a cool little smile (a hint of small white teeth, thin lips, sharp teeth) and said, "Yes, your headache. Probably the result of your years on the oboe."

I was baffled. How did she know I played the oboe? I must have looked a perfect oaf, standing there, staring at her in a mixture of desire and confusion, my hands groping the air as if they could grasp neither the fact of her nor the mystery of her remark.

Then, of course, I understood. My book! She had read my book! I was stunned. I was overjoyed. The image of her, this cool pale creature in green with her short red hair, filled me as totally as Juan's mad pneumatic raven-haired beauty had. I trembled with joy. I stifled a belch. Completely unconsciously, as I had done thousands of times before at Albert, I dipped my hand into my pocket and came up with a Bit-O-Honey, which I handed to her.

She took it, but she looked at it with an odd expression, as though I had handed her an animal dropping or, worse, one of my own. I stammered. I started to try to explain, but Dolgrum broke in (something about things to be done, some pointed remark or another) and led her away. She nodded at me, once, very coldly. She dangled the candy from two fingertips as they walked away down the long corridor. I believe I saw her show it to Dolgrum. I think I heard them share a laugh. I know I saw her toss it into a wastebasket just before they stepped into the elevator at the end of the hall and disappeared from my view.

I stood there, a blue shadow in the blue hallway, watching the empty silence for a long time. Then I came back here. To try to sort things out. To try to work. To try to live.

Fuck Albert!!!!

Women.

The whole problem. I remember walking Alice's dog, a pooch of some sort or the other, shaggy brown and white, small. (Have I mentioned that Alice was the woman I lived with? Should I? Or should I depersonalize it all? Or use false names? Alice = Carroll (Carol?). Or Alice = Elise?)

Get this right.

I was walking a small dog, shaggy little fellow, brown and white, eager-nosed, friendly, when we met a few blocks up the street two black dachshunds. They ran down their closely clipped lawn like two wiggling sausages (has that been used?) or two torpedoes, straight for the pooch and me. The first, a male, sniffed at my dog, who sniffed back; they maneuvered themselves properly head to tail, both tails wagging stiffly and steadily. No problems. But the other dachshund suddenly moved forward; my dog turned to meet the approach. The second dachshund, with no provocation, just that same wet nose, that same wagging tail, snarled, snapped its teeth, darted forward and back, began to bark angrily. The first dachshund then joined in, abrogating whatever treaty he had worked out with my small pooch. The second dachshund was, of course, female, a bitch.

Should be able to add a good deal to this. Not the overworked black widow tale. The mantis is too close to me, too deep, to use, to waste in anything other than the book. Must look around for other examples.

Why am I so angry? Tried to read Band's article. Again could not focus. Settled down with von Frisch. Found my quotation quickly. Wrote my notes in here. Then settled down in an armchair in the philosophy library (where no one seems ever to venture) by a narrow window facing the woods and the bog. And read her piece. It shouldn't bother me. Is this just frustration from the whole complex of emotions which were betrayed by my meeting with her? Or am I annoyed that the author (I am tempted in my anger to say authoress) of this garbage should be invited here to ITS to work with men like Juan Cortapiedras, Gilbert Austin, Hector Collembola, myself?!?

I stared out of the window toward the bog but saw nothing. I have been planning a reply, an article, a popular piece for a popular magazine (should I try *Playboy* or *Penthouse?*) exploding her thinking and her method. Turning her own guns on her. The bitch!

I must get back to my work. I'll try to read Fabre and think about pine processionaries.

Real advances. Real advances.

The whole thing has come together this evening with extraordinary clarity. I read Fabre's chapter on pine processionaries. To keep my mind working away from Sara Band and her abominable piece, I read the rest of Fabre, a remarkable book, the man a great scientist not so much for his observations but rather for his allowing his imagination to flow into those observations. He does not merely look at pine processionaries, he feels them. But, as I read on, I found a chapter on psyche moths, and (!!) I found the details of Band's piece practically intact. Without a word of acknowledgment, she has lifted Fabre's study of psyche moths and applied it to her own cheap purposes. I almost danced around the room. I felt freed of the need to refute her. She was a common thief. Why bother with an article in response, when a simple letter to the editor will do? If they accept letters from men.

But, in my elation, my excitement, my victory, I suddenly discovered my experiment with pine processionaries. It came to me in a sudden brilliant flash. I'll borrow the necessary caterpillars from Collembola tomorrow. It is so simple and so clear. The results will be irrefutable.

Tonight I will sleep deeply and freely, the succubus of Cortapiedras' imagining finally and successfully laid at last.

Woke up at 3 A.M., can't go back to sleep, too groggy to work. Memories of dreams, indistinct, disturbing, chilling. Was wet through my pajamas but cold. Had to walk around and around the room, slapping at myself, thighs and shoulders. Was she in the dreams, those cold eyes, cold hands? Were they sexual? I only remember struggle, furious struggle, an overpowering sense of being swallowed by something, smothering, drowning. Yes, and a distinct presence. Of Sara Band? I almost remember now.

Must do something. My nerves are fraying in the night. Will make notes on her article. Perhaps I can find a way to work them into the book, a rational solution to the dilemma she professes to describe.

"Psyche—Myth and Moth: The Bagworm as a Type of Oppressed Sisterhood"

Part One: a rehash of the Cupid-Psyche myth. Psyche as abused woman, how the gods conspire to hurt her because she has pride in herself and her beauty, how Cupid with typical male territorial and sexual instincts steals her away and forces her to make love to him in darkness, never allowing her to see him, his penis according to him enough reward for a life of loneliness and the fear of being turned over to a serpentine monster (as though he were anything other to her himself really) if she displeases him. This use/abuse of Psyche by Cupid is, according to Band, the heart of the myth, the terrible truth about woman's place in a male world. The rest is male cover-up, the business about Psyche redeeming herself by labors (the kitchen as path to salvation myth) and her final reward, immortality through the birth of a child called Pleasure (the myth doesn't mention the real labors of childbirth, which make the seed sorting and fleece gathering look like a picnic).

Her conclusion: that the Psyche myth unconsciously reveals a great truth about human behavior. The female, Psyche, is kept a sexual prisoner and made a virtual slave by male duplicity, and the only escape available to her, according to the male lie, is to accept the male penis in her as a suitable reward and bear a child as her only pleasure.

Part Two: a rehash of Fabre's chapter on psyche moths (bagworms). How the larvae, male and female, begin constructing houses, the familiar leafy bags that dot dying evergreens every summer, immediately after birth. How the caterpillars live in these bags, carrying them on their backs wherever they wander. But then they become moths. The male (and she quotes directly from Fabre without admitting it) "wears a costume of deepest black, all except the edges of the wings, which, having no scales, remain diaphanous. His antennae, likewise black, are wide and graceful plumes." The female moth, however, is horribly ugly, wingless, a tiny head, vestigial eyes, tiny weak legs, her body pale yellow, the bulk of her body a bag swollen with eggs. This poor female, looking like a maggot, stays forever in her house; she does not break forth like the free, handsome male and fly in the warm night air.

Band really gets worked up here, drawing myth and moth together in her spidery web. The male, like Cupid, comes to the female Psyche in the dark and screws her. They do not even see each other. The female lowers her tail out of her bag home, and the male puts it to her. (Suddenly I understand Cortapiedras' joke about Band's "sticking her tail out the door." But where does he stand on her? Did he mean it?)

Anyway, the sex act over, the male flies, according to Band, happily away, to live out his life in the free air, a typical male chauvinist. The female, again like Psyche, finds her pleasure in her young. She never leaves her home for her entire life. She lays her eggs and ends what is left of her life in the doorway of her home, protecting the eggs and then leaving her poor broken body for their future use.

Part Three: Band's conclusion. That both Psyche the myth and the female bagworm (for even the moth is more worm than moth) are types of oppressed sisterhood. That the woman who submits to a man's gropings and pumpings, allowing herself to be turned into household drudge with no reward but his penisolate gifts, is as foolish and benighted as Psyche in the myth and as cruelly imprisoned and put upon as the female Psyche moth. The married and oppressed woman is in fact nothing more an a bagworm (she lingers over the appropriateness of the name and the uses of "bag" in male slang).

The only answer, she says, is for the female to throw off the shackles of male myth and nature alike. Refuse to accept the Psyche role imposed by male mythic romantic notions. And (this is the radical part of her piece) refuse to accept the bondage of nature. Refuse the house. Refuse the role of egg layer and child bearer. Whether by knife or pill, circumvent the power of the ovaries. By force of will, grow wings, soar away into the starry night, fly away to the heavens of freedom, free of children, free of the oppression of men, free of the bondage of nature itself. And by your actions make Mother Nature herself over into Ms. Nature!!!

Need I say more? I think now I can finally get some sleep.

Spent most of the day setting up my experiment in a corner of the biology lab, a huge room swarming with glass tubing and green plants, insects and animals—even the special air conditioning can't remove the strong traces of jungle atmosphere, musk and droppings, the steamy breath of plants, the buzz and chir of the bugs and clicking beetles. I am still astonished by Collembola, the absolute ordinariness of his appearance and the extraordinary vitality of his presence, the spring of his walk, the vigor of his expression. He gave me a procession of twelve caterpillars, a supply of pine branches with which to feed them, helped me fashion out of quick-drying plaster a cylinder with fluting which roughly approximates the one used in Fabre's famous experiment.

Should I explain Fabre's experiment, or is it too familiar? Maybe very briefly, how the processionaries follow a thin silken thread laid down by their leader (a random leader, simply the first caterpillar in line) out from and then back to their nest, each caterpillar leaving a fine silken thread of his own, all of them forming a slim shining pale white trail along the way. Fabre set a group of them going round a large palm vase (or, rather, they climbed the vase, and he tricked them into following themselves around and around it). The caterpillars all faithfully followed their leader, each one of them both leader and follower, all of them going nowhere, around and around. For seven days they walked stupidly around the vase, eating nothing, always walking, going nowhere. Fabre was struck by "the lack of any gleam of intelligence in their benighted minds." In short, they are the perfect type of mindless Darwinian nature, life going nowhere with steady concentration, living beings bravely following their natural leader round and round that vicious circle when that leader is quite simply not there. Fabre's experiment is a favorite of Darwinians and reductionists who are seeking easy proof of the mindlessness of nature.

The answer is, of course, that they are not leaderless, but that each little caterpillar is himself the leader, able at any moment to launch out on his own, to lead all the others to safety. Each tiny caterpillar has the potential, given him by the very nature that seems to have doomed him to mindlessness, to become transcendent. And if they seem, as Fabre shows, incapable of making this leap on their own, then it is clearly our responsibility as the bearers of mind into the world to supply them with the necessary information and stimulus to make that leap from mindlessness and purposelessness to thought and direction, from worm to *Überwurm*.

Anyway, we made the plaster cylinder and, after some minor difficulties, succeeded in getting the small procession of twelve caterpillars crawling in a wavering line around the cylinder's rim. No tiny trail, after some careful rubbing, remains that could lead them down. Round and around they go. I shall let them continue their pointless journey until tomorrow or the next day (I must remember to ask Collembola how long he thinks I should let them go in order to establish the hopelessness of their plight, the mindlessness of their condition). Then I shall by intercellular communication alone instill them with the mental power to see their situation and to correct it. I shall give mind to the pine processionaries and bring them down to their feeding place (without, of course, any intercession of ordinary physical apparatus, stick, string, or tweezer).

I am confident that I shall be able to repeat my success with the spider in this controlled experiment under laboratory conditions. I have no doubts. I am filled with a strong sense of power and purpose.

Saw Sara Band at dinner tonight but resisted speaking to her, mentioning Fabre and article in the same breath, watching her realize the trap into which I have forced her, her rising panic and sinking despair. Instead, I ate alone. She did not appear to notice me either.

The others are like birds stretching out their wings to display their plumage or frogs ballooning their rubbery throats out into airy splendor. Six men at her table, and despite the stern presence of dour Dolgrum, all of them laughing loudly, waving their arms, talking at once, their noise echoing around the room like (again) a chorus of summer frogs, burp, boom, and harrumph. Cortapiedras, so clean shaven, so smooth, brushed, and combed, so polished that the light seemed to dance off him and dazzle the air.

And her face, always between someone's arm and someone else's shoulder, triangular, her red hair like some sort of dark flame, absorbing light, surrendering no warmth, her eyes hidden and expressionless behind large round dark glasses. She nodded at their jokes, never laughed.

I paid her no mind. Have come back to my room to read, relax, retire early. Tomorrow may bring real excitement in the lab.

Of course, no sleep. Only nightmares. Only book to read, since I had read Fabre, was von Frisch. So I read about bees, then put the book aside and drifted into an awkward and uneasy sleep, my hands clenched on my chest.

And dreamed of bees. The room full of bees. Buzzing and humming, dancing in a huge circle, wagging their wings and tails, telling me something, something I could not decipher. What could bees be telling me?

Then from the whir and confusion a hideous scene with workers driving the drones away from the queen. The drones battered and bleeding, almost wingless, their wings shredded down to the stumps. The queen an enormous bee, her eyes huge and black, her body, furry body, glowing deep orange, dark red. The drones buzzed horribly as the workers swept them away. Then the queen turned those horrible eyes toward me, to me, turned to me, her head huge and enormous, I could not run, felt numb, heavy weights pressing me down, the workers holding me, her huge head, her mouth, she began to chew at my face, my ears, she began to eat me alive!

I woke up, sweaty, both arms asleep on my chest from elbow to hand. I tried to fling myself up but could not rise, could not throw off their weight in the darkness. I struggled but always sank back, drowning in myself, my own dead weight. Finally heaved myself over, threw my legs out of the bed, knees hitting the floor with painful thumps, my arms dangling like lead sinkers by my sides.

Finally restored circulation, turned on light. Decided to write all this down, clear my mind of bees and dreams before I dare try to return to sleep. But I must sleep to gain a clear head, purity of mind, for tomorrow.

Slept late. Of course. Am noting this in an attempt to keep the shape and detail of this eventful and major day absolutely clear and fresh in my memory for the book. For posterity? At this yawning and stretching moment I can only hope.

The rest of my sleep was, for the record, dreamless. I seem calm and alert. I shall go to lunch and then to the lab. Will most likely see Collembola at lunch, ask his advice and assistance. And now to my toothbrush.

Can I write this down?
Has ever man been so sorely tried?

I think I can write it now. The sun is down. I spent the evening in the woods, far from the walls of my study, which I kicked and pounded until their yellow was scuffed and scarred and my hands red and aching, far from the society of men, far from that one woman, that bitch, that whore, far from the lab, from the green slaughter of innocents.

And now I am in my room. I am calm. I can think. I can write.

I went to lunch. Collembola was not there. I did find Juan Cortapiedras, who said that Collembola had been there briefly, had been quite upset about something, was seeking out Dolgrum to complain about something, something to do with Sara Band. And then, of course, her name mentioned, he swerved away from the subject and onto her. Had I made it with her yet? Had anyone? Promises that he would himself do so soon, that he would tell me all immediately, that I would in fact be the first to know. Good stuff, yes, good stuff. On and on. His eyes shining like jet black gemstones, a fire gleaming somewhere in their stony depths. I was almost nauseous with his intensity.

I excused myself and walked the graveled paths to the lab. I swung the green metal door in and entered the large room. Aware only of a strange and heavy silence, I at first thought I was alone. Then I heard the sounds of someone moving briskly about, someone humming, no tune, just a humming, steady and monotonous like that of a small child at vague play or the pointless droning of an insect.

"Hector?" I called out, sure that it must be Collembola puttering over one of his experimental arrangements.

But it wasn't he. It was she. Sara Band, her hair tied up in a bright (bilious) green bandana, in a green smock and pants, sweeping vigorously with a broom, a dust-pan dangling at her side, hooked to her belt like a slide rule or a pistol.

"Oh, Doctor Cotswaldo," she said, apparently surprised, with an edge to her voice, a slight one, not sharp enough yet to cut. That was to come later. "Oh, Doctor Cotswaldo, Doctor Collembola isn't here just now. Just me. Just tidying up."

I tried to say something, failed, stood there, my hands in my pockets, my feet probably fidgeting, probably scuffing the floor like some cinematic adolescent's, the urge to reveal my knowledge of her duplicity growing stronger second by second, my awkwardness in her presence (some residue, no doubt, of Juan's desire still burning in my bloodstream) keeping me there, keeping me silent.

She went right on.

"He was here though, though how he could stand it, I can't imagine. Actually I can—enjoying with typical male pleasure the mess he was making of a perfectly orderly situation."

Why she was so voluble when before she had scarcely said a syllable was beyond me. Nor did I understand, then, what she was talking about.

"So I cleaned up. It made him furious. Seeing a mere woman on his turf, invading his precious territory." She laughed, and the cold I had felt before in her presence knifed through me again. A clear crystalline little laugh.

I nodded, nodded only.

"Aren't you proud of me?" she went on. "Don't I win at least an M & M?"

I almost staggered. I may have leaned back into the door. But she turned and was gone before I could utter a sound, even swallow. I looked after her, green and small and (I admit it) shapely, as, carrying her broom and pan dangling, she walked across the lab and through the other door to the service rooms beyond. Only then, the room finally mine alone, did I realize what was wrong with it before, why it had seemed so particularly empty. The familiar and busy chir and whir of the insects, Collembola's various experimental insects, was silent. The room was quiet as a tomb or killing jar. Not a shrill or chitter.

I moved across the room, almost numb with a rising fear, to my plaster column. And it was, as I had feared, clean, smooth, dusted, and empty of life. Not a single tiny caterpillar marred its blank surface. Even the silken record of that small procession was gone. No pine boughs lay at its foot. Everything sterile and clean.

I stifled a roar of rage and ran across the tidy lab to Collembola's large glass terrarium, the one in which his pine processionaries had been making their explorations the day before.

And it was empty. Clean. Polished. Empty.

She had killed them all. I could feel it in the very air, vibrating with soundless intensity. She had killed them all!

I heard a sound behind me and whirled around. Now minus broom and pan, she was standing there, smiling at me. Again I was struck dumb, speechless, and doubtless slack-jawed.

"This place was literally full of worms," she said, calmly and with no little pride, "worms and bugs and litter. But no more. How anyone could have worked here is beyond me. I surely couldn't have, but now," and she paused and smiled, showing her small, even, pale teeth, "but now, I'm sure I can."

I haven't written in here for three days. For three days I have walked alone in the woods, eaten alone at meals, kept to my room from sunset on. For three days I have been so nervous and uneven in mind and spirit that I have not cared what I saw or did, scarcely saw what I was looking at or even looked at anything worth seeing. I have avoided the lab. She is, I am sure, there all of the time. Collembola has left ITS, left angrily, threatening all sorts of things. I don't know what Dolgrum said or didn't say. But the lab is hers now, and, for all I care, hers alone for the rest of the summer. I certainly shall stay as far away as I can.

I have been walking in the woods again. That and lurking in Austin's office, near mine but far enough away to avoid unpleasant confrontations should anyone (she) come looking for me. Austin has been away for the last week and won't return for another two.

I was going to describe things I have found and seen in the woods and by the bog, but I am drawn to describe that office briefly. It is a yellow study like mine. I think I call it an office (which I have been doing quite unconsciously) because he has moved into it so thoroughly, bookshelves along the walls, framed degrees, a picture framed and carefully hung by the window. The bulk of psychologists I find annoying and objectionable, whether luring you onto their couches of forbidden memory and pain or giving you vacuous grins and telling you how okay they are and you are. But Austin shows great evidence of mind, of curiosity, of thought.

I examine his books, the usual shelves of clinical studies, but others as well: Bergmann's *Meaning and Existence,* Dewey's *Experience and Nature,* even (!!) McTaggart's *The Nature of Existence.* The range pleases me: Wilson's *The Occult* by Becker's *On Justifying Moral Judgments,* Heisenberg's *Physics and Philosophy* alongside Velikovsky's *Earth in Upheaval.* His own books—*Homage to Edmund Husserl; Life, Being and Language; Miscellanies.* Lying on a table by the window (overlooking the woods, the bog) a copy of *Darwin's Bassoon,* the back bent as though he has read it, some annotations in pencil which I lack the courage to examine.

The picture on the wall: six stern psychoanalysts peering at the camera as though attempting to see into its inner recesses, Freud with his cane, a cigar in his fingers, seated clutching his hat tightly, looking almost as though he were ready to burst into neurasthenic tears; and on the other side of stern ancient Hall, close-cropped Jung, squinting at the camera, holding his hat delicately and carefully, glasses clipped to his narrow nose. If I should remove the photo from its frame and fold it precisely down the line of Hall's nose, Freud and Jung would meet face to somber face, beard to mustache, eye to eye to eye to eye. I am tempted to do it. What sparks would fly, the paper curling back like the fine gold leaves of an electroscope diverging with the charge of that old antagonism.

I am sitting in that congenial room now, the late afternoon sun warming the small window, gleaming off the table, the jacket of my book, the picture of Freud and Jung dimmed by its pleasant glare. The entire room, yellow walls and warm wood, glows in the sunlight. It warms me in some primal central way despite the sealed window, the whispering air conditioner. I shall turn into myself, into my memories, away from the buildings and frustrations of ITS and into the woods, the bog, the swarming vital natural world.

The path down to the bog winds through the vegetation, the

pines and persimmons and maples, the broadleaves and conifers, the sweet patches of honeysuckle and strangling kudzu, the undergrowth of bulging mayapples and shiny poison oak and ivy. Horned beetles doze the soil, rummaging for sustenance, steady and hard-shelled. Mole tunnels wrinkle the path, sinking with a surprising softness under your bootsoles. Birds whistle and chuckle in the leaves, invisible, always audible, occasionally startling the eye with a flutter and flurry, a quick winging away, a dart of blue or red or rufous brown. The heat of midday enfolds you even in the shade of the trees. In the clearings the sky lies hazily overhead, a dulled blue as though it were moist with the warm breath of tall trees.

You are alive in this living world, but it tempts you in its steadiness to surrender your mind, the edges of your thought, to its dullness, its enveloping physical malaise. You stir within yourself; you press out into this natural confusion; you focus it like an eye or the lens of an observing instrument.

A young rabbit, pale brown, a white fluff of tail, the eyes large and almost frighteningly open, still as a bush or tree, watching you: a small frail creature, the sunlight behind it. The light flows through the thin membrane of its ears; you can see the blood moving in the large blood vessels in those ears, the pulse and rhythm of life even in those delicate bunny ears. And then you see the ticks, three swollen pale gray blobs, leeched onto those thin ears, drinking out the life as you watch it. You start to think yourself into the rabbit, into that small round head, to urge it to you, to let you pick those repulsive suckers off and out. But it suddenly darts away, stung by your mind or startled by some movement of which you are unaware. The tall grasses tremble with its passing and are still. The sun sinks in the late afternoon sky; the tree leaves blink and stammer in your watering eyes.

You turn away. A dead bird, more a mash of feather and down than a real corpse, sinks slowly back to earth by your foot. The air is caught by the soil as the sun sinks down and down. A spider web ensnares your face. You brush it away with a startling violence. You shudder and are suddenly afraid. Not of spiders or of ticks, not of the sunning copperhead stretched like a curved bronze knife by the path, not of dead birds or dying rabbits. But afraid of the enormity of the task you have set yourself, which you demand of your fellow man. To give mind and meaning to this, to this mass of snarled being, of life and death woven like a tangle of vines, the sweet white blossoms almost lost in the choking leaves. You are afraid, and you run for home, for life.

It has grown dark in the study, and that dark has worked itself into my prose. I feel weary and weak. This friendly room seems now alien and dangerous. I must go back to my room, to my bed, to my dreams such as they are.

No dreams. None that I remember.

I am walking more and more. Good for my lungs. They buoy me up and bear me on. My legs no longer feel the swells and hills. Down to the bog, circling in through the high brush and wet soil, around it, narrowing my compass every day. Stepping occasionally into the water, concealed by the weeds and reeds, and limping back to ITS with a wet boot and sopping sock.

Bagworms, Sara Band's psyche moths. I doubt she's ever seen one. I am collecting a set of empty cases, former homes of male moths now flown away. Aided by Epps's *Guide to Familiar American Trees*, I am categorizing the materials of their construction: one made of the eastern spruce, the shell a brittle gathering of the four-sided needles, sharp and hard and somehow Nordic, spiky and gothic; another formed of red cedar, the flat faintly sticky brown leaves giving it a soft southern texture, rounded and classical; another, the home of a worm strayed away from conifer to wild cherry, the case an almost pathetic shanty of crudely cut leaves, like a tattered shawl pulled over poor shoulders. She probably wouldn't even know what they are. If I left them on her desk, she would probably squeal and mash their sturdy architecture, or sweep them with a squeamish notebook into the wastebasket.

The bitch.

I am so happy that I don't think of her anymore.

A wet dream last night. A reminder that I am still flesh as well as mind. I don't remember the precise terms of the drama. I felt as though I were in some soft cocoon or pressing into one. Flesh and flesh in a silken web, and then I awoke damp and dissatisfied. I must free myself from this necessity, from necessity.

I have it! The source of sweet revenge! I shall destroy her with the best weapon at my command. My own mind. The knowledge I have gained from my experiences with Cortapiedras. The power of sex channeled this time not into good work but into damaging disarray, hers, hers.

The plan: Dolgrum, the director of ITS, despite his apparent delight with Ms. Band, is a stern and puritanical man. He expects nothing but solid work from the fellows here at the institute. He is, I am told, easily shocked by rough language even when no ladies are present (the usual condition at ITS). There has been speculation, but mainly by Juan, about his doings in town on his frequent absences, but they are merely speculations. No proof at all has been offered. He is a cool and aloof man. He is the key to my plan.

I remember a comic *fumetti* that I read years ago. In it an idle young man, an office worker, while attempting by psychokinesis to cause a banana on the desk before him to peel, unknowingly causes a voluptuous secretary behind him to strip off her clothes. I forget how it worked out, but it and Dolgrum's grim nature gave me all the clues I need.

The next time Ms. Sara Band goes into Dolgrum's office for a conference, which she does from time to time, I shall manage to be in the next room, a small conference room adjoining his office with a pleated plastic folding door between. I shall tune in on her sexual nature, repressed no doubt but surely there, and I shall, by mental suggestion, by willing it, direct that energy to the front of her consciousness and by guiding it cause her to peel, to strip off her clothes in the director's very office!

Then, then, I shall be avenged!!!

I have won. And lost. Must every action be holonic? Is the real as absurdly confusing always as it has come to seem this summer?

The time came sooner than I had expected. Band and Dolgrum, alone in his office. And I, secreted in the silent conference room next door. I could hear them talking through the sliding accordion door, but I could see nothing, not even a shadow or pair of silhouettes. I had never before worked my will without the direct medium of sight, of visual connection, but I decided the stakes were high enough to press on, to risk failure and the feeling of foolishness.

I crouched by the door, listened to their innocuous chatter. Some conference. She complimented his tie. He spoke well of her dress, claiming always to have preferred that shade of green to all others.

I focused myself on her voice. I ceased hearing words, only the voices, the voice itself, hers. I tuned myself to the rhythms of her voice, and I began to think, slowly, carefully, coldly, thoughts the precise temperature and intensity of her own. "Strip off your clothes," no, nothing so crude . . . only sexual tension, I felt it in myself, rising, rising, the fury of Cortapiedras' sex, my own, hers (I am sure—hers). And I aimed it into her, into her voice, the shadow I could not see, the cool hard flesh of her body. Sex. Sex. Sex.

And then, knowing the climactic moment in the very sinews of my own crouched flesh, I forced the thought of stripping into her, a rape of will and spirit. Strip. Strip. Throw yourself at him. Tear the buttons of your blouse off in your frenzy. Pull down those tight green pants. The underclothes (how I wished I knew what they actually were, form and texture). Everything off, baring your teeth, cross to him, to Dolgrum, fling yourself on him, naked, naked, naked.

In the fury of this exercise of pure directed will, I fell over backward on the smooth carpeted floor. For a moment, I feared discovery, the shame of being considered an eavesdropper, a cheap voyeur. But then I realized that I had nothing to fear. The only sounds from beyond that plastic barrier were animal sounds, grunts and wet smacks, a growl, the sounds of territorial confrontation, the battering of Rocky Mountain rams, the snorting of sea lions.

She had done it! She had done it! I could still see nothing, but the sounds made everything clear. She had assaulted him. Sara Band had assaulted Dolgrum. I lay on the red carpeted floor, weak from the effort, my will thoroughly spent, listening to my victory, to Sara Band skewered on the spear of her own sexuality.

But the sounds went on too long. And with too much monotony. Breathings and shufflings. Did something (a foot perhaps) actually touch the pleated door right beside me?

I backed quickly away, scuttled across the red rug like a startled tree crab, crawled up the wall by the exit door, straightened my clothes, smoothed them, and went out.

I won. She stripped herself and threw herself at Dolgrum. I know she did. I know it. But instead of responding as he should have, of reprimanding her or leaving the office or even striking her, he responded sexually. That is the only explanation of the quality and duration of the sounds.

Did I accidentally, in the intensity of my concentration, in the absence of eye contact, impose that sexual explosion on Dolgrum as well as Band? Or have I simply misjudged him totally? After all, I scarcely know the man. He is just a stiff, flat image to me. We have never exchanged confidences nor even spoken seriously to one another. Could he have simply been ripe for the occasion, ready for her to leap bare into his eager lap? I must find out. I am whirling in doubt, sinking in confusion. Cortapiedras will hear all the gossip. I'll venture out to dinner tonight instead of ordering it anonymously delivered to my room. He will know.

No Juan at dinner. When I asked Miller where he was, he only winked a broad stage wink, nodded his head toward the director's table, and said, "You know." Dolgrum was eating alone at his table, no Sara in evidence. I certainly didn't know what Miller was winking and nodding about, nor did I particularly care. I'll stop by Austin's office and borrow a book from his shelves and read myself to early sleep. Then I'll catch Cortapiedras at breakfast. By writing these notes now at table, I have successfully avoided conversation. One advantage of ITS: even the appearance of work is respected by all.

By all but one, I should have said. The bitch.

Saw Juan coming out of Band's study as I was walking to Austin's. Tucking in his red shirt, straightening his yellow trousers, grinning like an ape. He may have seen me. I think he winked at me, or then again he could simply have been blinking. I ducked into Austin's.

The whore. She fucks them all. Like some kind of voracious spider. Juan. Dolgrum. Maybe Miller (his winks and nods?). Disrupting decent experiments. Driving a good man like Collembola away. Driving me half out of my mind. I probably had nothing at all to do with her taking off her clothes and throwing herself at Dolgrum. It was probably her own doing entirely. Probably wasn't even the first time. She wears that green jump suit or whatever probably just so her lovers can have easy access to her tail. Just zip open here and insert organ.

I raged. I circled the room in a tightening circle. I could feel the blood beating in my twisted face. My nails dug a path of grooves across each palm. Bitch! Whore! Slut! I cried all those names and more to myself, to the walls, the darkening room. The red sunset was turning its pale walls a deadly orange. I circled in it like a sick fish dying of whirling disease, spinning on my nose in a mad dwindling pirouette of pain. My throat filled with the harsh jelly of hate. I wanted to explode.

And then, suddenly, filling me with a terror that made my nerves race with electrical shock for minutes after, something did explode, with a terrific bang. Glass and bits of paper and wood showered me. The force of the explosion actually knocked several books out of their shelves, and it stopped me dead in my tracks. Electrocuted by the short circuiting of my own tension.

It was the picture of Jung and Freud on the wall by the window. It had exploded. Nothing had been thrown at it. Nothing was behind it except the injured wall. It had itself exploded.

I stood there in the gathering darkness, the orange room fading to a deathly violet, the water of my shocked nerves sinking in my body like draining water in an emptying tank. My knees felt wet and weak. I felt like settling to, even into, the floor.

I could hear footsteps in the hall, excited voices. I knew then in that deep purple room that I had caused that explosion, that my pent up fury and frustration had flashed out of my body, my raging brain, had smashed into that innocent photograph on the wall, had burst it like an egg, like a bomb. I had done it, and I was deeply frightened.

I managed to move across the room, to open the door, to move out into the brightly lit blue hall, to close the door soundlessly behind me. There was no one in sight. The search must have moved on down the corridor, around a corner. I realized that I was bleeding. There was blood on both my hands, no doubt on my face (there was). Sliced by the glassy shards of my own failure and frustration, bloody and empty, I slipped away, back to my room where I bathed and treated my ridiculous wounds. Where I am sitting now, absurd, beaten, afraid even to continue my work. What else will she drive me to destroy? What living creature will I explode like a firecracker because of her? Dare I even approach the living world in the state I am in?

I have returned to nature, to the natural world, to the woods and the bog. Chastened, humbled, no longer even sure of the correctness of my desire to give mind to blank matter. Perhaps it is better left alone. Or, at least, no longer sure that I can be trusted to do the job, even to begin it.

Am I in any way different from those slick frogs bulging and humping in the bog, slime-covered and squeaking, driven by no ideas but by blind frenzied impulse? I toss a stone into the scummy water at the bog's edge and watch them squeal and plop, scurry away through the green-webbed water, and I see myself, skittering across the floor in Dolgrum's conference room, creeping down the empty hall, dodging footsteps and shadows, plunging into my bed, sliding under the covers, and diving deep like a frightened child on a windy winter night.

What right have I to impose my mind on mindless nature when I seem unable to master myself, my own glands and juices, the frenetic pulsing of my own ragged nerves?

None. None at all.

But I have returned to nature, to the paths and underbrush of the ITS grounds, not so much to confront the facts of external being as to escape the facts of my own wretched self, unloved and unloving, ashamed to look Juan Cortapiedras or Dolgrum or Miller or anyone in the eye. Especially afraid to see Sara Band in her sleek green zippered suit. I know her secrets, her flaws, her weaknesses, and I cannot face her. So I shall examine the tendrils of climbing vines, the delicately arched paths of meadow voles, the cannibal feasts of my fellow frogs. I shall turn away from man (woman) to the landscape, and in that turmoil perhaps find the calm, the purity of vision, the understanding which I seriously need.

After you walk down the hill away from the silent buildings in the early morning, the leaves of the grass still pale and silvery in the slanting sun, the long shadows thin and almost transparent unlike their weary evening counterparts that lean so heavily the opposite direction—after you walk down the hill along the graveled path and enter the woods, a great silence as though the world were holding its breath, listening, watching for the sudden deadly move in the corner of the eye, the flicker in the ear, the faint scent of death. Still and ominous and terribly, terribly alive.

Tiny warblers plink through this awful silence, the sun filtering through the leaves to touch their golden feathers afire. And then you are by the bog, the steep hill behind you, circling the calm dead water, until finally you reach a nearly flat meadow, the weeds almost waist high now, steady and unmoving.

This morning I met a movement in those weeds, watched it come across the meadow, unwavering, steady, leaving a weedy wake like some land torpedo (have I used this?) aimed directly at me. It broke out of the weeds onto the path, a small (15 pounds?) beagle or small hound, a bitch, brown and black and white, the head mainly brown, the flat soft ears, the fairly small eyes dark brown, the nose damp black tinged with the pink of age. An old dog? I was not sure. She was a used dog, that much for sure, the double row of heavy black teats hanging uncomfortably under her belly, the weighty evidence of sex and birth and time.

She trotted right up to me, the brown and white tail wagging tentatively. I stooped to pat her head, to scratch behind her ears, and she looked up at me, those brown eyes filled with such extraordinary sadness that I felt the emotion flow through me, hand and eye, a heavy stoic sadness, surrender, acceptance, a sorrow of the very nature of things. I actually felt tears filling my own eyes. I understood there for that passing moment what it was to be alive, to be female, to bear the sagging bulk of your surrender to life on you not like a badge of honor but like the chains and weights of some ancient cruel prison.

I started to embrace the small dog, to hug her to me, but she broke away and trotted on down the path, her teats swaying beneath her, her tail wagging like a small white flag. I felt a confusion I have never felt before. I found a tuft of high ground, mashed down the weeds, and settled myself to write this, to attempt in the telling to see what I have seen.

That dog needed no infusion of my mind and thoughts, my feelings and values. She had a depth of life in her that filled me, or rather that drew me into her, into her experience, her knowing. Have I been coming at the whole question aslant? Is the answer to enter the natural world, to allow its cells to communicate with yours, to enter its flow rather than impose your patterns on it? It is true that my best results have been attained by attuning myself to some powerful natural force (Cortapiedras' lust, Band's perverse desires) and guiding that force, not by imposing thought on static nature.

This could be the breakthrough for which I have been searching, the moment at which all of the pieces of the puzzle slip suddenly together, the crazy chaos of color and shape become a peaceful if too brightly colored alpine scene. I must think this through. Stay here and think this whole thing through.

This day will go down into history. If I can capture it. I know I can't now, but I must get the shape of this afternoon down before sunset. I am afraid to wait until I get back to my room. I must try now.

But it requires a shedding of shame, of human limitation. How to confess something we have been taught from childhood (our own, the very childhood of the race entire) is evil, or at the very least is something to be experienced but never spoken of. At least in daylight or in a lighted room.

I sat in the meadow. I wrote in this notebook. I watched the day grow, the damp leave the grass, the grass stretch erect in the warmth, the buzz and dart of awakening insect life. The dog did not return although I thought of her, attempted to come to grips with what she had given me. And with the problem of how to analyze and ultimately to express what she had shown me. Who would listen? Perhaps an article, carefully phrased, the truth concealed (almost) in the language of the discipline, in the *Journal of the Association of Therolinguistics*. Then, after weighing the response (if any), a larger piece, one for a different audience, in *Mind* perhaps. Then the book, one designed to reach an audience as large as *Darwin's Bassoon*'s, but one carefully designed to blunt all professional attacks before they can be made.

I note all of this as evidence of my frame of mind. I was in no emotional state, was being totally (even coldly) practical. My imagination, in other words, was functioning completely as an adjunct to my reason; my emotions were behaving solely as a battery, a source of neural energy for the rational process.

The meadow had, for all intents and purposes, disappeared. I was aware of the rising heat, of the light, a vague sense of green grass, blue sky, glare. Then I became aware consciously of something at which I had been staring blankly for some time: the green weeds were glittering with flecks of gold, scattered over the stalks and mottled leaves, moving little but catching the light, a meadow of tattered leaves and fool's gold.

Once aware of what I was seeing, I tucked notebook and pen into my small pack and waded into the thick grasses, prospecting for gold. And what I found were clumps of *Popillia japonica*, Japanese beetles, on almost every leaf and rare blossom. Doing what, as far as I can tell, they always do. Eating, cutting the leaves, slicing small holes in them, chewing, swallowing (digesting, defecating), and they were screwing. Beetle on beetle. Their golden backs gleaming in the hot midday sun. Screwing on every leaf, male mounted firmly and to all appearances permanently on female, no wild mammalian humping, just this golden connection, beetle on beetle by beetle on beetle by beetles and beetles and beetles.

I have never had such an awareness of sex before. I have never (consciously) been in the presence of such a massive orgy before. A wide level field, a meadow of tall still grasses, stippled and studded with bright beetles, silent, unmoving, doing it.

My first response was laughter. In tune with my earlier thoughts of publication, I thought of a book title: von Frisch could have his *Dancing Bees*; I would sell rings around him with my *Balling Beetles!*

I leaned closer to one weed, some common plant with broad dull leaves, bearing no name that I knew but carrying a full load of orgiastic beetles. One leaf held fully seven pairs in silent ecstasy. I peered closely at it, wishing that I had Collembola here to explain the parts, the processes I was observing. Almost unconsciously I felt my way through that visual connection into one of those pairs of beetles, into the male hanging on the female's steady back.

And suddenly I felt the most overwhelming, explosive, shattering feeling of my entire life. I literally staggered back, fell onto the ground. From my ninth (?) year on, I have experienced literally countless orgasms, with and without partners, asleep and awake. All men have. But never had I experienced anything like this. I lay back on the ground, my whole body numb, every muscle in my arms and legs fibrillating wildly, an invisible tremble that jangled on and on and on. And I knew that this was the beetle's orgasm, that this blast of sexual fury was going on all around me thousands upon thousands of times, and that this furious orgasm would last not for anguished seconds but ecstatic hours!!

I could not stand it. I rolled over on the weedy ground, dragged myself to my knees, and crawled away, crawled through the high itchy weeds, the golden backs of beetles glinting all around me, by my arms and legs, over my head on high wavering stalks.

I finally gained my feet and staggered to the path, ran down it, fell twice to my hands and knees, paused finally here by the bog, seated myself on the flat stone outcropping by the willow where I often settle and write, paused and caught my breath, calmed my nerves, settled my soul.

I was right. This day has given me that. Not to impose myself on nature, but to think myself into it, to join it. To guide it from within. I could have guided even those thousands of beetles, but they caught me by surprise, a sneak attack on my sensibility. But even then, out of control, in a wild nose dive, I found my answers and the clue to my rewards. The rewards are enormous. I still cannot fully face them. I can't bring myself even now to write the whole of what I felt in that field. No man alive (possibly no man who has ever lived) has ever felt a tenth, a hundredth, a millionth of what I have felt. No Casanova, no liver of secret lives. I was a god incarnate; I was more than a god, I was a world, a universe, the cosmos.

Sitting in the combed pebbles, the smooth warm white and tan stones spread over the patio behind the central building at ITS, crouched like a yogi, cross-legged, in a pool of light, yellow light from a yellow study spilling out into the moonlight, mingling on these stones, on me, my blue clothes almost green, on this open notebook—the moon round and almost full (tomorrow, full), pale and pure. Love. I love the moon, each stone, each particle, each wave of light, the notebook, the pen, every vibrating cell in my body, in the night, in the world.

Don't dare go in, leave this night, the ecstasy which still fills me. I am literally trembling, trembling from head to toe. I think I understand for the first time McTaggart's contention that (I have it memorized, no need to go to Austin's study and the black volumes there) "when love reached or passed a certain point, it would be more good than any possible amount of knowledge, virtue, pleasure, or fullness of life could be." More good. More good.

I am in love. I could hump the moon. I finally understand the odd behavior of pet dogs, how sometimes they go mad and hump everything, other dogs, cats, human feet, chairs, everything. Not mad. Not mad. In love. Loving.

I can't believe it. My nerves are still in full spasm. I am full and emptying at once. I want the trees, the buildings, every frog in the bog, the moon, the stars. I want to hug the earth, the whole earth. I want to fuck the world.

Feel foolish. Want to stop. Want desperately to go on. Am outside the dormitory building. Her light is on. One shadow on the blind. Alone. The moon is swollen, glowing in this hazy sky. The ground, the hard earth, is like a dream. I am going in. I will surrender. I will be firm. Am going in.

I have been running all night, down the hill and into the trees. Into trees themselves. I have a cut on my forehead somewhere. It has stopped bleeding now. Maybe oozing, but not running wet down over my eyes. I can see. The dawn has come and caught me down and done for. Sitting by the bog. Trying to write it all down. The comedown. The fall.

I knocked on Sara Band's door. Pale green door, like mine, like everyone's. She opened it, dressed in her usual green pants suit, shiny and clean, her red hair, green eyes, pale face. No make up. No surprise.

"I've been expecting you, Cosmo," she said, stepping back to let me enter. "Wondering when you'd drop by."

I may have said something, thought something. All I remember is walking in, turbid with stirred emotions, shaking like a loose roof in a storm.

I heard her click the door shut behind me, heard her say, no mockery in her voice, something else: "Come to give me a Big Time?" I turned to her. "Or maybe another Bit-O-Honey?"

I felt my hips tug forward, my cock tauten of its own volition. I looked for the cold green of her eyes, but their pupils were swollen, the eyes full and dark and black and deep. I reached out for the ice of her touch, took her shoulders, the cool nylon of her suit, drew her to me (or did she draw me to her?), was kissing her lips. They were not cold, were hot and moist and opening.

She stepped away, unzipped her jumpsuit, pulled it back from her chest, tiny breasts, huge nipples. How can I write this without falling into the language of cheap sex, into pornography? I don't know that I can. Could anyone?

I remember this: my surprise at her nakedness, my surprise at how she did not seem to care whether I was clothed or bare, even my jacket still on, my surprise at how hot her body was, at how quickly she had manipulated me into her, at how smooth and firm her skin was, hard body, grinding at me, holding me down when I struggled to pull away, to gain control.

We lay on the floor, turning and turned. She moaned, a long low cry, not a moan, a sound, a cry, a call. I tried to focus my eyes on her face. All I could see was green, a reflection in the moisture of her face of those cool walls, pale green, and those enormous black eyes, like buttons, those huge black eyes looking at me, turning to me, looking at me.

She pulled my head to her, making that low low sound, twisted it around and began to nibble, to chew on my ear, her mouth wet, and the sharp teeth biting my ear, my head.

I struggled to escape. She gnawed at my head. I fought. I hit at her. I punched at her stomach. I threw myself back and away from her. I felt no more sexual pressure, not even release of pressure. Only fear of those huge hungry black eyes.

I ran away, ran out of that room, down that long hall, out of that building, down the hill. Battering from tree to bush to tree. Splashing the edges of the bog. Battling my way under the moon, away from the melting moon, into the trees. Finally here. The sun stealing up on me. I can't stand it anymore. Must get on, get away.

I am in the bog. I am calm, writing this down so that I can throw it, if need be, to the shore, an agonizingly few feet away. I am calm. I am in the bog. Quicksand. It is sucking me down. I struggled against it for a while, but now I am calm. I am writing this to help me wait for someone to come this way, to pull me out. There are plenty of fallen tree limbs about. I can see five or six. Six. I can see six from here. I am on my back. My feet are gone. But from the knees up, I am still relatively free. I don't seem to sink much so long as I don't move too much. I ran right into the bog. The first thing I knew was that I heard the frogs squeaking and plopping. Are there snakes here? I am in the bog.

I will will myself free, impose my will on the very molecules of this bog. I will start slowly, focus on the water and scum until they become as solid as muscle and skin. I will flex them then like an arm, push myself up and out like the contents of a swollen pimple! It will work! It will work!

Why am I hung here? Not floating like a vessel on the stream of time, but bogged down, half earth already? My head aches with the force of my thinking. This scummy, this goddam bog lies here, this ooze, this stinking goddam ooze. Why isn't it solid? *Contact! Contact! Who* are we? *Where* are we?

Sinking. Surrendered. Poor Moe, betrayed hound, Dark's sunk dog, brother in name and flesh. I was going to raise your bones, make them clatter across the surface of this bog like you doubtless once skittered, all comic toenails and eager motion, across the kitchen floor or waxed hallway. Poor dog. I've come, am coming to join you, a set of old bones, frog food, in the slimy bottom of this bottomless bog. No hope. No one is coming here. I will never know what I could have done. What Austin wrote in his copy of my book. Who Sara Band really is. The rain and fog will ruin even this notebook, pulp it back into the mushy ground from whence it came. No way to win in this mindless mess. No way.

Sunk deeper in, half in. It is pleasant now, the warm bog water, still, silent. It holds me like a mother. I am floating like a sigh, an unfocused memory easing down in amniotic delight. Mindless. Wordless. Content.

Do I know what it is to love others? Did I ever know McTaggart, understand him, feel him? To love others. To reverence myself for loving them.

I am holding to solid things now. To Juan Cortapiedras. To Hector Collembola. To Sara Band. Yes, to Sara Band, neither cold nor hot, just Sara Band, slow time, soft fact, hard truth. The walls of ITS. These trees guarding my blue sinking self from the hazy yellow sun. The even surface of this deadly bog, green shading to dark green shading to brown. The frogs bulging their steady ways along under its surface. The birds skipping the green flat surface, beaks open for bugs, for death, for life.

Something stirred in the weeds on the shore. My heart jumped for a second like a startled frog. Whatever it was, groundhog, fox, weary small hound, it went away.

I am holding to solid things, their being there enough, letting them be, being there and here.

This is all so absurd. Not philosophically. Simply silly. I am eating a Zero bar, last thing in my pockets, living for a short time longer on the last paper-wrapped remnants of my ridiculous past.

Oddly enough I am not drawn back to my past. A drowning man, I am not reliving my life. No need. It's done. And the world is still here. The trees are buzzing with life, insects sawing the rhythm of the spheres. Mayflies skimming the damp air, the moving light. That is enough.

I am sunk too deeply now even for help to help.

What strength I have's mine own.

Myself. My self. Do I survive in others' minds? In Sara Band's? In her anger, her laughter, her scorn?

Remember Broad's saying once that a human being is a long event. My long event grows shorter. The world within, without. The sun has crossed the treetops, is sinking, too.

My mind has returned to me, has reached out into the world around me, this bog, this sinking. I do know now what I missed all along. I am sharing all this life, second by long second, brief moment. My event is long, long as all men, all memory, long as the world, as all time. My flowing is that larger flowing; my stillness is that larger calm.

This living world did not need my mind. It had it all along. Yours, too. All of us. Self and self and self, infinite, endless, immortal. Self and self.

Am nearly under. Back first. Will soon be breathing bog. Must toss this book ashore. Am floating in a music of blood, yellow light, a harmony of cells singing. Cosmo Cotswaldo joins the cosmos.

As if he'd ever been away.

I am walking on water. I am sinking in sand. In either case, both cases, I shall, late or soon, be swimming in air.

Their Wedding Journey

It seems days that they have been traveling across this powdery expanse of smooth white snow, but Lorna knows that it cannot really have been that long, cannot have been very long at all. The country church where the wedding is to take place is, after all, only a couple of hours' drive from home.

It must be the silence, she thinks to herself, that is making time slow down or speed up or whatever it is doing. The road is unplowed, but the snow is so powdery that the tire sound of Syd's new radials is muffled completely. In the rearview mirror outside her breath-fogged window, she can see the clean arc of treadmarks stretching out behind them into the level distance.

Syd seems completely lost in thought, doing a deal or thinking about the bride's fresh young attendants whom he will hug and try to kiss with characteristic enthusiasm. Lorna has come to dread the occasional wedding to which they are invited, not because Syd makes a spectacle of himself—that he would never do—but simply because of that enthusiasm, that discreet expression of a dormant sexuality that she never sees at home in front of the children or recently even when they are alone or especially in bed.

The children are quiet, too. Tiffany and Michael began the trip noisily enough, poised in the back seat in their crisp clothes but soon quarreling and pinching each other, huddling to think up new ways to amuse themselves and annoy Lorna. Syd never seems to notice them at all unless at play one of them runs loudly into him or breaks something in the house that he has defined as his. But now they are quiet, too, staring out at the snowscape, their breathing as steady and quiet as if they are in a trance or a dream.

Lorna, tired of their squealing and giggling, had set them to counting things, cows in fields, bunched together against the winter wind, or dark birds on the power lines, or trees with their leaves still on in the bare, snowy fields. But not long after Lorna woke up from her nap or dizzy spell or simple lapse into automotive reverie, Tiffany complained that there was nothing left to count, and all Lorna could see when she looked was a snowy smoothness and distant irregular crenellations of hillocks and bushes buried in ice and snow. But before she could think of another game to entertain and quieten the children, they had lapsed into a stillness as profound as the silence in the snowy fields around them.

The insidious warmth of the car heater and the steadiness of Syd's driving make Lorna drowsy again. She wipes at the steamy window beside her with a tiny embroidered handkerchief, careful not to smear the glass with her bare hand and incur a sarcastic comment from Syd. She can barely make out the distant, steep flank of a white mountain before the glass steams over again, and for the briefest of seconds, she thinks she sees high, high atop the tiered white precipice two distant, gigantic figures, side by side. Like a bride and a groom, she thinks, as if some local Ikhnaton had decided to erect on the nearest mountaintop a vast monument to the perfection of his marriage to an unchangingly beautiful and perpetually sensitive and loving Nefertiti. I must already be dreaming, she thinks, as with a slight jerk and a contented sigh she does drift into an unclouded sleep.

Syd is not thinking of the bridesmaids he will see and meet at the wedding reception later this afternoon. He does always enjoy kissing the flushed faces of eager brides, and he does enjoy looking at and maybe even teasing and touching the clusters of brightly colored maidens who stand in lively prelude to the bride in the receiving lines. But he knows that if he does start thinking about them now, of young women sprawled easily over armchairs, bare lithe legs dangling appealingly from articulate knees just edging out from under skirt hems, or young women in crinkling bright gowns all in a row, their smooth small breasts tantalizingly veiled as they nod and bow in the stir of passing guests, knows that if he does start thinking about them now Dr. Dick might stir and shift in his trousers and Lorna, who never misses a thing that he ever wants her to miss, would notice for sure and as surely misunderstand.

He drives at a steady rate through the powdery icing of the snow, the road almost obscured but steadily arcing to the right around the flank of the mountain. He does not want to doze off or feel dizzy the way he did a few miles back, not even for a second, so he begins to think methodically of marriage in general, and of his marriage to Lorna in particular.

He remembers how desperately in love and how clumsily lustful they had been on their honeymoon, how after the bellhop had gone away into the Niagara night, they had gone back out into the hall and he had attempted to carry Lorna over the threshold into their rented room. They had been giggling furiously and were nervous of being observed, and Syd had started forward before he had Lorna completely lifted in his arms. As she had shifted and attempted to balance herself, he had tripped over his own foot and pitched forward into the doorframe, spilling Lorna onto the thick pink rug of the floor and splitting his right front tooth off practically at the root.

Syd stirs nervously in the car seat as he remembers the sharpness of the blow and the terrible finality of seeing his own tooth lying in his palm after they had crawled around on the rug until they had found it under the tip of the heart-shaped bed. There had been no blood and, oddly enough, no pain; only a jagged stump whose contours felt to Syd's obsessively probing tongue exactly like the shape of the abandoned rock quarry where he and Lorna had only the summer before fumbled and thrust their way out of frustrated innocence and ultimately into wedlock.

A funny thing, Syd thinks as he has so often thought before, the effect that broken tooth has had on my life. His thoughts move back again to his and Lorna's honeymoon, how they had stopped crying and laughing at the broken tooth, how Lorna had put it in her purse along with their traveler's checks and the xerox copy of their marriage license "just in case," and how they had rushed each other's clothes off and climbed onto the satiny slick red heart of the bed and begun to make love. Syd feels Dr. Dick stir as he remembers, but there is no holding back now as his memories rush over the precipice of his defenses like raging Niagara that night.

They had made love five, six, maybe even seven times that night, and always as they had rushed toward climax together his tongue had raked itself raw on the ragged contours of the stub of his tooth.

The next morning, dim and damp, the falls rumbling beyond the restaurant window, his tender tongue had plowed its way through the mushed eggs and bacon in his mouth to find the gap of the tooth, and he had had to rush Lorna back to their room, doubled over and feigning a stomachache to conceal his passion, and they had done it again and again all that gray day, Lorna once running her long tongue into his mouth and pushing his own tongue away from the tooth until she bucked and winged her away into an orgasm more powerful than any that had preceded it.

Dr. Dick is bent and shoving hard against Syd's fly as he glances guiltily to his right at Lorna, but her head has lolled against the window as she is apparently dreaming, her eyelids fluttering and her lips parted slightly.

Syd forces himself to think of his many trips to the dentist, of the needles and drilling, of the looming root canal specialist whose breath had been as foul as the tomb, so terrible that Syd had gagged and nearly choked right in the examination chair, of the curved apparatus filled with pink putty that had been forced up onto his gums, and finally of the shining and perfect new tooth that had been screwed into place in his mouth. As Syd goes over the terrible experience, Dr. Dick begins to subside and just in time as Lorna is stirring and sitting up.

Syd has no idea how long she has been asleep or exactly how far they have traveled while he has been thinking, but he does allow himself one more thought before settling back completely into the tasks of his driving. He thinks how since that tooth was repaired, he has never truly enjoyed sex with Lorna, not even the nights when he had sired Tiffany and Michael. He thinks, with some confusion and a great deal of wonder, how just when he achieves penetration, his tongue always seeks out the tooth and how when it finds the smooth German porcelain of his expensive crown all his pleasure seems to slide away on that perfect surface. I always complete my task, he thinks to himself, but I never enjoy it. And suddenly he feels empty and afraid and completely alone, as though Lorna and Tiffany and Michael were as unreal as their unnatural silence and as empty of meaning as the white untraveled road that stretches mindlessly before him, so he shuts off his troubling thoughts as completely as if they were just another gadget on the car which could be switched off with a mere flick of the driver's wrist.

Lorna has been dreaming of the giant figures she thought she saw through the fog on the window on the mountaintop.

She has always been a fan of gigantic statues. She had wanted to go to Mount Rushmore on their honeymoon, but Syd had insisted on a traditional wedding journey to Niagara. She has always felt that Syd would never have broken his tooth and brought them endless bad luck by dropping her on the threshold of their marriage if only they had been protected by those massive carved guardians in South Dakota. She buys and keeps every magazine she sees that features huge statuary on the cover: a *National Geographic* with the Sphinx dreaming in the desert or a cracked Olmec head tilted in the jungle, a Newsweek with stony Ferdinand Marcos staring unfinished at a land in turmoil, or a science fiction magazine with tiny awed explorers staring up at an overwhelming alien visage looming over a purple plain. She insisted that they buy a VCR, ostensibly so that Tiffany and Michael could take advantage of educational tapes, but really so that she could purchase her own copy of *North by Northwest* and visit the Mount Rushmore of her desires with Cary Grant over and over again.

So it comes really as no surprise to her that she has been dreaming of two enormous statues of a bride and groom poised high above her, and that in the dream she floated right up to them and hovered like a bird or mundane helicopter before their huge, placid faces: the bride's, veiled and distant and calm; the groom's, showing no emotion at all, staring straight ahead, the lips tight over his doubtless perfect teeth.

The dream had no plot nor even any distinct end. The only thing she is sure of is that it was completely unlike her earlier dream or swoon before the car and the snowy world became so silent. No, this was just a dream, a lovely dream with no unsettling qualities or even a hint of strangeness, just beauty and wedding wonder.

She looks at imperturbable Syd staring ahead at the white unmarked road and, over her shoulder, back at the two silent children, so clean and still, so distant in their own worlds in the back seat. It is almost as if she does not know them, her own babies, so far away do they seem.

She thinks back to that moment of giddiness or brief slumber before she had become so estranged to her surroundings. What a unique and special moment, she thinks, but one that seems strangely familiar. I can almost imagine what I looked like as it happened, she thinks, as though my amazed face were huge and perfectly carved in lasting stone, that dizzy moment held for the contemplation and awe of centuries to come. I must still be asleep, she thinks, if I am capable of such thoughts, and she shakes her head and begins examining her dress to make sure she hasn't mussed it in her sleep, for surely they must be nearly there.

And then, as bright and fresh as though it were happening at that exact second, Lorna suddenly remembers when she has had a strange experience like that before, remembers it precisely and exactly.

She and Syd were already in their traveling clothes, their wedding clothes safely in her mother's care, Syd's cutaway to be returned to the rental store and her white dress to be folded and pressed with sachets in crinkling white paper and reverently interred in a brassbound trunk in her mother's attic. They were standing together behind the wedding cake, facing a roomful of laughing friends and relatives and absolute strangers invited by their respective parents. They were holding a gleaming knife over the white three-tiered wedding cake, smooth and white and encrusted with sugary white decorations, doves and bells and looping wreaths of white roses. They were smiling and holding the long sharp knife over the surface of the cake while cameras flashed and clicked and whirred around the room.

It was then, just then, that Lorna felt the room blur for a second, felt her head spin, looked down at the surface of the cake as though to steady herself visually since she could not release her grip on the knife to put her hands down. And she was sure that she saw, just then, at that moment, a road in the middle of the wedding cake and a tiny car plowing its steady way across the powdery icing and even, she must have imagined, four tiny figures sitting silently in the tiny car. And just as she began to lean down for a closer look, she felt Syd's hand moving the blade of the knife down, and together their hands sped it down and into the cake and through the car and into her reverie. Everyone was cheering and laughing as the flashes split the room. And then everything was all right, and it was her wedding day, and she was pressing a large, uneven piece of crumbly white wedding cake into Syd's laughing mouth, smooshing it into his gleaming teeth, and she never thought again of that momentarily unsettling vision until this moment.

Lorna gasps and looks at Syd. He does not notice, is peering carefully through the windshield at the road ahead, at their unfaltering progress across the empty landscape. The children are still silent, and the flat world around them still and unchanging. Lorna is almost frightened, but she notices, stretching ahead of them on the familiar surface of the road, that now a single pair of tire tracks is preceding them, leading them toward the pleasures of the wedding before them. She feels a sudden warmth, a great and unyielding affection for Syd as though something has come full circle, a longing for him such as she has not felt for years, perhaps not since those delirious first days of their honeymoon. She glances around quickly at the children, who are both staring out of the windows at the monotonous snowy landscape, before she reaches her hand over to Syd's thigh, feels the muscular tension of his foot's steady pressure on the accelerator pedal through her fingers. She wants to speak to him, to say something that she has never said to him or to any living person before, but the silence of the car holds her in her own silence. She squeezes his leg, and just as Syd's startled face begins to turn toward her, she feels suddenly dizzy again, as though she were lifting out of her body and settling quickly back into it again.

Lorna senses Syd looking directly at her, feels his muscles tighten as he touches the brake and starts to slow the car in the treacherous snow. She senses that Tiffany and Michael are straightening up in the back seat, beginning to lean forward toward her. She has a sudden sense of terrible loss. Her eyes are a flutter of darting lights, the whole landscape seems to be flickering and shimmering as high above the car something huge flashes once and begins a terrible descent.

Syd and Lorna react to the burst of applause that greets their cutting of the cake by smiling, giving each other yet another kiss, and raising the clotted cake knife aloft in triumph. Lorna is blushing now after a brief moment of shy paleness. As they prepare to make the second cut amid the chatter of cameras and the hooting of friends, Syd allows his eyes to pass down the row of bridesmaids each at that moment prettier than the other, but Lorna looks only up at Syd. She squeezes his hand, and he turns his dazzling smile directly and only to her, but Lorna looks through and past the perfection of Syd's smile, past the room full of friends and well-wishers, past this singular moment in time to where the future stretches out before them like a smooth white road curving indefinitely into unending days of delight.

2

WAY DOWN YONDER

The Adventures of the
Butterfat Boy

Waiting for the Butterfat Boy

His left cheek was pressed flat against the tile floor in such a way that his tongue, fully extended, had he wished to extend his tongue or to do anything but lie there and wait, would have been able to tip lightly the flat white side of the tub. He was lying in his shame and could allow no thought but one to enter his reeling brain, could only say, over and then slowly over again, "Soon the Butterfat Boy will come and I'll be okay again." His fingers opened, stretched full length, tried to pull him across the floor, but failed. A bubble of air, long traveled, came forth then from his mouth, and he moaned once, rolled onto his back, and went completely out of focus.

Lunch

The motorcycle was running well. One tire was onion smooth, and the gas tank lid was held in place by black and tacky friction tape, but its roar was stunning and the cars he passed often trembled and nearly darted off the road and into the passing fields, almost all bordered with white fences. He had a pink, round face, plump little hands that scarcely covered the handle grips, and a leather jacket that was not black, but pink, the kind of pink that made him visible for hundreds of yards ahead and behind, as visible as the motorcycle's ruptured muffler made him audible. The motorcycle was red.

Hunger was by this time, for he had been on the road nearly ninety minutes since his last meal, which itself had been primarily bologna and bread, his central thought as he leaned into the wind and toward the cars he passed, showing his flat yellow teeth to the open faces in the receding windows and the back of his bulging pink coat, too. Hunger and the woman, whose lunch he had in a paper sack in the tool kit with the one greasy wrench and the plier (or, half of a pliers), that lunch liberally laced with a philtre which the Fat Lady had assured him would have astounding results, his own hunger and the woman, these filled his thoughts as he sailed, inches off the pavement, over a knoll and into view of EAT, a sign, and below it a gas station, a '47 Ford, and a tall man in a khaki shirt and trousers pumping gas into the Ford, or at least pretending that he was, for as soon as the red motorcycle skidded across the drive and to a stop in front of his door, he pulled out the hose, clamped it back into the pump, and walked over to the then silent motorcycle.

"Help you?"

"No, sir," the plump, pink boy replied, "I just felt a little hungry and thought . . . "

"I'll fill her up for you while you eat."

"Well, no, sir, I just . . . "

The tall man lifted the boy off the seat and, with one hand already opening the orange framed screen door, pushed him into the station and was back pulling the taped gas tank lid open as the boy discovered that he was not alone. Three men in blue denim bib overalls and white shirts, all paint-splashed in white and green, were lined up along the counter facing him. They were all chewing with deliberation and in unison.

"What'll you have, sonny?" came from behind them, and then, too, came a thin woman in a gray dress and laced shoes, rubbing her hands down her narrow hips and then down again.

"I was just a little hungry and . . . "

She was opening the top of the red drink cooler as he spoke, leaning in, her dress pulled up behind as the three painters' heads all turned to see her varicose veins, and emerging with a dripping bottle of cola which she, after closing the lid, opened and set down on the lid along with a curved, paper-wrapped disc, then turning and saying, flatly: "Moon Pie and RC."

The boy's eyes were open very wide, circles within the larger but just as round circle of his face, as he said, "I don't . . . " but could say no more, for the screen door slammed behind him and a familiar voice said, "That'll be two dollars," as the woman repeated, "Moon

Pie and RC," and the boy could only say, "But," as the man dug into his, the boy's, pocket and pulled out his billfold, counted out three dollars, saying, "That'll take care of your lunch," and pushed the wallet back in and, with some care, buttoned the pocket flap down, and still the boy could only say, "But."

"Have your lunch, boy," the tall man said with a jovial hand on the boy's shoulders.

"Looks like he don't take to Moon Pie and RC very highly," the woman said as she hammered the cap, which she had fished out of the cap box on the side of the red cooler, to the cautious accompaniment of the painters' eyes, onto the bottle and returned the Moon Pie to the rack.

"Don't like our food, huh."

The three painters watched silently.

"Well, sir," the boy said, "I never . . . "

"Well, boy, if you don't like it, we ain't agoing to make you eat it. No, sir, we ain't going to do that."

The woman had returned behind the counter when the tall man took the boy by his coat collar and belt, lifted him to the tips of his toes, and danced him to the door, kicking it open with his boot and bouncing the boy out onto the greasy pavement by his motorcycle. The pump hose was once again nuzzled into the Ford. "No, sir, boy, we ain't agoing to make you do a single thing that you don't want to do," the man said as the screen door slapped shut.

A Quaint Pair

The woman was enormous, at least five hundred pounds, and she seemed even larger because of the neatly dressed man arranged on her lap, his feet, the shoes carefully having been removed and placed on the floor next to hers, on her knees and his head cushioned somewhere between her breasts and the top fold of her belly. Both of their heads turned suddenly to the right where a thumping sound began and as soon ended beyond the door there, and the fat woman began to laugh, softly at first and then harder, jiggling the little man on her lap up and down, his ugly face split too with laughter, until he began to bounce and turn, the two of them roaring finally, the dwarf dancing over her lap like a water drop on a hot griddle, until, their laughter subsiding into giggles and then stopping, his head was on her knees and his feet wedged under her breasts and into the cloth covering her fat, this causing the laughter to start again, the little man bouncing crazily up and down and tears rolling over the bulges of the fat woman's face.

Over the Mountain

The motorcycle's roar had changed in pitch but not in volume as it had started the long climb up the mountain. There were fewer cars on the side road which led to the mountain, so that the pink-faced boy had reached his maximum speed for most of the trip. Although he was drawing nearer and nearer to the woman, his thoughts were more and more centered on his hunger. For the last two miles, climbing steadily up the mountain, zigzagging back and forth, he had been writhing on the saddle and had even groaned in pitiful harmony to the motorcycle's roar.

Suddenly he went under a stone bridge and was at the top of the mountain, wreathed in clouds where a moment before he had been in bright sunshine. Baffled by the fog, he slowed and bumped to a halt near a stone water fountain which bubbled in silence even after he stilled his engine and paused in the quiet wind soughing through the pine boughs and shifting the cloudy fog about his head.

He climbed off the motorcycle, propped it against the fountain, and, after taking a sip of the cold water, wandered off in the fog. No cars passed on the mountain road, and he was alone. He bumped into something which proved to be a wooden picnic table, and he was then overwhelmed by his hunger. He began to cry, for he knew what he was going to do. Images of the woman, dressed, undressed, moving, lying still, whirled around him faster and thicker than the fog. Tears dripped on the saddle of the motorcycle as he opened the tool kit and tugged out the paper sack; he began to yowl as he stumbled back to the picnic table, and actually blubbered as he opened the sack and spread its contents before him, two sandwiches and an oatmeal cookie. The woman's face, mouth open, tongue darting in and out, eyes wide and glazed, hung before him as he tore the wrappers off and stuffed the sandwiches in his mouth, chewing hard and moaning in his throat. He shrieked aloud and pushed the oatmeal cookie in with the rest; all of the food tasted faintly metallic and even gritty.

A uniformed figure was suddenly standing opposite him in the fog, sinister, as, whimpering, he started to his feet and ran backward to his motorcycle. The figure was shouting at him as he cranked his motorcycle, which caught easily and suddenly.

"Hey, buddy. Hey, you, clean up this trash."

But he was away, roaring and backfiring, rolling into the downgrade, out of the fog and into the sunlight, the valley gleaming rich and green below and before him, a crazy grin on his face, and the town where she waited almost under him as he pressed forward, down onto the handlebars, and picked up speed, going down, down, down into the valley.

A Face in the Window

The sheer cliff of the tub side loomed over him, and above it, the impossibly high wall, and in it, far over his head, the window, as far as the peak of Everest and as difficult to attain, but he decided to try, pushed himself over on his belly and, after a long pause during which he could hear crazy laughter beyond the door, up onto his hands and knees, then hooking one arm over the edge of the tub and then a leg so that he was astride the tub rim and then standing up, a foot in the tub, the other on the floor, his hands pressed to the wall, his head to the window. His breath spread a cloud of vapor on the glass before him, and, impelled by some memory beyond recall or specific statement, he scrawled a tiny face into the dampness, two arched eyebrows, a pair of questioning eyes, a crooked nose, and a mouth open in surprise or wonder. His finger moved to sketch a circle of head around the face, but the vapor was diminishing too quickly; already the right eyebrow was gone and then the right eye. The cheeks were disappearing, the left eye; the nose faded slowly and only the shocked mouth remained when he stepped back, bumping into the wall and sliding down into the dry tub, three words forming on his lips, unuttered, "The Butterfat Boy," as he glided flat into the tub, one leg dangling over the side and into the room.

The Assignation

The motorcycle was parked, the nickel in the meter, and the boy, who by then was trembling all over, sweat icing his pink brow, was feeling most particularly the need for a men's room. A girl in tight shorts and a halter made from a man's wide and obsolete tie walked past, brushing lightly against the boy's hip, and he leapt forward, his face flushed, dashing past the astonished farmers and businessmen on the sidewalk, across the street against the light, and into the town hotel, his pink coat winking out of sight through the door and into the musty gloom.

Once in the men's room, shaking violently, unable to open his fly, he tugged his pants violently down, just as the stream of pale urine began to pour out. Only after several minutes did the shaking subside and was he able to pull has trousers up. An old man, toothless and bald, sat in the corner under the frosted glass window, whittling at a mop handle, a small cushion of shavings already around his feet.

"You must have quite a bladder there, sonny."

But the boy was gone, the doors still bumping back and forth as he reemerged into the light, seeing her then across the street in the drugstore, seeing her notice him, and then dashing back into the hotel, flinging the doors of the men's room open again, this time managing his fly, and filling the urinal once more. The old man's jaw fell slack as the boy zipped up and ran back through the swinging doors. He folded his knife, brushed the shavings off his trousers, stood up, propped the mop against the wall, put the folded knife into his pocket, crossed the room, and reached the street just in time to see the plump boy dash out of the drugstore across the way, waving his arms and shouting after a black Dodge which was pulling away from the curb, a hard, pinch-faced woman at the wheel and a young woman of about twenty (twenty-five? thirty?) seated beside her, neither of them noticing the noisy boy in the pink coat and the greasy trousers.

The boy ran down the street, hopped on his motorcycle, kicked its engine alive, and, with a bellow, spun out into the street where the red motorcycle slid onto its side, flinging the boy off and into the opposite gutter while the motorcycle spun slowly around on its side in the center of the street, its engine still sputtering, its rear wheel spinning, touching the street just long enough at a time to keep the machine revolving. As the plump boy got up, poking at himself for broken bones, a small boy in sneakers and blue jeans ran out of the gathering crowd into the street and up to the turning motorcycle, snatched the gas tank cap off by its taped binding, and dashed away whooping. The plump boy, a shoulder of his pink coat ripped open, limped over to his motorcycle, then dribbling gasoline out onto the street as it turned, and moved to the saddle, but just as he reached out the wheel gripped the pavement for an instant and the motorcycle spun like a roaring top just released from its string. The crowd laughed as the boy leaped away, but then they were amazed, even the white-haired, waddling policeman who was shouldering his way through them, as the boy jumped again, was on the moving motorcycle and away with a sputtering bellow up the street, smoke swirling from the exhaust, obscuring everything but the glow of the receding pink jacket.

Revelations

The fat woman had, at first, laughed at the suggestion, but then, as the dwarf stood on her lap and continued in a low whisper directly into her ear, her laughter stopped and her ears flushed and, once, she had to move the dwarf's foot quickly from where it had wandered and back to her massive thigh. Finally she agreed, and then, with mounting enthusiasm, she grasped him under the arms, lifted him out in front of her, and turned him around before her eyes. She began to hum a low and rumbling tune as she placed him on his back on her trembling belly, her fat fingers probing at the buttons of his coat, his fingers assisting as, first the coat, then the trousers were tugged off and tossed to the floor; then the white shirt and finally the underwear, tiny, even tinier in her huge hands, and immaculately clean, until he lay naked and aroused in her lap, her hands gliding gently over him.

"Why, you're as hairless and smooth as a baby," she said and raised him up to her breasts, his hands stretching for the buttons on her dress as her kiss half-covered the side of his twisted face.

The Confrontation

The sun was already low over the mountain and the mountain's shadow approaching the turrets of the stone house when the motorcycle weaved across the road, the gravel shoulder, and onto the grass of the lawn where it coughed and became silent as the boy slumped forward in the saddle over the open gas tank, dizzy and drunk with the gasoline fumes which had nearly smothered him for the few miles from the town to this house, her house, a trip made maddening by fleeting glimpses of black cars which had lured him down side roads only to become Pontiacs or Plymouths and once even a Kaiser, luring him away from this house and the woman who had looked at him in the drugstore with horror, who, as he had tried to explain, had run past him as her companion, hard and forty with steel-rimmed glasses and a black hair bun, had elbowed him hard in the stomach and he had felt, for the third time in five minutes, again the need for the men's room but had run out after them and had only then, as the sun was already low, found the car sitting in the drive of the turreted house.

The house was dark and silent, and he could hear his heart beat as he staggered across the lawn and up the steps; it seemed abnormally fast and he still feared that he would wet his trousers. His knock sounded hollow and somehow foolish, and he was turning when the door banged open beside him, a gray face over a black dress appeared in it and shouted, "He's here, Emily, hurry, hurry!" and he heard another door bang at the rear of the house. As he wobbled back down onto the grass, he heard a car start and saw the black Dodge, the same two figures in it, spin out, spraying gravel behind it on the lawn, into the street and, picking up speed, down the road.

The boy stood quietly, his eyes open and glazed, until he heard the voice again, this time right beside him, saying, "Here, Emily, I'll hold him, hurry," as her bony fingers clutched into the glowing pink of his jacket. The boy turned to see another woman, fire in her eyes, advancing toward him, squirting a tiny stream of liquid into the air from a large needle, and then turning to him. In the distance, he heard a siren, even over the old ladies' screams, as he pushed the one holding him into the other who was still waving the needle in the air, ran his motorcycle across the lawn as it coughed into life, and roared down the street from side to side, turning finally into the shadow of the mountain.

Discoveries

The pink coat seemed indecent in the room, which was scattered with clothes, a tiny dark suit coat, the billowing sheet of a dress hanging from the curtain rod and down over the window. It was so pink and the Fat Lady's flesh was so sallow, blue veined like a road map left floating on a vacation lake, faded but still lined. Her breasts were unbelievably huge, even in relation to the rest of her, with massive brown nipples swelling from them. Her face was blank and she was moaning; fat folded her privates into decent seclusion, but the dwarf, naked and smooth, ran around her on his bowed legs, poking at her with his tiny silver-knobbed cane, poking her as she trembled and moaned.

    The plump boy crossed the room quickly, moving beyond their notice into the bath, opening and then closing the door behind him. The trembling had finally subsided during the long walk through the night from where the motorcycle had finally run out of fuel. He emptied his bladder again, this time with no audience, and turned to the window. He could see the two trucks behind the motel; one of the trucks had burned out its clutch coming over the mountain the week before.

    The boy puffed his breath on the glass to blot out the scene and was not too surprised to see a face appear, arched eyebrows, startled eyes, crooked nose, and mouth open to scream. He watched it as it began slowly to disappear, and then, as he heard a shrill animal cry from the room behind him, he slumped to the floor in such a way that his tongue, fully extended, had he wished to extend his tongue or to do anything but lie there and wait, would have been able to tip lightly the flat white side of the tub.

The Road

A MODEST FINAL CHAPTER FOR THE
SOUTHERN LITERARY RENAISSANCE
WITH RESPECT TO
ELLEN GLASGOW, T. S. STRIBLING, STARK YOUNG,
DUBOSE HEYWARD, ELIZABETH MADOX ROBERTS,
CAROLINE GORDON, MARJORIE KINNAN RAWLINGS,
WILLIAM FAULKNER, ALLEN TATE, THOMAS WOLFE,
ANDREW LYTLE, HAMILTON BASSO,
ROBERT PENN WARREN, JESSE STUART, EUDORA WELTY,
TENNESSEE WILLIAMS, CARSON MCCULLERS,
PETER TAYLOR, ELIZABETH SPENCER, TRUMAN CAPOTE,
AND FLANNERY O'CONNOR
&
WITH A WINK AND A TIP OF THE HAT TO
ERSKINE CALDWELL AND RALPH ELLISON

Prologue

In spring of youth it was my lot
To haunt of the wide world a spot
The which I could not love the less—
—E. A. Poe

It was a gentle spring, warm with still skies and alive with peepers. That year it had rained only lightly, but the field rising to the hill behind the grandfather's house shimmered with pale and new green life, the trees filling and the grass growing tender in the morning sun. Even the dust from the narrow dirt road seemed to hang low over its own boundaries, not yet spreading out to smother the grass and the porches and closed parlors of the big house as it had all the last summer and the ones preceding, especially those since the first automobile had bounced and hee-hawed down the valley only a few years before.

The sun was still low over the round hills across the road before the house, winking the windows on the second floor above the sloping porch roof, and the mists had not entirely risen from the pasture and the branch which ran between willows, rare rowans, and wide oaks across it. The grandfather was standing alone on the lowest porch step, dressed in white, his vest buttoned, hatless and white-haired, a cigar slim and dark in his fingers, watching the easy progress of the dawn, the sifting of the mist, and then, in a clatter and erratic roar, the arrival of his motor car, polished and steaming, bouncing up to the steps, coughing to a halt, and puttering out just as he raised the cigar to his lips.

"Tom, God blast you," he said, "you lazy darky, you have stalled that machine again!"

The old colored man at the wheel bowed his gray and woolly head in shame, not even attempting a defense, humbly surrendering to the knowledge of his wrong. The grandfather puffed slowly on the cigar and then stepped down onto the grass, across to the car, and, as he climbed up and into the rear seat, said, "You, boy, come here and crank this thing."

Two boys appeared at that moment, the one popping from the front door and out onto the porch shouting, "Grandpa, Grandpa, wait for me!" and the other suddenly crawling from under the front steps, black and smiling, his teeth bright and "Yassuh" perking and repeating from his lips as he ran to the front of the motor car. The first boy, a small pale lad, tidy and shining in his best clothes, a black string tie around his soft collar, ran to the car and clambered up onto the seat beside his grandfather, as the colored boy, watching the driver of the car for his signal, stationed himself by the cranking lever.

"Now, Uncle Tom?" he called out, with a flash of teeth, as the driver turned to the grandfather, who nodded and puffed again on his cigar. The little boy in the rear of the car leaned forward in anticipation as the driver called out, "Now, Rastus," and the small black boy stooped to his task.

He spun the crank heavily over, once, twice, and then with a bang and wild roar once again, when the engine caught and spun the crank suddenly backwards, yanking the little boy down and under the car. He reappeared in a second, his left arm dangling and crooked, a tooth missing in the twisted rictus of his mouth. Hopping up and down, his arm flopping and the skin of his face pulled tight and yellow over his grinning skull, he skittered and teetered to the steps, where he was soon smothered up in the dust of the car's departure.

"Sonny," the grandfather said, the smoke of his cigar swirling back into the car's billowing trail, "that boy's got a natural sense of rhythm."

The little boy was very pale and frightened in the noise and movement of the car, and he sat very close to the grandfather and stared at his clasped hands, watching neither the passing green countryside nor the impassive back of the driver's woolly head.

The car moved slowly up Slote Valley toward its northern neck — a fertile valley, stretching north and south, a long oval separating the low hills, itself divided by a narrow ridge, Clytter's Ridge, which loomed behind the grandfather's house and split it from the western part of the valley and the colored community there. The two halves of the valley mirrored each other, roughly equal in size, both with a branch of the same stream named with Biblical thoroughness by the early settlers, Gihon on the west and Pison on the east; the two halves were alike, one black and one white, one with small weathered houses and the other with the grandfather's large, white house, New Garden, but in nature alike, green, rich in soil, and quiet in the vital spring.

The little boy huddled by the grandfather, who finished his cigar and snuffed it in the carton of sand by his foot, as the car bumped its way, a cloud of dust in the growing day, up the valley, across Pison ford, through the upper neck and out onto the newly paved road leading into the county seat. When it finally paused, it banged into the curbing of whitewashed wooden railway ties and jolted the boy and the grandfather up and into the back of the front seat. They were before the courthouse, a square white building with a green cupola and the Confederate soldier, stone erect on his pillar, looking south toward Slote Valley and beyond to the lost land.

"You, Tom," the grandfather hissed at the driver as he stood beside the car and held open the rear door, "you black devil," and then he could add no more as two ladies passed, smiling and fluttering hellos, on the walk. The old negro hastily began to brush off first the grandfather with a tiny whisk broom, shoulder and back, lapel and knees, and then the little boy, a quick and dusty flitter up and down, following the two of them up the steps but not into the open doors and the dim, dry halls.

The small boy clung to the grandfather's coattail and hung close to him, peering around him at the dark walls and fat men with their cigars and red faces, all laughing with the grandfather, none of them appearing to notice the small face with its open eyes and mouth, the tightly clenched hand on the white cloth, or the skinny legs, naked and very fragile in those adult precincts.

"The big day," they said among the laughter, and, "the suspense," big laugh, "is killing me," and, "That old Coon is shaking so hard in there you can hear him rattle," and, with great guffaws, "They're so pale we oughta call them 'whiteys' instead of 'coloreds.'"

The little boy began to relax in the laughter, feeling the force of the grandfather's laughs shaking the coattail, but then they moved on, the two of them, away from the laughing men and into a small office, sun pouring through its windows onto the one desk and the floor and a group of standing figures, black and white.

A hand tousled the boy's hair gently, and he looked up, not far, for the figure was bent with age onto a cane, at the wrinkled face of a very old colored man who was saying, "Hello, boy, how is you?" and the boy replied automatically, "Just fine, Uncle Abraham, and how are you?"

"Tolerable, just tolerable," the old man answered, never looking away from the boy's eyes, his dark brown hand trembling on the smooth head of his cane. "I got the epizooty something terrible today, and it's a long road to town." He gave all signs of going on, but then turned away and walked slowly to a cluster of colored men, two of his sons and some of their friends, all of them from the other side of Clytter's Ridge in the west of the valley, turned away as the enormously fat white man behind the desk began to speak and the uneasy silence in the room became an attentive one.

The fat man's head was bald, but it was covered by a damp handkerchief, knots tied at its corners to help form it to the round smooth head; his face was red, as red as the men's in the hall, but he was not laughing. The sun splashed around his bulky figure and onto the wall behind him where a newly framed photograph of Herbert Hoover hung, that face in its high stiff collar familiar even to the little boy, who had seen it each day of the preceding autumn on the small brass-rimmed button which the grandfather had screwed carefully into his lapel each crisp morning.

"Gentlemen," the fat man began, his round fingers thumping arhythmically on his desk blotter, leaning forward, circling the room with his earnest gaze, "we are here, as you know, to announce on my part and to hear on yours the final decision of the County Road Commission as regards the paved road to traverse Slote Valley north and south, whether it is to pass east or west of Clytter's Ridge. Am I not correct?" He paused to mumbles of assent and a shuffling of feet from the colored side of the room. "Is there anything further you might be wanting to say before I announce our decision?" His fingers continued to tap their erratic tattoo.

The grandfather cleared his throat, and the little boy watched him speak in awe. "I think there is very little to add that we have not already made abundantly clear. I only wish to express my total confidence in our County Road Commission and its distinguished chairman," as the fat man nodded his head, the knotted handkerchief flapping at its corners, "and to assure all here present that I and my family and neighbors shall abide cheerfully and wholeheartedly by their just decision." A brief spatter of applause startled the hot air and subsided as the little boy clutched the grandfather's coat again, this time with pride and a sense of ownership.

"Why, thank you, Colonel Edwards," the fat man replied. "It is your kind of confidence that makes the sacrifices of public service seem worthwhile." Then he turned in his groaning chair to look out the window at the dusty square and the shimmering heat dancing over the paved street. "And you, Mister Coon," he said over his shoulder without looking back, "have you anything you wish to say?"

The old colored man looked around the room, turned his faded and tattered hat around and around by its dusty brim, and could only say, "Yassuh, your honor," and then, "yassuh, it would surely be a pleasure to be able to sit on my porch and watch them automobiles go by."

The other colored men looked as one at the floor, their heads bowed in unison, as the white men in the room all laughed, not harshly as they had in the hall, but in tones the little boy recognized from the times he had said clever things to his aunts when the family had gathered together for Sunday dinner. The old colored man smiled wide and broad and said, "Yassuh, it surely would indeed."

Then the fat man spun abruptly back to his desk, picked up a sheet of paper and read it out: "On this third day of April, 1929, the County Road Commission expresses its intention to extend the paved county road numbered 666 south from its present conclusion through Slote Valley and"—here he paused long enough to stare around the silent room—"east of Clytter's Ridge."

His voice was drowned out in hasty talk then, and the little boy could not follow the conclusion of his reading for all the distraction of hand-shaking and the movement of the grandfather's coattails as he turned back and forth to the men near him.

"Gentlemen, gentlemen," the fat man was saying as he stood up and thrust the sheet of paper reversed out onto the desk before him, "I must request a little silence," and then as the hubbub settled down, he added, "Will the spokesmen for both halves of the valley please sign this paper on the dotted lines?" as he unscrewed his large fountain pen and made small black *X*'s by the sides of two lines.

The grandfather stepped forward and took the pen, signed the paper with brisk bold strokes, and turned, holding the pen out, to the old colored gentleman. The little boy could see the large name, ADAM LEE EDWARDS, glistening as it dried on the first line, and he watched as the old man traced the hesitant letters of his name under it on the next line, large wobbly letters but clear ones: A. COON.

The fat man took the pen back from the old man, and the grandfather then shook the old man's hand warmly, saying, "Uncle Abraham, you may not believe it now, but this is a fine day for us both." Then the little boy's interest wandered to the rows of black and yellow bound books arranged in large shelves along the wall, and he only idly paid attention as the grandfather took his hand and led him back through the crowded hall and congratulating men to the door and the bright outside.

"Sonny," the grandfather said to him as they paused on the curb, watching the old chauffeur and a small black town boy coax the open touring car back to life, "I envy you your youth today as much as you must envy me my years." He paused and struck a spurting match, lit his newly unwrapped cigar, and puffed slowly as he flicked the match away into the street near the little boy struggling with the crank where it burned slowly down in the hot sunlight. "You will live to see the results of my efforts which have culminated on this April day."

The engine burst into a roar as the little negro stepped back barefooted onto the hot match, yelped once and started hopping wildly around on one foot, holding the other high in both hands. The grandfather shook his head slowly from side to side and flipped a penny to the sidewalk near the black boy's pounding foot as the little white boy climbed up into the back seat of the car and settled down for the long road ahead.

I

But if with travel, toil and pain
Worn out, we're hastening home again,
Our fancy has a knack ...
—R. H. Wilde

It had been a long, hot summer, and Abel Boyd drove the rented car fast, whipping the hot air in the open windows, making the plastic bag on his suit flap and snap in the back seat. He had driven slowly through the town, wishing in the slow heat that the car agency had had a model with air conditioning, around the square and the courthouse, which still looked the same as ever except for a billboard by the front door which listed in large and movable red letters the toll of traffic fatalities in the county that year. Cars and pickup trucks of all ages and sizes were parked aslant all around the square.

And he had turned south as the Confederate soldier indicated with his gaze and was soon out of town, onto 666, gaining speed and wind in the hot, still afternoon. The hills seemed blurry and lower as he had expected them to, the woods more sparse and scraggly, but the mouth of Slote Valley seemed oddly wider, worn and loose around the hard, heat-dancing highway. The road cut a flat gash down the valley, unhealed in thirty-eight years, raw and red, clay banks and dusty shoulders.

The white marks darted under the front left fender, becoming briefly double, yellow and solid as the road veered left of Clytter's Ridge, and then returning to a steady broken white, straight down the valley. Abel Boyd saw the lines and the road, but he was watching the hills, higher to the left, and the ridge on the right, swollen and huge for one second and low and small in the next, slipping in and out of focus in the sun's glare. The car crossed a small bridge so quickly that he could not see any water between the scrubby creek banks. And then, suddenly, much too quickly, on the right, back behind a low cinderblock building painted bright fluorescent pink, the old white house stood, neglected and falling to slow ruin.

Abel Boyd quickly braked the car down and turned into the gravel parking lot before the pink building which blocked the old house from view straight on. He parked by a 1947 Ford with its rear end jacked up, enormous wide tires on its rear wheels, and a foxtail hanging limp and matted from its radio antenna. He got out of his car, slammed the door behind him, and stared up at the sign painted in large and clumsy letters across the front of the building over the one large window and the door:

HONK-E-TONK
(CURB SERVICE, JUST BLOW)

He walked over to the screen door, crunching through the loose gravel, tugging out the wet seat of his trousers and smoothing down the wrinkled back of his black and white striped seersucker coat, pulled the door open by its tin Red Cap Ale crossbar, and walked with the slap of the door into the dim interior.

The first thing he saw as his eyes adjusted to the dark was another sign, this one on the wall over the mirror behind the bar, beside the usual fly-specked WE RESERVE THE RIGHT TO REFUSE SERVICE TO ANYONE sign. It read, WINSLOW "PUKE" GUFFAW, PROP., and under it a big man was grinning and wiping out a beer mug with his damp apron. "What'll you have, old buddy?" he was saying, and Abel Boyd looked nervously around before he answered, sure then that the big man was speaking to him, "A Red Cap Ale."

"Shit," the man answered, still grinning but setting the mug on the counter bottom up, "I ain't got any. Haven't for years."

"Schlitz?"

"None cold."

"What've you got, then?" Boyd's voice was trembling despite himself. He stared at the black bird tattooed on the big man's left forearm, bare to the rolled-up sleeve above the elbow.

"You like my bird?" the man said, and then, leaning over the counter, winking to someone sitting farther down the bar, flexing his pale, freckled muscle so that the black bird on it fluttered convulsively and unconvincingly, "That's a buzzard, and you know what a buzzard'll do if you get him mad? Huh? Well, I'll tell you. He'll puke on you" (big laugh, two bursts, haw, haw), "and" (thumb over his shoulder toward the sign) "that's me, Puke Guffaw, biggest damn buzzard in all these parts!"

He laughed harder then, his eyes flicking up and down the bar. "We got good old Dixie beer." And, turning his back, he fished into a bright red cooler tank, produced a dripping bottle bright with the Stars and Bars, turned back to the bar, popped the bottle's yellow top, flipped the mug before him right side up, and poured Abel Boyd a mug brim full of good and foaming Dixie beer.

"That'll be forty cents cash."

Abel Boyd fumbled in his coat pocket, the nylon change flap torn and frayed and the coins jumbled in with his keys and a tube of mints, put a quarter and three nickels on the bar, and raised the mug for a tentative sip. Guffaw moved away as he drank, and he set the mug back down on the bar with relief. Alone, sitting in a dingy dive, hearing but not listening to the talk in the room, Abel Boyd watched the faces and forms in the mirror directly opposite him across the bar.

First, there was a face looking directly into his, neither an uninteresting face nor very interested, ordinary, the hair neat, graying unevenly, the eyes wide and ingenuous, belying the fifty years that had shaped the face, begun its almost imperceptible sag and wrinkle, no excessive features, even nose, steady mouth, chin neither large nor receding, in need of a second shave that day, shadowed, the clothes rumpled, seersucker jacket, tie and damp collar, not a face to hold a gaze, his own, his very own, familiar from every day but so unobtrusive as to appear to belong even in this bar, this foreign place.

And then, the rear of Guffaw's close-cropped and balding head set square and thick onto the bulk of his back, and two more faces farther down the damp bar. A boy, long nosed with a little chin, pink cheeks, a mountain face, pale blue eyes, pimples, narrow and alert, and an old man, hollow cheeked and toothless, wet eyes and thin hair, gray, both with beer and both talking to Guffaw.

No one else at the bar. A teenage boy and girl squirming in a side booth, giggling, the boy in white, paint-spattered bib overalls, the girl in orange shorts and a red halter, wrapping her pink mottled legs around the boy's under the table, and in another booth under the window, two heavyset men in blue overalls, round faced and squinty eyed, laughing and talking to a fat woman in gingham and cheap plastic shoes, the uppers composed solely of peeling white straps, Madge, she was called, loud and often.

And that was it. Outside and through the streaked window, cars flashed by on the road. On the wall by the door, across from the large Wallace poster, the familiar and belligerent little Confederate refused to forget. Abel Boyd looked down at his beer and the settling foam; he began to listen to the room.

"You boys," this was Guffaw, less loud, conspiratorial, "coming to the meeting tonight?"

"No," the boy.

"Going to be a good one, I promise you. Hot speaker coming in all the way from Danville."

"No," again the boy, "got a load tonight. Don't get them that often anymore that we can afford to pass one up."

"Shit," Guffaw.

"Shit, shit!" the boy. "Not since those goddam yankees have been coming up six-sixty-six in those damn black Lincoln limousines. Hell, John Law wouldn't no more stop one of them big-ass Lincolns than they would kiss your fat behind."

"No, no, I know," said Guffaw, "I just meant that it's too bad you can't come to the meeting. That's all."

"Hey, Puke," from the booth under the window, "Madge here..."

"Now you shut up, R. J., you big loose mouth you," Madge, laughing, shrill with mock terror.

And R. J., continuing, "Old Madge says hers is bigger than your whole fist."

"Now, R. J." big squeal, the sharp smack of a slap, laughing.

"Is that so, Puke?"

"Shit," said Guffaw. More laughs.

"I tell you one thing though," the boy was saying, his voice a thin drone like a locust's, steady through the interruption, "I got one thing on those yankee bastards."

"What's that?" Guffaw.

A howl of almost hysterical laughter from the booth under the window.

"I know six-sixty-six like the back of my hand. Better, in fact. You ain't never going to catch me missing that damn curve down there where that last yankee bastard wrapped himself around that tree. You see that, Mr. Guffaw? Whooee! Hot damn! That dude come tearing up the road like it was the Martinsville 500 with the law hot on his ass and smacked right into that tree. Bent the front of that damn Lincoln cross-eyed. Oh man and God alive! What a crash! Bet you could hear it all the way up here. Kaboom! Whiskey all over the road, and the law sliding and squealing up, and that damn yankee in his fancy suit hanging up in the tree like a damn scarecrow. Whee doggie!" A slap on the thigh, and the old man wheezed in his beer.

"Hey, Madge, did you ever see a black one?"

Guffaw: "There's more than just that guy hit that tree. Hell, somebody gets killed on that curve seems like every other week."

"Hey, Puke," from the booth under the window, "old Madge here says that she allows as how black ones is bigger and better."

Guffaw, then, loud, angry: "Now you shut that shit up in here. You shut it up or I'll kick your asses right out of here."

In the embarrassed silence that followed, Abel Boyd swallowed the last of his beer, glanced once again at the gray face before him in the mirror, backed away from the counter and off the stool, and walked down the room, not looking around, almost invisible in the quietness of his passing, past the boy and the old man and the booth under the window, past the other booth where the boy and the girl were huddled over the table and the remnants of their cheeseburgers, her freckled back split by the red halter, and their voices audible as he passed.

Hers: "If poppa finds out I was here with you, he'll whip my fanny red."

And his: "Will he take your pants off?"

And Abel Boyd passed through the swinging door marked MENS and into the smell of urine and stale disinfectant. Lit by a small bare bulb in a ceiling socket, the dim yellow room contained a commode, seat up, a grim white basin, and a rusty green towel dispenser. The walls were stained and covered near the commode with familiar graffiti: IN CASE OF ATTACK CRAWL UNDER THE POT ITS NEVER BEEN HIT YET and WATCH OUT THE CRABS CAN SWIM UPSTREAM HERE and the usual organs, drawn quickly and huge, speaking for themselves in their blunt simplicity with no slogans or captions.

Abel Boyd made water and turned to wash his hands. On the wall over the basin, in the pale rectangle where once a mirror had hung on a single bent nail, someone had copied out some verses in pencil and a small tidy hand:

> Maud, with her venturous climbings and tumbles and
>   childish escapes.
> Maud, the delight of the village, the ringing joy of
>   the Hall,
> Maud, with her sweet purse-mouth when my father
>   dangled the grapes,
> Maud, the beloved of my mother, the moon-faced
>   darling of all,—

And, in the same hand, JUST ASK AT THE BAR.

Abel Boyd cranked the small handle on the side of the rusty towel dispenser, but it was empty and he had to dry his wet hands by rubbing them on the sides of his shirt under the coat. After checking his zipper, he shouldered his way back through the door and walked past the booth in which the teenagers had been sitting. They were gone, leaving only two greasy paper plates, crumpled napkins, and paper cups still containing Coke-stained ice. Madge and her two friends were still laughing in their booth, their embarrassment apparently forgotten, and Guffaw was leaning on the bar still talking to the boy and the old man.

"You'd be amazed," Guffaw was saying, "at the trouble I have to go to just to get my robe cleaned. It's that satiny green cloth, so I can't just throw it in the wash here."

Abel Boyd walked on by them all; no one noticed; he walked out the door into the bright air, the heat, and the parking lot. The screen door banged to behind him, and a big diesel truck, heavy tractor and Fruehauf trailer, blasted by on the road, General Lee shaking General Grant's hand on its shiny side. The sudden wind of its passing whipped dust into Abel Boyd's eyes, and he turned away, walked past his rented car and around the edge of the pink building.

A narrow, dusty path led him past the building and the rusting hulk of a burnt-out car in the weeds, past a smaller building, also of cinder blocks and painted pink but with tidy white curtains in its windows, led him through brambles and flowering vines to where he could see the big house, still white but long unpainted, columns and blank windows, paneless and hollow on the upper floors, boarded clumsily over on the lower. New Garden, old at last, empty and forgotten, locust and sumac trees sprouting with tropic urgency along the walls, a jungle of weeds and tangled honeysuckle, no doubt alive with rats and snakes, hollow, barren, and useless, one last graying ghost in the shadow of Clytter's Ridge, held from total shame only by the concealing shield of the Honk-E-Tonk.

Abel Boyd stepped off the narrow path which led on back toward the low ridge and picked his cautious way through the weeds and snares to the first wooden step leading up to the porch and the boarded front door. As he put his foot on the step, he heard the unmuffled blat of a motorcycle on the road behind him, and he hesitated a moment before putting his full weight on the foot and the step. The wood gave way with a snap when he did, and he almost fell face first into the remaining steps. Small animals scurried squeaking under the porch.

He carefully extricated his foot from the broken step and turned around to make his way back to the path. The afternoon was waning toward evening, the sun moving down toward the ridge. Abel Boyd made his way back to the path and began to walk away from the road and the Honk-E-Tonk, away from the pink outbuilding, and past and away from the ruin of New Garden, following the dusty trail as it wound into the shadows of the trees and up the easy flanks of Clytter's Ridge.

II.

Honoured and old and all gaily apparelled,
Here we shall meet and remember the past.
—R. L. Stevenson

Out of the trees of the ridge and onto the two smooth and hard-packed ruts of the dirt road, Abel Boyd felt the present glimmer and fade, for he was in the past, his past, the green grass in the late afternoon sun, the small frame houses far up the road, clean with smoke spiraling in thin lines up from the kitchen stoves, no sounds from the highway, the clatter of a towhee in the leaves behind him, and ahead from a pool of shade and a wide green oak the opening and tentative trills of a mockingbird's evening song. It was August in Gihon bottom, a dog was barking somewhere to the left, and Abel Boyd, still in seersucker, felt himself in knee pants and bare feet, knowing that Noble was in the tall weeds, snuffling at rabbit paths but ready to come, tail awag and loose ears, at his slightest whistle. A little boy, free on a summer afternoon with his dog, walking to see Uncle Abraham, to roust out Rastus for a game of catch, warm in the summer air and the dust powdering his bare legs and puffing between his toes.

Just ahead, from out behind the first small house, a voice was singing, a woman's, and past and present in truth fused to become one:

> Ol' Molly Har
> Watcha doin' dar?
> Runnin' through de cotton patch
> Hot as I can tar.
> Rather be here
> Dan to be up a tree
> Wif ol' popguns
> Poppin' at me.

Aunt Aggie, he thought, though she was long dead and in the ground at the little cemetery by the Abyssinian Baptist Church on Gihon near the foot of Clytter's Ridge. Aunt Aggie, thin and rich brown, the clean and unmistakable smell of her house, sitting in her rocking chair by the window with the afternoon light on her white hair, spreading her pale and pink palms before her, gesturing as she sang; Aunt Aggie in her chair, the big double bed and the patchwork quilt, the large photograph browning with age of her and Uncle Abraham on their wedding day, young and handsome and pretty, with the boy's grandfather in a white suit and sleek black mustache standing between them with his arms around their shoulders, all three of them grinning and staring out into the room from the ornate frame and the wallpaper of newspapers plastered neatly on the walls and the ceiling with news headlines and photographs of Hoover and Franklin Roosevelt and ads for Mercury and DeSoto and Star automobiles; Aunt Aggie, nodding her head in the afternoon sun and singing about Ol' Molly Har and good night to Mister Whipperwill and hi my rinktum and a plane tree that's planted 'side the water.

Dreaming, a small boy who would finally sit, shy and ginger on Aunt Aggie's thin lap, he walked around the yard by the small house and found a young woman, rich brown and in a red dress of flour sack calico, and she was singing Aunt Aggie's song. She was no one he recognized, so he slipped away from her bright red back and returned to the road.

He walked on south, down the road. Ahead, leaning lazily against the trunk of a maple, dark in the shade, was a man, well-dressed, a suit, a narrow-brimmed hat, blue both of them, a middle-aged black man but a face which Abel Boyd did not know. He walked slowly into the tree's shade and up to the man, who looked straight at him but did not move.

"Excuse me," Abel Boyd said, "I wonder if you could help me?"

"If I'm able," the man said, still leaning against the tree but with no unfriendliness.

"Could you tell me . . . where do all the Coons live around here?"

"The what?" the man said quickly, standing erect and putting his right hand into his coat pocket.

"The Coons," Abel Boyd replied, resisting the sudden impulse to turn and run, to dash back to the woman in red, to interrupt her song and ask his question of her.

"Why, you . . ." the black man said, his face twisting with dark emotion as he drew a small black revolver out of his pocket, cocked it, and swung it directly under Abel Boyd's nose. "What do you mean using a word like that to me?"

Abel Boyd could feel the cold metal and smell the gun oil, but he could look only at the hard face and angry eyes before him. He was rigid, scrotum tight, unable to move. He could feel the sweat running free from under his arms and down his sides, the water of his knees. His heart beat slowly and painfully in his ears. He could not even swallow.

"Answer me, you mother," the black man said roughly and nudged the gun into Abel Boyd's nose.

And the fear broke from stasis into words, words that spilled around the black revolver and over the black fingers and the black hand. "What do you mean? I don't understand, you have no right, it just isn't right, all I did was ask where the Coons live"—the gun twitched—"and what's wrong with that? I know the Coons, I grew up here, I'm not the police or anything, don't pull that trigger, don't, I know the Coons, really I do, I grew up with Rastus, we're the same age, I used to hear Aunt Aggie sing and sit on her knee," he began to his surprise and shame to cry, big tears wetting his cheeks, splashing on the gun, "and all I wanted was to know where the Coons live, that's all, that's all in the world I wanted," he said, convulsively sobbing, gasping and trying to stop, shaking all over, "and you had to go and pull a gun on me."

Abel Boyd could see, feel, smell, and hear nothing, only the intensity of his own anguish, the explosive rush of his accumulated sorrows triggered by this last straw of experience, but somehow he knew through it all that the gun was gone, back into the coat pocket and even out of mind, felt then a hand on his shoulder and a handkerchief on his cheeks and under his nose, and finally heard a voice, warm and understanding, saying, "Why, you're old Mister Edwards' grandson Sonny, and I didn't recognize you. Now hush your crying, and I'll take you home with me right now."

Suddenly ashamed and very confused, Abel Boyd stopped crying, blew his nose with a damp snort into the proffered handkerchief, and then, blinking his eyes and staring into the dark face so close to his, asked, "Who are you?"

"Why, Sonny, I'm your old playmate, Rastus."

The sky was blue again, birds sang, and the day was green. Rastus,

Rastus, Rastus, oldest friend and dearest playmate, and they were walking on down the road arm in arm as a redbone hound came out of the trees to their left ("Wallow, that's Pappy's dog, Wallow," Rastus said), and Abel Boyd, baffled but alive, confused but no longer afraid, almost began to dance for the bittersweet joy of it all.

It was Rastus, older as Abel Boyd had somehow convinced himself he would not be, smooth and well dressed, and he talked as they walked down the narrow road.

"Why, it's just like homecoming this week, what with my being here and Willkie's coming back from up north, but then I doubt if you knew he was even gone, he's so much younger than us and you've been gone so long yourself. And now you, too, Sonny, Sonny Boyd, here again, my, my."

"Rastus," Abel Boyd said, but his friend went on.

"Things have changed, Sonny. It's not Rastus now. You see, the old name got funny after the war, and it got in the way, so we had it changed. The name's Crown now, and my name's Royal Crown, and nobody laughs anymore. Why, I have a master's degree in business administration."

They walked on in light and shadow, Royal Crown talking and Abel Boyd listening and asking questions. The old people were nearly all dead now, Uncle Abraham and Aunt Aggie and two of their three sons, Tom and Richard. Of the next generation, Tom's son Tombo was still a farmer, living down by the church and the churchyard where the Coons were buried, and Richard's son Willkie, who was now twenty-six, had run off up north where he had sired two natural sons, was a leader in a movement, and had just come back to Slote Valley the week before.

They reached a brick house set back from the road, deep in trees and clean and cool. The sign on the mailbox by the road read HARRISON CROWN, and when they turned and began to walk across the fine bluegrass toward the house, Wallow began barking wildly and ran ahead to the porch.

"Is this Uncle Hairy's?" Abel asked.

"It is. Yes, it is," Royal answered, "and Uncle Hairy is Harrison Crown. Isn't that a fine and gentlemanly name?"

A young black man in black-and-gold suede trousers and gleaming black shoes with gold platform soles and heels, a gold ring in his left ear, and a yellow silk pullover with GOMANGANI written across it in large, black letters was lolling on the porch, his legs stretched down over the steps as he sat on the stoop. His hair was dry and bushy, and Abel Boyd realized that he must be Willkie, and his fear began to return ever so slightly. He had never really known Willkie, for Uncle Richard had been the black sheep of the family and had not been around New Garden very much. He remembered that Willkie had gotten his name because Uncle Richard had bragged that he wasn't going to follow nobody's lead when he named his son, Roosevelt or no Roosevelt. Beyond that initial fact, he knew nothing of Willkie except what Royal had told him in the last few minutes.

"Hey, Willkie," Royal called out with enthusiasm as they came up to the steps, "guess who this is?"

Willkie looked at Abel Boyd, but he said nothing.

"Why, it's Sonny Boyd, don't you remember him, old Mister Edwards' grandson?" Royal Crown continued. "Why, he and I grew up together."

Willkie grunted but made no move.

"Come on in, Sonny," Royal Crown went on, "come on in to the home of Harrison Crown. He'll be so glad to see you."

Royal Crown led Abel Boyd up the steps by Willkie, still unmoved, across the wide porch, and into the shadowy and cool hallway.

From behind on the porch, a voice, Willkie's, shouted "Crown, my ass!" but Royal led Abel Boyd through the dark hallway and into the dim parlor without replying or even letting on that he heard.

There was a television set in one corner of the room, and its blue light met the muted sunlight from the slanted venetian blinds more than halfway. Seated in a rocking chair under a framed color print of the slain Kennedy brothers and Martin Luther King, his feet in worn slippers and his hands knotted in his lap, lost in the laughter of an anonymous audience, Uncle Hairy did not notice their entrance. He was very small and nearly bald, cotton tufts, clean and fluffy, over each ear and fringing the back of his dark brown head, and he was leaning forward to peer closely at the jumbled face on the screen.

"That one's Arlene Francis," he said, "I'd know her anywhere."

A bell rang, and, "Well, Number Four," the voice of the television said, "who is our Mystery Face?"

"John Wayne," an excited woman's voice replied, and another bell rang, the audience clapped wildly, and the woman's voice broke into a shrill squeal as the slatted features rearranged themselves on the screen to form the familiar face of the cowboy hero.

"Huh," Uncle Hairy grunted, "huh. That surely enough looked like Arlene Francis to me," then, turning to whomever was in the room, "You know, Martin Gabel's wife," stopping suddenly at the shock of the pale white face and unfamiliar form of Abel Boyd.

"Hey, Pappy," Royal Crown said, his voice drowning out the television's mutter and applause, "guess who I've got here. Guess who this is."

The old man squinted and stared up at Abel Boyd, saying hesitantly, "Now let me just see, let me see. Is that the sheriff? Is that the sheriff there?"

"Oh, no, Pappy, no. It's somebody you know," and with a broad wink, "somebody you used to ride on your knee."

The old man muttered to himself and rubbed the top of his head with the palm of his right hand. He stared alternately at Abel Boyd and at his son, seeking the answer that neither of their faces supplied. Unable to arrive at a solution, he let his hand drop to his lap and became immobile, staring flatly ahead as the television laughed beside him.

"Why, Pappy," Royal Crown said, "I'm ashamed of you." The old man winced. "This is Sonny Boyd, don't you remember, old Mister Edwards' grandson?"

In one smooth movement Uncle Hairy reached out and snapped the television off, leaned forward in his chair, and opened his face into light, wrinkled with a great grin.

"Little Sonny," he said, his voice filled with the static of feeling, "how you have grown." The old man reached out his hands, took Abel Boyd's extended hand in them, and squeezed it long and hard. "Little Sonny Boyd," as his eyes searched the fifty-year-old face of Abel Boyd for the past and signs of the old gentleman who was his grandfather and the little boy's familiar face long lost.

Royal Crown snapped the blinds open wider to catch the early evening sun, but it was clouding over and a breeze had begun to toss the tree limbs outside the window and ruffle the fine grass across the level lawn. And in the shifting light, they talked and remembered aloud, brought up the old times and laughed together, were silent in the grandfather's memory and lively with reminiscence of him. And they talked of themselves, Royal of his business, Abel of his visit, and Uncle Hairy of his memories.

"The things I could tell you boys," he said, leaning forward again in his chair, "but even now I am worthy of the trust placed in me by the Pullman Company. Porters was always chosen for their discretion, for we was the men who met the people for the Company, we was their only contact with the people. Well, then, you understand how carefully we was chosen. We had to be able to talk and to think, and we had to know when not to talk, too.

"Why, when I was on the Southern Pacific line out of New Orleans—that was before I was married to Rhody—many is the movie star, many the actor and many the actress, I had to carry to their compartment and undress and put to bed, yes, undress and put to bed. But do you think I would say a word to anybody? Do you think I would say a name even now? No, sir. No, sir. We let the Pullman Company do the talking. Yes, sir."

He rolled his eyes significantly and settled back in his rocking chair. Royal Crown began, "Pappy," but Uncle Hairy was not through.

"And during the war, I met many foreigners, Chinamens and Frenchmens and Englishmens. I always liked the Englishmens. I always told them that they couldn't speak English proper and, my, how they would laugh. And I would tell them about Patrick Henry, the great statesman, a hundred years or more ago, and what he had to say to Daniel Webster, and they had never even heard of Yorktown or such things and listened most attentive.

"But the things I saw," he went on, more reflective, drifting off, "why, there was a champion fighter, a big colored man, you would know his name right off if I was at liberty to mention it. Well, his compartment and the one of this blonde lady, an actress she was, from Paris, France, they was side by side, and they had me to open the connecting door. He was all of six feet tall and a champion, so I obliged him. What went on in them compartments, upper bunk and lower, floors and all, I wish I could tell you. I wish . . . "

But then he paused as there was a chuckle of rain on the window, a banging of windows and doors from other parts of the house, and a young woman in bright green flared pants, a yellow blouse, and a yellow dusting turban looked in the door, checking the window. Uncle Hairy clapped his hand over his mouth and hunkered down in his chair.

"What is you up to, you old scoundrel?" she began, mock sternness coloring her voice, but suddenly noticing Abel Boyd, she stopped and turned to leave.

Royal Crown called out to her, "Hey, Nellreena, didn't I tell you it was going to rain? Didn't I?"

Nellreena nodded quickly and backed out through the door to disappear out of sight into the hall.

"It's my left arm," Royal Crown said to Abel Boyd. "It aches something fierce whenever it's going to rain."

While he was still talking and extending his arm as if for inspection, Willkie appeared in the doorway, shaking his wet head and slapping his arms against his sides, followed by a slow, silent, wet, black dog which shuffled over to the television set and lay down on the hooked rug in front of it.

"Get in there, Panther, goddam you," Willkie was saying. Then, to the room at large, "Dumb mother, had to drag him in out of the rain," and then, standing taller and curling his upper lip, "Been having a cozy little get-together in here?"

"We've been talking over old times," Royal Crown said, a tone of deep pleasure still in his voice. The old man and Abel Boyd both said nothing, staring at the young man in the doorway.

"White times," Willkie said.

"Old times," Royal Crown repeated, his voice even and suddenly very quiet, "good times."

"What do you think of the Crowns, elder and younger, white eyes?" Willkie asked suddenly, past Royal Crown directly to Abel Boyd. "I bet they're still just coons to you, huh?"

"Don't be that way, Willkie," said Royal Crown, the level of his voice rising as he got up out of his chair. "Can't you manage to be civil?" He walked quickly to the window and stared out through the level slats of the blind at the rain, which was hard, beating the grass flat and twisting the leaves.

"I'm so sorry, Mister Crown," Willkie said, whining and grinning. "Did I offend whitey? Would you like me to tug wool, Mister Whitey?" He grabbed a thick tuft of his damp hair and jerked at it and then said to Royal Crown's back, "Or would you like me to kiss Mister Whitey's slick ass?"

Abel Boyd was stiff with doubt and worry, rigid with fear. Uncle Hairy turned back to the television and stared at its dull, gray face. Royal Crown eased back around to face Willkie.

"Or would licking the pale, hairy back of his white hand be enough?" Willkie went on. "Fat lot of good all that kissing and licking done you now that your honkey friends have all forgot you just like all their other little fads. Huh? Huh?"

"Willkie Coon," Royal Crown said, but could add no more for Willkie's shouting.

"I am not Willkie Coon, damn you, Mister All Fine and White Sucking Royal Rastus Shame Crown Coon. My name is Willkie X and don't you forget it."

Royal Crown's voice was becoming shrill. "Willkie X! Willkie X! You're Willkie Dewey Coon, and you know it. X! X! X!"

"And what do you think you are, Mister Rastus White Sucker Coon?"

Royal Crown took one step away from the window, still thrumming with rain, and toward Willkie, who cocked his fist, the skin over the knuckles taut and tan as though he were holding something dangerous that only he and Royal Crown could see. He said, "Now, what's my name? Huh? What's my name, Coon? Hey, what's my name, Burrhead? Spade? Huh? Huh?"

Abel Boyd edged his chair back until it bumped into the sleeping Panther, who growled and thumped his heavy tail on the polished floor. Abel Boyd sat stiffly, feeling the dog's hot wet breath and cold nose on his leg, between trouser and sock, unable to move, his eyes hung on the face of Royal Crown.

The eyes were cold and hard in that dark face, sweat catching light in the wrinkles of his brow, and the eyes were watching the fist wave in the air as Willkie continued his chant.

"Hey, what's my name, Mister Royal Crown Pepsi Cola Doctor Pepper Coon? Huh? Hey, why don't you give yourself a real white man's name, huh? Why don't you call yourself Coca Cola? Huh? Hey, what's my name, huh? It's X, and you better believe it. X, baby, X."

And then Royal Crown made his move, jumped across the room, grabbed Willkie by the wrist, and spun him up against the wall with the weight of his rush.

"You can't do that to me," Willkie shouted, but Royal Crown held him there, pounding the tight hand against the wall until it went limp and slack.

"Quit it, Royal," Willkie was saying. "Now you quit it. I'll go tell Aunt Rhody."

And Royal did let go and stepped back. Willkie left the room instantly with no backward glance, only saying, "I've got more important things to do than fuck around with some nigger."

Panther grunted, yawned, rose up hind first, left Abel Boyd's leg, and walked slowly after Willkie. And Abel Boyd, too, got up, was standing when Royal Crown reached him, apologizing and saying that Willkie didn't mean any harm by any of it and asking Sonny to stay to supper.

But Abel Boyd left, said good-bye to Uncle Hairy, who promised to tell him about the Great Northern and the Glacier National Park the time they found three suspicious Japanesemens in one of the crevasses when he would come calling again, and left the home of Harrison Crown.

Royal Crown accompanied him out into the fresh dusk where the rain had stopped abruptly and the setting sun glowed red and orange in the flat clouds over the low hills to the west of Gihon and across the narrow valley.

"Now, Sonny, don't let none of this upset you," Royal Crown said. "Willkie is just a hot-headed boy. He'll cool down when he gets a few more years behind him and sees how things really are."

"I think I understand," said Abel Boyd.

"And you're sure you can't stay? Mammy will be down for supper, and Tombo would certainly like to see you, and the farm's within an easy walk after supper. Tombo Coon. He wouldn't change his name for all the reasons in the world; he don't want anything to change. He's just like Uncle Tom. He'll surely miss seeing you."

They paused by the mailbox, and the low sun made them glow against the darkening green of the trees. Lights were blinking on in the house behind them.

"And be sure not to worry about Willkie and the race thing. Why, there's a brand new Howard Johnson's over by the interstate north of town, and we can eat there with no questions asked. Pappy loves fried clams, can't seem to get enough of them. I drive down here in my Torino, and then we go over together all the time.

"In fact, places like the Honk-E-Tonk over by New Garden are the onliest ones where we can't get served, and frankly, who wants to go to the Honk-E-Tonk?"

He put his arm around Abel Boyd's shoulder and laughed.

"No, Sonny, don't let your heart be troubled, for the lamb and the lion are going to lie down with each other. There is no room in this world for more violence, but there is much room for understanding. There'll never be any violence between us."

They parted as the sun touched and splintered the edge of the ridge into burning pines and blurred maples. Abel Boyd looked back once as he moved up the road, almost as if looking for a sign as he walked in the grassy center to avoid the mud. Royal Crown was a trim shadow with one hand raised in a gesture of farewell, a salute, still and blending into the dusk. The sun sank behind the ridge, and a single shaft of light, a green flare, rose for a split second and was as suddenly gone.

When he passed the wide oak where he had met Royal Crown earlier that afternoon, Abel Boyd felt his groin tighten and prickle, and his brow became cold and damp. A growling and rush of weeds burst into the open beside him as he passed the house where the woman had been singing, and two dogs, red and black, Wallow and Panther, raced round and round, wagging their tails, growling and chewing at each other's ears and throats. Abel Boyd paused for a moment, wiped his face with his handkerchief, tucked it back into his hip pocket, and just as the last light faded seriously into darkness, he turned onto the path and walked into the deep woods.

III.

O! darkly fair!—yet beautifully bright,
I know now how to call thee, sweet unknown.
—R. H. Wilde

Winslow "Puke" Guffaw was laughing and cracking jokes, sloshing tap beer into mugs, and popping the tops of beer bottles when the state policeman came through the door and walked heavily up to the bar. His uniform was powder blue, and he carried a crash helmet slung by its strap in his left hand. The noise lessened for a moment as he walked across the room, but as soon as he leaned against the bar, laid his helmet on it, and asked for a beer, the Honk-E-Tonk roared again with the racket of a hot summer Saturday night.

Abel Boyd was sitting at the bar right beside the policeman. Clytter's Ridge had seemed larger and less manageable in the dark on the way back over, a jumble of high weeds and wet vines, of stones and boggy depressions, so he was now finishing up a cheeseburger and another mug of Dixie beer with relief. He watched the policeman in the mirror and listened to his talk.

"Another bad one," he was saying to Guffaw, and he wiped his big hand over his thinning hair and sweaty brow. "I guess that piddling little rain laid just enough of a slick on the road to fool them."

"What," said Guffaw, "was it the curve again?" He wiped off the bar in front of the policeman and around his helmet and set a mug of foaming beer in front of him with no mention of cash or charge.

"Yeah, and they should have known better."

"Who was it?"

"I don't rightly know their names, but you probably know them. They've been running whiskey up and down this road for years, both of them. I forget the name, got it written down on the pad outside in the motorcycle. Hell, I forget it. You know them."

Guffaw did not say anything.

"Killed the old one outright, windshield cut his head off. Took us all of twenty-five or thirty minutes to find it over in the field behind that damn tree what with the dark and the briers, but we thought the other one was going to live. He looked all right and was moaning, even talking a little, but he died before we got him in the ambulance. Just died of a sudden."

He drank half the beer off then and set the mug back on the bar with a bang.

"Why the hell," he said, "they didn't build that road down by Gihon so it would've run straight I'll never know. But, no, they have to run it down this side of the Slot and put that one kink in it that's killed God knows how many people. It's enough to make you sick."

It was making Abel Boyd sick, looking at the policeman's red and angry face in the mirror and then hearing a thin, crackling voice, that of an old man in a khaki work shirt and white and blue pinstriped galluses sitting on the other side of the policeman, his toothless mouth with puckering lips, bald head, and eyes that were honed sharp and needle black.

"I remember that," he said and wiped the foam from around his lips with a swipe of the spotty back of his right hand. "I helped work on that road, ended up supervising a gang of niggers, a whole gang of them."

The policeman finished off his beer in another long pull as the old man talked on, eager, his voice piercing the noisy air and his eyes alight.

"Yes, sir, I supervised that gang of niggers in moving the cemetery just where that curve is now, the old Edwards burying ground, and if we hadn't moved it that curve would be a lot worse than it is today, yes, sir, I tell you, a whole lot worse."

Both the policeman and Guffaw seemed to be paying the old man no attention, and Abel Boyd was the only one of the three who was caught by his glittering eye, dark as a moonless night in the crazy blur of colors and motion in the mirror behind the bar.

"And the things we found in that graveyard you wouldn't believe. I still wake up in a cold sweat sometimes if I think on it too much the night before." He paused and shook his head, but clearly only a pause and not an end from the very way he sat.

"Hey, Puke," a voice from the room, "now Madge wants to know how long it is from here to there."

"You shut up, dog nab you, Jeems Puckett," a shrill echo of the afternoon.

"We had to dig up all them graves and load the coffins on a wagon and cart them over Pison to the burying ground at the Slote Presbyterian Church, and them coffins was old, some of them over a hundred years I bet."

An argument boiled up, spewed and sputtered for a moment in one of the booths, and settled then into an ugly murmur.

"Another beer, S. 0.?" Guffaw offered.

"No, I've got no more stomach for it," the policeman answered.

And the old man went on, the interruptions diminishing the intensity and steadiness of his narration not a jot. "Some of them old coffins was just decay and gray dust, so we had to just scoop them into a feed sack and then dump them into the new graves. The state police put a guard out and wouldn't let nobody come near, so it was just me and them niggers, and it was so hot that they were sweating something fierce and the smells from them rotten graves was ugly as sin, but that wudn't nothing to what we found in one coffin that wudn't more than ten years old. It almost turned them niggers white, and I ain't been quite the same since, myself."

His pause this time was dramatic, for he had his audience; Guffaw and the policeman were still paying him no open mind, but they were caught even as Abel Boyd was, hung on the promise of the pause and the old man's jerking Adam's apple as he took on some beer for the finishing. Madge and her friends laughed loudly and in unison, but the bar hung suspended and silent to Abel Boyd as he waited for the old man to start again.

"I would have knowed it was a recent coffin," he began, "even if the gravestone hadn't been there, because it was a strong box, store-boughten and still looking almost new, and it was shut tight and if one of them niggers, Tom Coon as I remember, well, if he hadn't started letting on as to how it was his young mistress and crying and taking on and if he hadn't thrown himself on it when only three niggers had hold of it and was lifting it, we would never have knowed what was in it, but he did, and it fell over right on the ground and the lid opened with a big crack and the whole thing bumped back right side up but wide open in broad daylight."

"Hey, Puke," one of Madge's friends.

"Shut up," Puke said. "Shit, a man can't think, for you people."

"It was a woman all right," the old man said, talking lower, pacing himself more slowly, "and she was a little musty but still fresh, her dress was silk, but she wasn't in no blessed repose, no indeed, her hair was long and wild but her fingernails weren't, no, sir, they was all busted and torn and her face was all clawed and bloody and her clothes was tore to shreds, all that silk was in ribbons, and the inside of that coffin lid was clawed like a wild animal had been let loose on it, a panther or something, and her eyes was scratched out, all hollow and torn."

No sound, no sound at all broke into Abel Boyd's brain aside from that thin, low voice, going on and on, flat and steady.

"She had been buried alive and woke up in the dark screaming and she tried to claw her way out and when that didn't work she tore herself to bits, and we'd have never knowed it if that nigger Tom Coon hadn't been so damn upset about disturbing the rest of his young mistress. I mean she was tore to bits, like a wild animal clawing and clawing and her mouth was wide open where she had been screaming at the very end."

He stopped then, and his eyes looked down at his beer, and the room was noisy.

"What did you do about it?" said Guffaw, still not looking at the old man. The policeman was sliding his beer mug back forth, from hand to hand, looking only at himself in the mirror, squinting his eyes, testing his teeth in a grimace, looking rock hard and unmoved.

"What could we do?" the old man said, the fire gone out of him, the embers dying. "We nailed her back up and put her on the wagon."

Abel Boyd was truly sick, the room rotten in his nostrils, the air thick as gelatin, and the beer rose, the greasy meat and bread and cheese, all stale and foul in his throat and nose, and he got up from the stool, walked down the room past the booths, ignoring them and their dizzy noise, and through the door marked MENS.

The small toilet stank of vomit, and the floor was slick with it around the commode. The odor and sight surprised and settled Abel Boyd's stomach somehow and cleared his head. He stood in the center of the dim room, his eyes searching for something not quite lost in memory, and then they found it, over the basin, the fine handwriting and the praise of Maud. JUST ASK AT THE BAR, and Abel Boyd turned around and went straight back through the swinging door.

Madge and her two friends and a new one, identical to the other two as far as Abel Boyd could see, were still in their booth, sodden and disheveled, but loudly and raucously happy. She squealed in high ecstasy as Abel Boyd passed, and one of the men across from her turned bright red and yelled aloud as she groped him with her hands and arms under the table. The state policeman was gone, but all the stools were taken along the bar. Abel Boyd did not look for the old man, but went to the take-out counter at the end of the bar and waited for Guffaw to look his way.

He did not have to wait long before Guffaw was leaning on the counter, his large red hands gripping the edge, and his voice, big and personal, "And what'll you have, a couple of cold six-packs to go, old buddy? You're smart to buy now, because I'm closing early tonight."

"No, thank you," Abel Boyd said, his voice as cool and calm as his nerves were knotted. "I want to ask you about Maud."

"Well," said Guffaw, impatient and glancing back down the bar at the mugs which were empty in varying degrees, "what do you want to know about Maud?"

Abel Boyd stared at the black bird hovering on the flexing red forearm. And when he spoke, cool and calm, it was to no one, for Guffaw was back down the bar, snatching an empty beer mug from the raised hand of a thin man in a white shirt without a tie who seemed to have been preparing to throw it across the room.

"I ain't having none of that shit in here," Guffaw said.

"Aw, Puke," the man said, "I wudn't really going to throw it."

"The shit you wasn't."

"I wouldn't do that."

"The shit you wouldn't. Listen, Rafe, you save your energy for tonight and leave my bar alone, you hear?"

"Aw, Puke."

"Aw, Puke, hell."

And then he was back, leaning on the counter again, bulging buzzard and hot eyes.

"I'm just asking about Maud, about the sign, I mean."

"What sign?"

"The one on the wall."

"What wall?"

Abel Boyd stood stock still.

"Shit, old buddy," said Guffaw, "wouldn't you rather have a couple of six-packs of good, cold Dixie beer and head on down the road?"

"No," said Abel Boyd. "I'm asking about Maud. I want to know."

Guffaw grunted and reached over to the wall beside him and pushed a red button. He waited, not looking back at Abel Boyd, until a little grill above the button buzzed, once, twice, and three times. Then he turned back to the counter.

"You know the little building out back?"

Abel Boyd nodded.

Guffaw turned around then and walked back down the bar shouting, "Who needs a beer? You better get it in you now, because I'm closing early tonight."

Abel Boyd, not hearing the groans and complaint around him, stared at the red button for a moment, then pushed off across the floor and out the screen door into the hot night. It was dark beyond the red neon glow of the Honk-E-Tonk, and if there was a moon it was still making its way through the low clouds and was not yet in sight. His car was where he left it, although the '47 Ford was gone, revealing a pickup truck of indeterminate make and year, the usual rifles racked in the rear window. He had rolled up his own car's windows and locked it upon his return from across the ridge, too late to save the seat from a soaking but before anything could be stolen by the late night and heavy drinking patrons of the Honk-E-Tonk.

He walked by the car and the truck, illuminated for a few seconds by a passing car, its engine cackling and roaring with speed, a flash of light and sound soon fading into the dark, and he went around the corner of the building and onto the narrow path that he had followed earlier in the day. The old hulk of New Garden was a heavy shadow in the night before him, but bright and yellow light shone from the curtains and small windows of the low building to his left. Abel Boyd paused at the branching of the path and stared at those light windows. A trailer truck blatted its air horn on the road behind him, and he leapt onto the path and was soon at the building's dark door.

A mockingbird began to bubble and lilt in the night, and Abel Boyd hesitated for a moment, listened, and then knocked, once, twice, thrice, as the buzzer behind the bar had seemed to instruct. He listened for a sound from within, heard none, and then was startled and caught blinking and blind when the door swung suddenly in and the bright light cut a sharp rectangle in the dark. The light revealed only a silhouette, but a young and feminine voice invited him in.

"Come in," it said, "come in and sit right down."

Abel Boyd felt a cool, small hand pulling his left hand, and he went into the room and heard the voice continue, "That'll be twenty dollars in advance, please," as his eyes cleared and focused to find a young woman with brown eyes, pale brown hair cut shoulder length, a white ribbon bow at the top of her head and a white and gossamer peignoir through which, as his eyes grew sharper, he could see the firm and naked outlines of two small breasts, the sharp curve and angle of a hip bone, and the sly shadow of her nether hair.

And then Abel Boyd was sitting in a small rocker, ruffled and cushioned, saying, "Will a traveler's check do?" and she said, "Of course," so he pulled out the small, dark blue paper folder, opened it, took out his felt tip pen, and, balancing the folder on his knee, signed his name as boldly as he was able in her presence. He tore the check out and gave it to the girl, who placed it in her bureau as Abel Boyd restored pen and flat folder to the inner pocket of his seersucker coat. The room was yellow and the palest of blues, with frills and laces, all feminine and delicate, clean and innocent. The girl stood looking in the mirror at the flounced dressing table by the bureau, and Abel Boyd watched the fleshy curve of her behind through the pale peignoir and then looked around the room. There were no pictures on the walls, only needlepoint mottoes. The peignoir lifted over the backs of her knees as she leaned into the mirror; her legs were slim and firm and beautiful. The motto closest to him, in purple thread and pink, hung just over the bed. It read:

> My life has crept so long on a broken wing
> Thro' cells of madness, haunts of horror and fear,
> That I come to be grateful at last for a little thing.

As she turned and posed herself by the mirror, head back and shoulders, her small, round, and tipped breasts rising, Abel Boyd felt himself rising as well and knew the old and too long pent-up urging of the flesh. And she came across the room suddenly, arms extended, her movement flowing the peignoir back, revealing a smooth hard belly and the brown bush below, and then she was in his lap, the rocking chair humping backwards, and kissing him wet and hard in the left ear, her legs dangling over the right arm of the chair.

So Abel Boyd, wordless and wild, lifted her surprisingly without strain and carried her to the bed, arranged her on her back, and unzipped, untied, unbuttoned and unbuckled himself with only a passing thought of his wife, her moans and bites flashing for a moment in his ears and over his nerves, and he was in bed beside the beautiful girl, eyes open in the light and his left hand like fire and hot combustion tangling itself between her cool thighs.

Prepared by his wife for a warm and open space, a vast and featureless interior, Abel Boyd was struck still, caught rigid and unhinged, for in the bush was but a hard and tight-lipped line, the pursed and stern feature of a New England maiden aunt on a chill February's morning. His spirits fell as his fingertips sought out a chink, a cranny, and failed. He looked at her, spread on the bed, her peignoir askew, her breasts flat and soft and scarcely covered, the taut nipples and her smiling mouth and eyes.

And on the wall on the other side of the bed, in a small wooden frame, the needlepoint words in red and black, DEEPER, EVER SO LITTLE DEEPER, but he was stopped cold, and she said, "I think perhaps I should explain."

She pulled herself up and away from naked Abel Boyd, crossed her legs, and sat like Buddha, beautiful and now covered as well as her gossamer could. And Abel Boyd crouched and tugged at the yellow-and-blue coverlet and pulled it over his loose flesh and his shame.

"My name is Maud," she said, her voice alert and her eyes lively, "as you no doubt know. I've been here for nearly two years, and I have helped hundreds."

"Helped," Abel Boyd repeated.

"Yes, sir," she said, bright and interested in his interest. "You see I was in college at one of the Seven Sisters, I think maybe it was Smith although it could have been Mount Holyoke or Hollins, it seems so very long ago, and I said to myself, 'Maud,' you see my daddy loves Tennyson and thus the name and all my samplers," as she gestured at the room, "but, as I was saying, 'Maud,' I said to myself at college, sitting in my room, looking out over the quadrangle at all the other girls in their bright spring clothes, walking with boys or sitting on the millstones singing together in the afternoon sun, 'Maud,' I said, 'you have an obligation to life,' and I was right, for I did and I do as do we all, especially those of us favored with gifts or beauty."

Abel Boyd felt himself being caught up in her enthusiasm. He leaned forward, and his face with its rising interest urged her on.

"I knew I could do little myself about the war or the world, but a voice within me urged, 'Maud, go south,' for I am from the north, Ohio, 'go to that impoverished and forgotten land and bring them truth and love,' but I didn't know just how, and I argued with myself that balmy afternoon, sitting at my dorm room window, listening to the girls' voice drift up to me in soft harmony, and suddenly I knew. 'Maud,' I said, 'you've got it,' and I did and now I am, for I have come south in this guise in which you see me now, Maud, the Archetypal Golden-Hearted Whore."

As she talked, she was growing physically more lively, tossing her beribboned hair and leaning forward, toward recumbent Abel Boyd, toying with the long satin ribbons of her peignoir, once even running a fingernail lightly around the goosey flesh of Boyd's nearest ankle.

"I told all my friends what I'd decided to do. Most were shocked, some told me I was deluding myself and that I wasn't really evil but just thought so, but they didn't understand, because the ones who did (the ones, by the way, who really mattered) thought that it was a neat idea, and they encouraged me to stick to my convictions," her face grew determined and her little jaw stuck bravely out, "so I told my faculty adviser, and he said for me to keep careful notes because I could maybe use them as the basis for a thesis at M.A. school."

Abel Boyd felt himself suddenly renewed, thirty years younger, bright, trim, and erect, a college boy again, and he asked just the right question: "What's your major?"

"Social philosophy," she said, paused, then, proudly, "It was a special college major, just for me. What was your major?"

The past tense startled Abel Boyd for a second, but he answered, "Astronomy . . . at the University, and I met my wife at a Sweet Briar mixer," a startled pause, "I hope that you don't take offense that I mention my wife."

Her face became as soft as early April and as warm. "Not at all," she said, with enthusiasm flowing into gentleness. "Tell me why you're here."

Abel Boyd felt her concern around him, felt secure and at home in her delicate room, and knew that here he could release himself, be shriven, and find ease for his doubts.

"You are a whore," he said.

"With a heart of gold," she said.
"You are . . ." he said.
"I am a virgin," she said.

And Abel Boyd became all things at once, proud father and shy boy, doting lover and smitten youth, young and old, besmuttered and pure, and he spoke to her open and inviting face, told her of his youthful dreams and how they faded, of the collapse of his family after the loss of New Garden in the Great Depression, of his father's drunkenness and his mother's unending headaches, of his brother's angry threats and his mysterious departure to parts unknown after their last terrible argument, of his marriage and his children, of his wife's sensuality and lack of discrimination, of the break-up of their marriage, of his loss of faith in all young people and his fears for the country, and of his own journey home, away from the painful shards of his broken marriage, the bitterness, the threats, the frightening hatred, away from his own descent into approaching old age, back to Slote Valley, back to New Garden, back to that small and lovely world now grown loose and large.

"I often think I hear life in the old house," she said, "late at night when the moon is waning, and I look out of this window"—she pointed to one of the ruffled squires—"but I never see anything but the play of shadows in the vines and boards."

And he asked her questions:

"Why did New Garden come to this sad end?"

"For the same reason," she said, "that forsythia opens in the early spring and gnats live, for the same reason that you grew into a man and came into this room in all the world."

A great long screech of pained rubber broke the quiet, but it was followed by no thud or clattering smash. Abel Boyd pulled the coverlet to his chin, but Maud continued to look into his eyes, her eyes cow brown and daisy sweet.

"But why," he asked, still clutching the cloth high and hard, "is there, must there be a Honk-E-Tonk?"

"Mister Guffaw's grandfather," she said, prim and instructive, her fingers touched together forming a tidy steeple before her, leaning forward once more, "came south after the War Between the States, carpetbag in hand and very little else, disinherited scion of a fine and respected New England family, where he married into southern stock less exalted than his own but sturdy and vigorous."

Abel Boyd leaned forward, too; their foreheads were almost touching, but she said no more, just tilted her head, his eyes twisting uncomfortably following the movement, and smiled again.

"Then why," he said, as they both sat back and up, now touching knee to knee through the coverlet as Abel Boyd assumed her cross-legged stance, "did my playmate and oldest companion draw a pistol and point it at my head and then go on to say the things he said?"

Maud's eyes trembled with tears as she swung her legs away from his and out of the bed as she got up, a swift curve of bare hip and thigh, pulled the coverlet away from his clenched hands, took him by the arms, the soft folds of her peignoir spilling down over his chest and legs, and pulled him up and out. She hugged him tightly for a second, nestling her head under his chin, her stiff ribbon scratching his lips lightly, and then stood back, looking up at him, cupping her young breasts absently through the shimmering cloth with her gentle hands.

"We are," she said, tenderness and sorrow and love all informing her quiet voice, her brown eyes drowning in tears, "we are all moral octoroons."

And then quickly she picked up his clothes, all busy arms and legs, swift knees and sudden fingers, thrusting them at him, urging them on, helping, tugging and buttoning, zipping and tying, and saying, "You must go now, someone else is due any second."

Abel Boyd had noticed no buzzer nor seen any light blink, but he stood fully dressed and puzzled, an unanswered question still on his lips. Maud tidied her hair, straightened her bow and the ribbons of her peignoir, and then led him, pressing her small hand firmly to his elbow, to the door. He turned around to face her, and she put her hands on his chest, at first gently, but as he saw the door on the other side of the room opening, the door he had assumed to be a closet or toilet, she increased the pressure and pushed him out onto the narrow stoop.

"But I have another question," he said and saw for one keen second before her bright body blocked his view a black hand, the skin over the knuckles taut and tan, on the other doorknob.

"Good night," she said, still softly, gently, and he asked, "But why did you kiss my ear that way?"

The door closed then, quickly and with a bang. Abel Boyd thought he heard distinct dark laughter, but a passing truck confounded his ears. He thought, too, for a moment, to look in one of the bright windows, but the lights went out, and he was standing alone in the blue moonlight, listening to a solitary mockingbird, alone on a flat dirt path before New Garden in the moon's moving shadows and the night's unabating heat.

IV.

And oh for a man to arise in me,
That the man I am may cease to be!
   —Tennyson

The room was dim and red, illuminated only by the red neon in the wide window and one night-light behind the bar where Winslow "Puke" Guffaw was adjusting his slick and shining green robe. He was not alone. The old man in the khaki workshirt and striped galluses was still sitting on the same stool at the bar, and Abel Boyd had just come in at the door. He had passed Madge's three friends silently and grimly carrying her, heavy, loose, and limp, arms and one fat leg dangling, out to their pickup truck, and had decided to go in so that he could think a few things out before getting back on the road.

Guffaw was having some trouble with the catches on the inner front flap of his robe and was muttering under his breath.

"Shit," he said, "oh, shit."

"They kept her in a little shed out behind the big house," the old man said in his thin and crackling voice, as though he had never stopped talking, had been weaving his gothic spells without cease during the whole time of Abel Boyd's absence, "and I don't suppose more than ten or a dozen people ever knowed she was even there, yes, sir, it was a sight like none I've ever seen before or since, enough to make you sick indeed."

Guffaw tugged at the robe, and it popped open, loose and flapping all the way down.

"Oh, shit, shit, and double shit," he said.

"You just said a mouthful," the old man replied, and Guffaw glared at him, but started fumbling with his robe again immediately.

"I never seen so much dung, so much human dung, I mean, in all my life," the old man went on, and Abel Boyd walked over to the bar and sat down quietly on one of the empty stools.

"You see, the family never trusted the state asylums, because after all she was theirs and blood is thicker than water, so they just let on that she had gone off up north somewhere and fixed up the old shed back of the house with a pallet, and they put her out there."

Guffaw was at the point of surrender or uncontrollable rage, and Abel Boyd got up, walked down to the open end of the bar and around it. He turned Guffaw away from the mirror and began to hook up his robe. It was constructed just like an academic gown.

"In the winter, they put a little wood stove in the corner opposite the pallet," the old man said, "but they never did cut a window, and they always kept the door padlocked on the outside."

Abel Boyd hooked all of the hooks and snapped the snap at the throat, and Guffaw stood glowing, rustling, and green.

"Stay here a minute, will you, old buddy?" he said. "I've got to get my hood."

The old man, his eyes drilled black in the red glow, continued, apparently not noticing Guffaw's departure into a back room, "Well, laying in there in the dark with nothing to do but sleep and think crazy thoughts and yell and carry on and eat, she got fatter and fatter and big and white like something that lives under a log, and it got so that when anyone come around, she would holler and squall so that they took to leaving her alone, only sticking food in three or four times a day, because they had cut her a hole in the floor to do her business in, so they didn't have to worry about that."

Guffaw came back carrying a shiny green hood, peaked and pressed, which he tried on in front of the mirror and asked Abel Boyd to help him get straight.

"Then," the old man said, steady and level, never slowing down, "there come a day when she was too fat to move, or too lazy anyway, so she fouled her pallet without getting up and laid in it for two or three days until they noticed the smell, so they hosed the pallet out without bothering to move her, and then they beat her good and hard so her bones would remember, even under all that fat, what would happen to her if she fouled her bed again."

"Thanks a whole lot, old buddy," Guffaw said, neat and in order, and then, "Why don't you come out to the meeting tonight? Ought to be a good one, and you look like a fellow who would appreciate a good discussion." He winked at Abel Boyd broadly.

Muttering an apology, Abel Boyd turned, embarrassed, to a glass counter beneath the mirror. He stared into it without seeing its contents as the old man droned on and Guffaw, obviously disappointed, busied himself with striding about in his robe, letting it settle comfortably to his frame.

"And she learned her lesson, never messed up her bed again, but somehow she got all mixed up what with being crazy and in the dark all the time, so she took to digging the dung out of herself and flinging it across the room at the walls. Took them a long time to figure out what she was doing, they could smell it but they couldn't find it—and when they did, they hosed it out and beat her black and blue, but they never could make her figure out just what for."

"Well, old buddy," Guffaw said, "I'm closing up for good now. Anything I can do for you?"

Abel Boyd, lost in himself and in the irony of Guffaw's question (what could anyone do now?), focused his eyes through the glass of the counter and found a gun, a snug black pistol, short nosed and heavy, an outlawed Saturday night special, almost hidden in an array of pocketknives of various shapes and sizes.

"They finally, " the old man said, "had to hang up quilting on the wall that they could take down and clean regularly, because it was too much trouble to hose the room out every time, especially in winter, since she was practically impossible to move by then, and, I tell you, yes, sir, that place sure stunk, even in the winter when the stove was hot, worse than the hottest day in summer."

"Is that pistol for sale?" Abel Boyd asked.

"Now you know it ain't, old buddy. But," he looked around the room, at the empty booths and stools in the wavering red light, "I can let you have it for fifteen dollars real money, and I'll throw in a load of cartridges for good measure, but we got to hurry, because it's nearly meeting time."

Abel Boyd stood still and quiet for a moment and then said, "I'll take it if you'll take a traveler's check."

"Ain't you got enough cash?" Guffaw replied, suddenly suspicious, worried.

Abel Boyd took out his wallet and counted through the bills in it.

"When she finally died, of a heart attack I bet from all that fat, they got together and dragged her out at night and buried her in a secret place near a big pile of rocks in the pasture and never let on that she still wasn't up north, happy and contented." The old man finally paused, but then went on into a fast finish: "And they burned the shed down that very night, pallet, stove, and all, and that's the God's truth. It ain't very pretty but it sure is true."

"All I have is twelve dollars."

"Sold," said Puke Guffaw and opened up the case, lifted the pistol out, and checked it to see it if was loaded. It was.

"You could see the flames for miles around, they whooshed up in the sky like a big furnace, roaring and shooting big fiery sparks up in the night, flaming ashes come down all over the farm, and they had to hose down the house roof for fear it would catch fire and burn down, too."

Abel Boyd took the pistol in exchange for all his cash and weighed it heavy in his hand, black and oily and smooth.

"Well, old buddy," Guffaw said, friendly and proudly green, "I've got to close up now."

Abel Boyd walked back around the bar and over to the door, dropping the pistol into his right-hand coat pocket. The old man seemed to have disappeared or to have already gone out, for the room was dim and empty as they went through the door and Guffaw snapped off the red neon tubing.

"The meeting's just down the road a little piece," Guffaw said as he shut and locked the door behind them. "You sure ought to come on down. Turnout hasn't been too good lately, and a new face, fresh blood, would do us all good. Just head on south here for a few miles past the curve till you come to the gap in the Slot and turn left at the first white fence. You can't miss it, and," he laughed, "you can't very well miss me neither in this get up."

He climbed into his car, ignoring Abel Boyd's noncommital silence, bending his head carefully to protect the order of his hood, slammed the door, and started the engine. Then he leaned out the window, pulling his shiny green sleeve up to reveal the sharp talons of the black bird, and said, "Might even some spades show up, and you could use your new gun." He winked and laughed and waved good-by as he backed the big Cadillac out onto the road and scratched out, leaving twin streaks of hard black rubber smeared down the highway after him.

Abel Boyd looked around in the silence after his wild departure. The old man was nowhere in sight, long gone. The moon was gibbous and white, turning the Honk-E-Tonk pearl pale and giving the woods beyond on Clytter's Ridge a silvery glow as light and shadow hung flat and luminous along its flank. He walked around the building and onto the path again. The twisted frame of the burned-out car took on abstract form and no longer seemed out of place so near New Garden, rising itself white and calm in the moonlight, cool and asleep, waiting for a new dawn in the east to wink its windows awake and spill its life over green lawns and fresh spring grass.

The low building in front of it was dark and silent, nearly invisible in the shadows. Abel Boyd began to walk slowly up the clear path to New Garden, to his room and to bed, to a dreamless and refreshing sleep, but the blat and stammer of a lone motorcycle on the highway jerked him back and awake, drew him to his car.

He walked around it once, thumping idly at the tires with his toe, his tires, his car only for a rented week, and then he unlocked the door, opened it, and slid onto the damp seat.

The whole interior was musty, and he rolled both windows down into the front doors. He was alone again and in the car in the loose gravel of the parking lot of the Honk-E-Tonk. He blew his horn, loud and sudden, once, twice, three times for service, but no one came, so he pulled the pistol out of his coat pocket, where it had hung heavy and awkward.

By the muted light of the moon filtering through the bug-spattered windshield, the gun was a vague shadow, ominous and ambiguous. He pointed the gun at his nose and turned the cylinder carefully around.

The faces of the day turned beneath his empty gaze, the old man and the boy at the bar, the teenaged boy and girl squirming in their booth, Madge and her fat friends, old Uncle Hairy, the woman in red and her song of the peaceful past. But, no, there were only six, the heads of the bullets, blunt and dull, catching none of the faint light on their dark surfaces, all identical, all the same, six: Winslow Puke Guffaw, in order, click, Royal Crown, another click, Willkie X, and, click, Maud, click, the old man in the bar who talked and talked, then, click, last, between that old man and Puke Guffaw again, first and last, himself, no different, Abel Boyd, all the same, all turning, click, click, and click, around and around, black and white, dull, all dull, dark, and the same, click, click, round and round, in the moonlight, in the car, in the cylinder of Abel Boyd's gun.

He tucked the gun in his belt then, started the engine, and backed the car around in the crisp gravel, pointing it south, parallel to the road, pointing it toward the curve and Guffaw and the lower mouth of the Slote Valley, below Clytter's Ridge where the split into two halves ended, where Gihon and Pison met and flowed on together to the sea.

He pulled out onto the dark highway in a spatter of gravel, and he could feel the insistent prod of the pistol from his belt into his groin. As he drove into the moonscape, his headlights cutting only narrowly into the pale night, he wondered idly whether the gun could discharge accidentally as he drove and whether the wound he would receive would be in the flesh of his thigh or would be more serious.

He picked up speed, heading farther south, going deeper into the night, running between dawn and sunset, sunset and dawn, lost past and puzzled future, nearing the curve where the road recrossed Pison and cut sharply, where once his ancestors had been laid to rest and where now only a scarred tree stood. Abel Boyd pressed down on the accelerator, heard the engine whine in response, and drove on under the moon, gathering speed and plunging free into the long lost and always promised land.

That's What I Like
(About the South)

The defining characteristics of southern fiction:
    Roy has gotten thirsty again, and, recognizing that it is after all another long hot day in another long hot summer, Shirley sighs loudly for Roy's benefit, continues to streak down the flat two-lane blacktop, but takes the dusty unpaved right-hand fork just beyond the rattling explosion of the bridge over Cross Creek. The bright red Bronco slips sideways for a brief second on the dirt and gravel, straightens out, and speeds on down the back country road, raising huge battle flags in the dust that has just begun to settle down from the last car or truck that recently broke the heavy stillness of the summer heat.
    Two miles past the fork, three tiny black boys crouch in the shallow bottom of the ditch by the side of the narrow road with a plastic milk jug half full of water, making tiny mud buildings for a town that their plastic cars can visit and that the next rain will destroy like a major flood. They scarcely glance up at the dusty Bronco roaring by, but their angry big sister shakes her fist at Shirley from the open window of the small pink house and then slams it shut as the thick dust billows toward it. Shirley laughs out loud, reaches over and turns up the volume of Lyle Lovett on the tape player, and pushes the accelerator even harder to the floor.
    Shirley knows from experience that a Coke Slurpee is just what Roy has in mind, so the Bronco swings right again at the hardtop state road by the forge and then pulls in abruptly onto the hot pavement of the South Fork 7-Eleven. The red and white SLURPEE banner hangs limp and unmoving in the heat, and Roy wishes out loud that the sun were in Capricorn and the air cold and crisp. But the sun is in Leo, and Roy feels almost faint as Shirley bangs the Bronco

door behind them and they wade through the heat toward the 7-Eleven.

Roy leans against Shirley, and he hugs her with his big bare arm, pulls her tight against his side. They make their way together across the shimmering pavement, Shirley in his sweat-stained straw hat, worn jeans, and mirror sunglasses, and Roy, sturdy and small in her carefully pressed jeans and eggshell blue blouse.

deep involvement in place,

Shirley releases Roy and pushes the glass door open for her, putting his hand flat on her firm, smooth back as he urges her into the cool interior of the 7-Eleven. She smiles up at him and steps quickly into the store. Not for the first time, Shirley notices how sure of herself Roy always seems to be, how she moves steadily and unswervingly past the island of the checkout counter, nods hello to Glenn, who was a cheerleader at Roy and Shirley's high school and who is tugging at her bra under the green-and-red smock she wears when on duty at the store, and walks without a hitch or falter right by the metal, freestanding candy and snack rack, swerves to the left, loops the island, and ends up right between the ice cream refrigerators and the Slurpee machine.

There is something unsettling to Shirley about Roy's single-mindedness. It is not something he can put his finger on, but it worries him from time to time. He is not sure whether it bothers him because it seems inappropriate to a woman (*his mother, for example, would have stopped dead in her tracks just inside the door and looked nervously around for a long time before she would have taken another step*), or because it is so typical of a woman (*he, for example, always likes to stop and scope a room before deciding which way to move through it; get the lay of the land, so to speak; be aware of alternative routes*). "All of Roy's choices," he thinks, "seem to be made before she makes them."

He stands in the doorway, peering at the shadowy room through his sunglasses, glances at the abbreviated aisles with their bright variety of colors and shapes, the leaning tower of straw hats and gimme caps to his right, his eyes skimming all around the room, but then lighting on the rack of bright magazines just to his left by the island, their covers lit up with the luminescent tanned skin, long legs, and lithe arms of slim women in bathing suits. He moves right to them and picks up the one nearest to him as he always seems to do every time he visits the store. He pulls off his sunglasses, folds and slips them into his workshirt pocket, and settles himself back on his heels for a good, long look.

Roy pulls a medium-sized paper cup, red and white with Slurpee written on it in blue, from the torpedo rack of cups by the machine. Without hesitating, she places her cup under the spout for the Classic Coca-Cola Slurpees and gently eases the smooth metal handle forward. The icy brown coil spills out and into her waiting cup, and she can almost taste its cold freshness as it spirals to the top.

"Nothing's as refreshing as a cold Coca-Cola on a hot day," she thinks happily to herself as she plucks a spoonstraw from the rack and turns to Glenn behind the counter to pay.

"Roy," Glenn says as she watches Roy pop a plastic top on her cup and then strip the red spoonstraw and insert its scooped end into the X-slit in the center, "don't you want to buy Shirley a 7-Up or something and answer the Question of the Week?" She winks at Roy and punches the cash register, stuffs Roy's smooth dollar bill into it, and fingers out twenty-four cents change, while pointing with her other hand to the question printed on the familiar sign on the counter: IF YOU FOUND YOURSELF IN LOVE WITH ANOTHER PERSON, WOULD YOU TELL YOUR CURRENT LOVER?

The big round numbers which Glenn has carefully inscribed in magic marker on the slick plastic total board by the question read: YES 27% NO 73%.

A cold chill runs through Roy's chest as she takes her change, and she stops sucking the pulpy, sweet ice of the Slurpee through her spoonstraw and takes a deep breath. Glenn glances over at Shirley by the magazine rack and looks eagerly for Roy's answer. She is obviously disappointed when Roy says that she wouldn't even consider answering such a question.

"These questions," she says, "are just too silly. I mean, as though anybody would know what they would really do anyway. Or tell 7-Eleven." Roy laughs, but really she is shocked by the number of people, people right around here, people just like her and Shirley, who would lie to their current lovers. She, too, glances over at Shirley, but he is completely lost in a well-thumbed copy of *Swimsuit International* and doesn't notice.

Roy strolls back around the store, mainly to get away from any further inquiries from Glenn, who is tugging uncomfortably at her bra again, probably trying to get Shirley's attention away from his magazine. Roy is looking at a display of refrigerator magnets with American and Confederate flags, little red-white-and-blue signs saying THESE COLORS DON'T RUN, and Ninja turtles in odd poses, when she begins to slurp noisily at the bottom of her Slurpee. She peels the plastic top off, extricates her spoonstraw, and slips the top tidily in a waste receptacle marked FEED ME AND SAVE A TREE.

Roy looks across at Shirley, who has put his magazine back on the rack and is talking to Glenn, laughing about something, and suddenly and unexpectedly Roy feels dizzy again. She looks down at her spoonstraw, and she cannot decide what to do with it. Is she supposed to spoon the rest of her Slurpee out in tiny little dips, or is she supposed to guide the scooped end around the bottom of the cup while she sucks like a mini vacuum cleaner? She is filled with doubt and indecision.

She hears Shirley say he needs a cold drink, and she finds herself walking quickly over to see whether he will vote YES or NO, but he disenfranchises himself by choosing and paying for a chocolate YooHoo in a bottle. She doesn't know whether to be annoyed or relieved, and the whole store begins to seem huge and alien to her, as though she has been translated to another dimension like a character on a Twilight Zone rerun but can still see back into the one where she formerly resided.

"You ought to ask people," she hears herself saying too loudly to Glenn as she grabs Shirley's arm and pulls him toward the door, "what they do with these dumb spoonstraws. Now, that might be useful information."

Shirley has put his mirrors back on and is chug-a-lugging the YooHoo as they reach the door. Roy looks back and waves, and Glenn calls out good-bye and starts impressively rearranging herself once again. Roy turns back to the door and notices that, as Shirley holds it for her with his back as the last of the YooHoo disappears, with his straw hat on, he measures exactly six feet, two inches tall against the robber ruler by the door.

"I never even knew how tall Shirley was before," she thinks as the heat folds itself around her in the parking lot, and she does not allow herself to think how many other things about Shirley she does not know.

family bonds,

It is only when they are back in the Bronco that Roy notices two odd things. The first is that Shirley did not buy a Lotto ticket. She knows that there was not a winner at the last drawing, that the jackpot must be eight or nine million, and that Shirley has not yet bought a ticket or surely he would have told her. He always buys the same numbers (1-11-12-22-23-33), and he always shows her the ticket, has her hold it or even kiss it for good luck. She wonders what there was about this visit to the 7-Eleven that was different, that made him forget.

Roy glances over at Shirley, who has cocked his straw hat back on his head and is singing to himself, but the words whip out the open window in the hot wind. She wonders just what is making him so happy, but then she thinks of the other odd thing. She remembers that the whole time she was in the 7-Eleven she never once thought of her Uncle Vivian.

When Roy was a little girl, there was a strange man on all the 7-Eleven ads with such an odd, funny voice that everyone listened to those ads as if they were a regular comedy show and talked about them, too. She remembers her father saying one day that the man on the radio sounded like almost as big a sissy as Vivian. Her mother, Vivian's sister, told her father to just hush, but from that moment on, Roy has associated 7-Eleven with Uncle Vivian. And, until today, he has always come to mind whenever she goes in the store.

Uncle Vivian was a musician, a precise, round little man, with close-cropped hair and a shiny cherubic face, who always answered her many questions with "Oh, my dear, no" or "Oh, my dear, yes" with the same inflection, as though both answers were exactly as upsetting and vaguely dangerous. He taught piano and was by reputation a very demanding teacher. He always told stories that kept everyone laughing about his students' failings, how they stooped to folly, calling them always by the same names, Little Miss Muffet and Little Master Bates. Roy's mother would always get red-faced with laughter and tell him to just hush that kind of talk in front of the child. Roy never understood why her mother was so worried;

she just knew that she loved Uncle Vivian and admired him and thought studying the piano with him would be the most frightening and wonderful thing in the whole world.

But Roy never got her wish and never even learned to play "Chopsticks" on the piano, because one day Uncle Vivian came home from a vacation to Key West and everything was suddenly different. Roy still remembers that she was in the living room, drinking buttermilk and playing Parcheesi with her best friend, Dale, who was one of Uncle Vivian's beginning piano students and who was surely, given Dale's miserable progress, Little Master Bates in more than one of Uncle Vivian's tales. Roy had been blocking Dale for a long time, and even Dale's patience was beginning to wear thin, when Uncle Vivian burst through the door, his face burning like a Key West sunset, wearing orange Bermuda shorts and a bright pink-and-orange Hawaiian shirt unbuttoned almost to his stomach. A gold chain around his neck seemed almost painful against the flame of his fiery skin.

"So red the rose," he cried out to anyone interested in hearing, "no redder than I. Kiddies, I'm home."

Roy still remembers her mother's shocked face, how she almost stepped right in the middle of the Parcheesi board and did, to Dale's relief, scatter all the pieces. Her memory stops short there, probably because she and Dale were encouraged to go play outside, but the image of the new Uncle Vivian still burns in her mind's eye. He continued to dress as he had in Key West, so that Roy had ample opportunity to observe the new diamond earring in his right ear ("Zircon," Uncle Vivian had conspiratorially whispered to her one afternoon in his empty studio). He wore flip-flop sandals and an ankle bracelet with his name engraved on it in curlicues, and he began to come over for dinner much more frequently.

"Oh, my dear," he said at the table one evening to Roy's grimly silent father, "I just don't know where Little Miss Muffet and Young Master Bates have gotten off to. I hope they're not up to anything." He still gave lessons, but the student population had dwindled dramatically, so his comic tales began to be repeats, and then he began to brag about one of his few remaining students, Bonnie.

"Bonnie is so charming and so naughty," he would say, "I just let her make mistake after mistake without correcting her. Though correction is just what she needs." These remarks just weren't funny, and Roy could tell that even her mother was disappointed in Uncle Vivian.

And then, as suddenly as he changed after his trip to Key West, he was gone. Just gone, leaving an empty studio and a dusty piano, an empty apartment. Dining rooms all over town rang with the eager voices of speculation and gossip, but Uncle Vivian had clearly gone on to other voices, other rooms. And then, a few days later, it began to be known that he had not gone alone, that he had taken his favorite pupil, Charles Edward, with him, quite without the boy's family's permission. They had found a note addressed to "Bonnie" in the boy's room, noting the time he should be waiting at the studio with his bag packed.

Roy is startled to discover that the Bronco is pulling up at Shirley's house and that she has been thinking about Uncle Vivian for the whole trip there. The 7-Eleven does, she thinks, in one way or another, still remind her of him. And then she realizes for the very first time that she has never quite trusted anyone as fully as she once trusted Uncle Vivian. When he was arrested in Memphis and Charles Edward was returned home to be sent off to military school, Roy was crushed and very confused, and now she realizes that her injury was greater than she has known.

She flinches when Shirley bangs the Bronco door, and she thinks how strange he looks, standing impatiently on the sidewalk, his straw hat tilted forward now over his nose, his hand on his hip, waiting for her to get out and join him. She shakes her head like a dog coming up from a creek, pushes the door open, and climbs out to Shirley, who is, she knows as her eyes squeeze into a pained squint, standing there like an invisible man in the blinding glare of the sun.

celebration of eccentricity,

Roy pauses on the walk under the tree in the yard to let her eyes adjust, but Shirley's hand on her back urges her on toward the rooming house. Shirley has been living in a room here ever since he graduated from high school. Both he and his parents agreed that life in the trailer had just gotten too cramped for them all.

Roy and Shirley climb the steps and nod to the women on the porch, three of Shirley's fellow roomers swaying back and forth in bentwood rockers in the shade, before passing through the screen door and into the hall.

Roy goes on up the stairs and into Shirley's room while he takes a trip down the hall to the bathroom, and as she sits on the clumsily made bed and looks around the room, her eyes pass over Shirley's things as they have done so often ever since she and Shirley found each other suddenly last summer.

The one genuinely neat part of the room is a set of shelves Shirley has constructed out of boards and cinder blocks along one wall. On the shelves he has placed his collection of books and valuable objects. She notices the little black-and-white Scotty dogs on magnets, the multi-colored sets of dice, the salt and pepper shakers that echo each other in tidy rows.

And the books that seem to have no connection one to the other until Shirley explains his interest in doubles, in things that repeat. The Ed McBain mysteries with Detective Meyer Meyer, the copy of *Catch 22* with a character named Major Major, the copy of *The Last Days of Pompeii* that Shirley bought at the annual AAUW book sale by Edward Lytton Bulwer-Lytton, Lord Lytton, a paperback copy of a book with the queer title *Poe Poe Poe Poe Poe Poe Poe,* and a little book on the philosophy of James McTaggert Ellis McTaggert. Over the shelves, Shirley has taped on the white wall a picture he cut out of a book at the high school library of his favorite actress, Simone Simon. He has not been able to explain to Roy just why he likes these things so much, but he surely does. Whenever he takes to Roy out to eat at the Top of the Catch Restaurant and Lounge, she notices that he always orders "Mahi Mahi, the Fish So Good They Named It Twice."

Usually Roy does not worry about this oddness in Shirley's character. In fact, she finds it interesting and attractive, proof that he is not just another good-looking guy in a battered straw hat. But in the strange mood she has found herself in today, she almost feels another chill come over her in the stifling heat of the room, so much so that she glances at the limp blue curtains at the open window to see if a sudden breeze has come up.

When Shirley appears in the doorway, leaning against the doorframe, his hat tilted forward and his lower lip pushed out, instead of running to grab him and tickle him the way she usually does, Roy tells him she's feeling a little queasy and asks him to take her home so that she can take a cool bath, lie down in darkness, and have a little nap before they go out later in the evening.

a strong narrative voice,

Well, you can git up an' mosey long ef you wanter, but I'm gwineter tell dish yer tale ef I hatter r'ar my head back an' shet my eyeballs an' tell it ter myse'f fer ter see ef I done fergit it off'n my min'.

"Are you really Uncle Ben?" the little white boy asked politely, more like a girl in his refinement; all the boyishness had been taken out of him by that mysterious course of discipline that some mothers know how to apply.

She, the young mother, thirty-something, suntan smoothly glowing against her severely cut, white linen sundress, was standing by the looming display of brown-and-white rice boxes that the manager of Phar-Mor had constructed for the Grand Opening celebration. She was watching the little boy and me (in my Uncle Ben costume complete with tufts of cotton hair) very closely, so I knew I had to be very careful what I said.

"I speck dat's so," I remarked, "an' a ole nigger dat oughter been dead long ago, by good rights. A pity—a mighty pity."

The mother's face reddened, and she grasped the boy's hand and spun him abruptly away from me. She marched him quickly down the aisle, but her head was scanning from left to right as though she were looking for someone in authority. I decided it was probably a smart time to take a break, so I put my sample tray with all the little cups of hot rice down by the hot plate on the card table next to the display and started walking toward the employees' lounge at the rear of the store. I was in a hurry, naturally enough, but I did remember to shuffle along with bent back, in character. I may have an attitude, but no sense losing a good job on the first day, even if it does only last three days.

"When you wanter be hardheaded," I muttered half to myself and half to any interested on-lookers, "an' have yo' own way, you better b'ar in min' de 'oman an' de dinner pot."

I was nearly back to the prescription counter when I saw Shirley looking at a copy of Playboy in the book section. I hadn't seen him since I had gotten home from the summer semester at college, so I decided to see whether he would recognize me in the Uncle Ben getup. I shuffled up to him and prepared to give him a goose, as though we were still in middle school together when I was the voice at the back door every morning, calling him to shake a leg or we'd be late again. But before I could get in range, his name boomed almost unintelligibly out over the store loudspeaker system, and he jumped, looked around guiltily, put the *Playboy* back on the highest shelf of the magazine rack, and bolted for the prescription counter. He didn't even see me in the rush, just another black boy or shadowy native son standing around, looking for something not to do. I shrugged my shoulders dramatically, spread my pale palms wide, and continued to shuffle my way to the lounge.

At the prescription counter, I saw Shirley and a slim blonde woman about our age, talking animatedly. So I sidled alongside to see just what was going on.

"That's my prescription," Shirley was saying to the blonde, who was clutching tightly in her hand the little paper bag the pharmacist had given her.

"Then why," she asked, "does it have my name on it?" And she shoved the bag under his nose.

Shirley actually blushed and then said in a tense low voice, "That is *my* name!"

The blonde squinted at him, a mean hard squint, and then she popped the bag open, pulled out a blue-and-white tube, and said with some bitterness, "I suppose you use Monistat regularly."

Shirley blushed again, and this time looked confused and baffled to boot. The blonde was by this time as flushed as he was. Just then the loudspeaker boomed out his name again, and he turned to see the pharmacist holding another smaller bag with his name on it.

Shirley looked back and forth from the bag to the blonde to the bag and back to the blonde, and then he said, with a voice touched with what I felt to be genuine awe, almost a whisper, "We must both have the same name."

I hate to inject the teller in the tale here, but before she could answer, I noticed the little boy was tugging his mother my way around the corner of the vitamin shelves, and I decided it was time for my feet to continue doing their stuff. The mother looked strained and almost in tears, but the little boy was very far from crying. He suddenly broke away from her, seized this old darky's hand, and went skipping along by his side.

I led him in a slow curve back to his mother, handed him over to her, and bowed from the waist, before shuffling through the lounge door and out of sight. I could still hear him whining shrilly to her, but I did not falter for a second. I did not look back.

Ain't dat de way you does in books?

themes of racial guilt and human endurance,

The noise and confusion of the Merchants Association Annual Dixie Days Ball makes Roy almost want to shout, it is so loud, but when it falls suddenly silent as the skirling of a bagpipe cuts sharply through the hubbub, she almost wishes the noise would continue. She squeezes Shirley's hand tightly as the piper marches sedately across the center of the dance floor toward the bandstand. He is playing, as he does every year, "Amazing Grace," and everyone is standing at excited attention. His appearance always marks the formal opening of the ball.

Roy does not share the excitement, however, for a terrible sense of guilt sweeps over her like a cold fog swirling down over the scattered sheep and bare crags of the mountains of Glencoe. The icy notes of the bagpipe stir her Campbell blood to a boil, and her face burns with the guilt of the terrible massacre in that pitch-black early morning of February 13, 1692. No Campbell, Roy thinks, must ever be allowed to forget the burden of that guilt. She knows that everyone in the crowded room must be staring at her, so she releases Shirley's hand and, without explanation, pushes her way head down through the mass of excited couples to the ladies' room.

Only after she can hear no trace of the piper's laments does Roy venture out of the lavatory and back onto the floor of the ballroom. The band has begun to play, the lights have been lowered, and the dancing has begun. She looks around for Shirley but does not see him where she abandoned him nor on the dance floor. She does see a clump of Shirley's friends over near the punch bowl, so she heads in that direction.

She has not seen Allison, one of Shirley's best friends, since he went away to college on a big minority scholarship, so when she spots him in the group, she goes up to him and gives him a big hug.

He is dressed in the striped outfit and little striped hat of someone on a chain gang, and he has even got a chain of black cardboard links trailing between his ankles.

"How are you?" she says. "You're looking so good. What are you doing here in town?"

"You're looking pretty good yourself, Roy," he says, smiling at her, holding her by her shoulders at arm's length. "Haven't you heard?" he continues. "I'm playing Uncle Ben at the new Phar-Mor, yassuh, yassuh."

Roy is as confused as always by Allison and as happy as always to see him, but she remembers that she is looking for Shirley. When she asks Allison if he has seen him, Allison grins, pushes a couple of their friends aside, and points to Shirley, who is hunkering on the floor in his riverboat gambler's costume by the punch table, along with three or four other boys they knew in high school.

"It's a hunkering contest," Allison says. "They're going for the championship by seeing who'll last the longest. And there squats Shirley," he says, with a sweep of his hand, "a veritable fireplug of strength."

Roy stares down at Shirley's confident, determined face, and realizes that he will spend most of the dance hunkered down, waiting for one or another of his friends to fall over, stiff and groaning. She starts to complain, to pull Shirley up right now and get it over with, when she suddenly has a vision for reasons she cannot explain of Dale, sitting in his Great Aunt Sidney's kitchen, sipping buttermilk out of a thick glass tumbler and solving a complicated chess puzzle, missing the dance of the year to take care of her as he does every Saturday night.

Roy stares at Shirley but doesn't really see him. She hears Allison's witty voice but doesn't really hear him. She knows something very strange is happening in her life, but she doesn't know what it is.

local tradition,

Shirley is still one of the two remaining hunkerers when the lights flicker up and down and the announcement for the formal dances and the arch figure blurs out into the room. Roy is dressed as Julie in *Showboat,* and her crinolines and hoops swish and switch as she decides enough is more than enough and pushes through the few remaining observers to Shirley's side. She plants her small patent leather pump on Shirley's shoulder and gives him a good shove. He cries foul as he falls over backwards onto the floor, but his opponent, a thin boy whom Roy does not know with a face red with raging acne, leaps upward with a bounce and shouts in a high-pitched voice, "All right!"

Shirley lies on the floor in a horizontal squat, moaning, until Roy takes his hand and pulls him erect. He crawls up onto his feet among the catcalls of his jeering friends. He is angry, but he also knows that Roy is right, that Julie cannot be expected to walk through the arch without Gaylord Ravenal at her side. All around the room, couples are forming two long lines that, when the band begins to play "Can't Help Lovin' Dat Man," will begin to snake through the Dixie Days Arch of Love, which is bathed in golden light near the bandstand. The local tradition is that young lovers who pass through it together and in perfect step will be wed within a year. Many is the couple that has stumbled out of step at the last moment as they entered the arch, but Roy has every intention of strolling through the arch with Shirley and of not being even the tiniest bit out of step.

As they take their place in the line behind Billy Joe and Billy Jo, the couple in high school voted the cutest couple but who somehow haven't made it through the arch together yet, Shirley winces and stretches his legs and grumbles until he notices a pretty blonde young woman dressed as an antebellum belle in a pale pink hoop skirt, standing right beside them. He blushes suddenly and involuntarily, nods at her, and turns to Roy, who is looking up at him with considerable interest.

"Roy," he says, putting his right hand on Roy's smooth, sturdy back, "I'd like you meet somebody I just met," and he puts his left hand on the blonde woman's back, noticing how delicate and frail it is, how aware his hand is of the tracery of her spine and shoulder blades.

"And the funniest thing, the most amazing thing," he continues, nervously and quickly, "is her name."

"Roy," Shirley says, "I'd like you meet Shirley. Shirley, Roy."

Roy feels Shirley's hand almost tremble against her back, and she looks straight into the other Shirley's pale blue eyes, feeling for a second almost as if she were about to float right over the arch and away, when the lights all go out except for the single gold spotlight, and the band begins to play, "Fish gotta swim, birds gotta fly ... "

a sense of impending loss,

The line begins to move forward, slowly and rhythmically, and the other Shirley, who is unaccompanied, walks alongside Shirley and Roy, chatting about the dance and the arch. Roy has never seen her before tonight, and she wonders whether this new Shirley is visiting in town or has just moved here or has been here all along like a copperhead, dangerous and silent and unseen. She cannot see her china blue eyes in the dim gold light, but she knows they are focused on Shirley. "Like a smart bomb," she thinks.

The succession of couples moves steadily forward as the music yearns and turns on itself.

Shirley turns abruptly to Roy and tightly squeezes her hand, which until now has been lying limply in the loose coil of his fingers. His eyes are like bright metal in the gold light, and he says to her urgently, "I forgot to get my Lotto ticket. Roy, how could you let me forget my Lotto ticket?"

There is an intensity to his voice that Roy does not like or understand, and his grip seems more like that of a vise than a lover's caress.

"I just know," Shirley is saying to Shirley, "that my numbers are going to come tonight when I don't," and he squeezes Roy's hand even tighter and hisses through his teeth, "even have a ticket."

Roy knows that Shirley is nodding sympathetically to Shirley as well as she knows that the heat in her face is caused by the rising of her Campbell blood. The golden blur of the approaching arch seems to her like the dawn that finally rose over bloody Glencoe and the scattered corpses of the MacDonalds. She grits her teeth and pulls her hand from Shirley's hard grip just as Billy Joe and Billy Jo step through the arch together, but also just as she hears her father's voice in her ear.

"Roy," he is saying, "I hate to spoil your evening, darling, but there's been a death in the family."

He pulls her out of the line just as she and Shirley are poised to swing through the arch. Shirley and Shirley step out of line on the other side of the arch and look back at Roy and her hovering father.

The line of couples falters behind them, unsure of what to do.

"Who is dead?" Roy says. "Mother's not . . . "

"No, no, Roy," her father says quickly, "don't worry, darling. It's your Uncle Vivian. We just got the call."

An icy numbness sweeps up over Roy, the arch seems to grow and sway, and the loud mourning of the band reduces to zero db in her deaf ears. Once again, she feels as though she is floating right out of herself as the room grows larger and larger in the silence. And just as she feels herself falling back into her father's arms and swaying toward the floor, she sees Shirley and Shirley, in perfect synchronization, rush toward her through the golden arch.

a pervasive sense of humor in the face of tragedy,

The long night passes from death to morning, and all night long Roy tosses and turns, dreaming fitfully of Uncle Vivian and Shirley and Shirley, mixed-up dreams of a wolf at the door and the iron baby angel by the cemetery gate, a descent into the maelström of dreams and nightmares, Uncle Vivian's voice, and the voice of the 7-Eleven man, and a sound of voices dying all around.

"Follow me down to one of the dark places," Uncle Vivian says to her, and when she tries to follow him, Shirley and Shirley stand in the arch and laugh at her. Dark laughter. Or are they crying for her? She wakes with a start and finds her mother, her red cheeks streaked white by tears, standing by her bed.

"Roy, we're going to have to take care of the funeral and of each other this week," she sobs. "Your father never did like Uncle Vivian, always called him a sissy. And after . . . and after . . . well, you know, after Vivian left town, things just got worse and worse. It's up to us, Roy. Vivian loved us, and we're the ones who loved him."

Roy sits up in bed and hugs her mother. She is crying, too, now, and throughout the next three days, whether she is sorting through the family linen and silver for the reception after the funeral or helping her mother buy a new dress or keeping peace at the dinner table, she finds herself crying unexpectedly and often.

She has not noticed that the winning Lotto numbers were 2-22-23-33-34-44, so she does not comment on it when Shirley calls her and offers to take her for a ride or something. In fact, she is unable to talk to him and coldly dismisses his offers. He calls again the next day, but the next couple of days he doesn't bother.

The morticians pick up Uncle Vivian at the tricounty airport and lay him out in the mortuary in a bright yellow sport jacket, an open-collared pink shirt, with the gold chain gleaming around his neck. He looks very pale and thin, especially with the rouge on his cheeks and lips. Roy weeps when she sees him, terribly and hard, and then she suddenly stops crying, becomes cool and distant and very clearheaded.

Uncle Vivian's partners, two singers called the Romantic Comedians for whom he played the piano, arrive in town the morning of the funeral, two nondescript bald-headed little men with strange smiles.

"I'm Tweedle," one of them explains to Roy when he discovers she has never seen their act, doesn't even know anything about it. "I play the Man, and Dee, my partner, plays the Woman. You wouldn't believe it, but she looks marvelous in drag. We sing the old songs, the great ones, 'Tea for Two,' 'Miss Otis Regrets,' 'Can't Help Lovin' Dat Man,' 'Let's Call the Whole Thing Off,' you know. And of course we camp them up quite a bit." He tosses his hands in the air in a helpless gesture of mixed sorrow and delight.

"Vivian was such a dear," he continues, and Dee chimes in, "The best pianist we ever had." He sighs, looks down at his hands, and then suddenly cracks his knuckles with a sharp clatter.

At the graveside, despite the oppressive heat and without warning, the Romantic Comedians begin to sing a medley of songs. Dee pulls a long purple feather boa out of his pocket to indicate that he is the Woman, and Roy is surprised by how good their voices are. They sing "After You've Gone" and "Ev'ry Time We Say Goodbye" and "The Man That Got Away" and close with "There Will Never Be Another You" and "Too Late Now." As they are singing, Roy's mother begins to sob uncontrollably again, while her father and the minister both stand in stony, grim silence.

The Romantic Comedians are singing "The Man That Got Away" when Roy looks up, past the solemn boy with the close-cropped hair and the gray sergeant major's uniform, to find Shirley standing with Shirley at the back of the assembly of family friends among Vivian's former piano students of various ages. Shirley looks hot and uncomfortable in his blue suit, and Shirley looks particularly delicate and almost transparent beside him, her hand perched gently on his sleeve.

Dale is standing beside Roy, and she takes his arm and presses her face into his lapel as the sight of Shirley and the sound of the Romantic Comedians segueing into "There Will Never Be Another You" triggers another bout of tears, just when she has begun to think that she will never cry again. Dale hugs her to him, and the sight of his serious, concerned face when she looks up again causes her to break out laughing. Laughing and laughing and laughing.

an inability to leave the past behind.

The rain, which has been threatening all day, begins in the early afternoon. It washes the dust off the leaves of trees and bushes all over the county and causes windows to be hurriedly closed that had been open throughout the entire heat wave. It settles the dry sod into place on Vivian's grave and washes the petals off the few sprays of flowers still tilting on their wire frames.

Shirley is perched by Shirley's window as though poised for flight while he stands behind her. They are looking out over the wet treetops and watching the rain dance on the sidewalk and the top of the red Bronco parked in the street. He wraps his hands around her waist, and she turns her head up to him for a kiss. He is still amazed at how thin she is, how her breasts seem to come out of nowhere and press into his chest, how hugging her is like embracing air or an image in a mirror. A gust causes a mist of rain to spray through the open window and onto their faces and hair, and just for a second Shirley remembers hugging Roy in this window on a rainy evening last spring and how she seemed so substantial and so permanent. But Shirley presses herself into him with such urgency that he can think of nothing else. He wants her so badly and, when she finishes her prescription, maybe, just maybe she will be his. He wants to shout, but she is kissing him so hard she is taking all his breath away.

Roy is sitting across from Dale at his family's kitchen table. They are drinking cold buttermilk and playing chess. The door is open, and the rain is dancing on the flat painted wood of the back porch and on the rambling rose that winds up the porch pillars. The blooms are bright pink, and the rain makes them dance and nod, but Roy finds herself thinking how a killing frost will one day make the whole plant dry and brittle. Roy has Dale backed into a corner, but she finds her attention wandering. She licks a white rim of buttermilk from her lips and finds herself suddenly wishing she had a Coke Slurpee, wishing that she were at the 7-Eleven with Shirley and that she were making him answer the Question of the Week, making the total rise to 74%. She feels her eyes swimming in tears, and Dale's serious, puzzled face seems far away as though she were looking up at him from deep underwater.

"Fish gotta swim," she finds herself singing out loud. And then she repeats it, "Fish gotta swim." And then she starts to cry again, saying to Dale over and over again, "I'm sorry, Dale. I'm sorry. I'm really sorry. I'm so sorry."

Allison is looking out of the window of his sister's small pink house at his little nephews jumping up and down in the rain by the drainage ditch at the side of the road. Water is raging in the ditch, and they are screaming, "Flood, flood, flood!" His sister is in town at her job, and he has agreed to watch the boys all afternoon. The rain is washing away the dust from the road that always coats the house and makes his sister often keep the windows closed even on the hottest nights. They are open now, and the rain is splashing in on the floor. Allison does not close them; he can always mop the floors later. He is supposed to be working on his honors paper on the uses of African-American folk tales in southern literature, but he can't help but watch the boys leaping around the muddy yard.

"'Twouldn't 'stonish me none ef we wuz ter have some fallin' wedder," he says aloud. "'Tiz e'en about ez much ez I kin do fer to keep fum laughin'."

3

WALKING ON SHALLOW WATER

The Death Eater

My intention is to portray a truly beautiful soul.
—Fyodor Dostoevsky

 I swipe at the formica counter top with a short mop—one of the manager's bright ideas, he's full of them—among other things—a short wooden handle, a cluster of synthetic pink sponges—a toilet mop for the slick counter where people eat—appropriate enough. I watch them chew and swallow, talk to each other with their mouths stuffed with half-chewed food—pasty bread and grainy burger, split pickle and oozing ketchup, a swirl of mustard, crinkles of lettuce in the mushy mix. It's enough to make you want to wipe them off, mop them out. Chewing, chewing, chewing all their lives, at their lives, chewing at things that were once alive, things that were killed solely so that they could chew them, swallow them, eat them—pale dimpled lettuce leaves, as green and delicate as a spring day, calves wobbling on their spindly legs, cows running and leaping like colts across a hillside pasture, wheat blowing and waving in an easy wind like the flowing sea, tomatoes swollen on the hairy vines, red and yellow flowing over their even green like a vivid sunset. Their throats are jerking like spastic things with a life of their own, passing death on down the tube, juicing it up with acids and biles, squeezing it out as steaming piss or rank shit. At least they don't come in here and drop their trousers or hike up their skirts and do *that* in front of me.
 I swab the shiny top and put my mop away in its bucket of antiseptic poison. Someone sneezes down the way, the splutter diving into his food or bouncing damply across the gleaming counter

top. I stare at him, death in my gaze, little skulls in my eyes. He doesn't even notice, doesn't even look up, shoving the burger in, chewing, chewing—a rim of grease and smeared mayonnaise around his flexing lips—the eggy slime of aborted yellow chicks. A guy in a red plaid jacket comes in out of the snow—the doorbell clapper dings and hangs there swinging. He orders a burger all the way, taking off his jacket and hanging it up on one of the little hooks lined down the opposite wall, looking around for a stool—chooses one up near the register—his face hard and open and eager, death in his eyes, death on toast. A relief anyway to turn away from all those mouths, to smack the cold damp meat on the griddle, to split the mealy bun and put it face down on the edge of the griddle with the iron on it—to heat some fresh death for the guy on the stool with the open hungry eyes. Hot death—coming up—going down.

A burlesque joke. Man says to girl: "Come on, let me kiss you, honey." She replies, coy: "Where do you want to kiss me [tilting her head], on my cheek?" He says: "No, honey, on the mouth." She says (raising up her hands, shocked): "On my mouth—where I eat?!?"

Love. Sex. How can you love anybody that eats? Death on the lips, death on the teeth, death on the tongue—the furry red tongue that comes out and licks the greasy lips. Death on death on death—hot death, cold death—death in sealed plastic, death crimped in aluminum foil—death warmed over, reheated in the microwave—regurgitated death, heartburn, the upward eruption of stomach juices and deadly acids into the esophagus—death any way you want it—gourmet death, home-cooked death, take-out death, convenient fast death.

I slip the spatula under the sizzling meat, flip it over—squeeze the grease out of it with a hiss and spreading sigh—take the iron off the bun—lay the bread on a white plate, face up, hot and dry, smear on some mayonnaise, a leaf or two of lettuce—two—a slice of pale winter tomato, tasteless death. I slip the spatula under the meat, lift it onto the bun. One hamburger, all the way. Not far. Not far to go either—through the lips, into the teeth and jaws and tongue—down the hatch. I scrape the grease across and off the hot griddle with the end of the spatula—mop it off with a damp rag lying on the counter by the griddle. I listen to them chew and gulp and swallow.

Just think of it: the lips press together—four lips, two mouths—

tongues that licked the grease of dead meat greedily off those lips, maybe only a few minutes, a few seconds before—the tongues press against the teeth inside each mouth—the bacteria swarming between those teeth, stinking like a garbage dump, eating, eating—the tongues probe out between the lips—the tongues touch—he moans—he loves it—she pushes her tongue into his mouth—where he eats!

Maybe it's just this bad winter—snow everywhere that won't go away—even in the brief thaws, lying on the banks, beckoning, drawing more snow to it—the furnace running all the time, even with the thermostat cut down to 65°, to 40° overnight. It's not too bad though, working over the griddle—but I think it's been getting me down—making me more touchy. All that talk about fossil fuel running out—not even enough dead things left to burn—we eat every dead thing so fast there won't even be any fossils left by this generation to be fuel—we eat dead things faster than we die. Some say a new ice age is coming—others claim we're turning the whole planet into a giant greenhouse—no more winter, no more trees, no more food sooner or later. Whichever's right—fire or ice—maybe they both are right—fire and ice—the whole world is dying—and who'll be here to eat it? Only the sun. I remember once in class a teacher telling us about the sun—trying to scare us, I think, for some reason, with the end of the world—how one day the sun would swell up like a giant hot orange and devour the earth. And it was pretty frightening, even if this wasn't supposed to happen for billions of years—I remember looking at my hand, a nick on the knuckle just scabbing over, a cracked nail, and thought of it—finger and knuckle and thumb—swelling and blackening, bursting and dissolving in the greedy sun. But there was one girl in the class who wouldn't buy it—I can see her face now, puzzled, eyes wide, incredulous—"How can it eat the earth?" she said—"Why, it doesn't even have a mouth."

Until the sun opens those red hot lips and gulps us down, though, I know who'll do the eating. We will—we, the omnivores—we'll eat anything, whether it moves or not—and if there's nobody handy to eat us when we die, crack our yellow bones and suck the fatty marrow, we'll eat ourselves—all those enzymes living happily in our cells will get hungry and eat us on the spot. Breakfast, brunch, lunch, tea, dinner and supper—all in one sitting—smack, smack, smack!

For that matter, the sun probably does have a mouth—has just been keeping it closed—just hasn't had anything to say—waiting. Probably has a tongue, too. In fact, I saw a picture in a magazine not long ago of the sun licking its lips—a huge flare of orange flame licking out—ready to slurp us down—the mouth splitting the fiery face of the sun—tongue lapping out—out hundreds of thousands of miles—hot hot death.

Some fat guy in a black overcoat is standing by the cash register, waiting to pay for his chili dogs, for his crime. He'll look at me now—no shame in paying for it—not like sex—but he wouldn't meet my eyes while he was eating it down—looked down at the plate or out the window at the snow or, out of focus, into space. Couldn't face me while he did the deed. It's too bright in here. It's like fucking in daylight with the shades up. Some people just won't do it. Have to do it in the dark—so it's not so personal. Like those restaurants with the high prices and the dim lights—dark to cover up the guilt—so he can murmur to her over his hot meat, and she won't have to notice what he's doing—shoving it in, chewing it up, gulping it down. Eating death in the dark. How romantic.

This place is called the Bright Spot—THE BRIGHT SPOT IN YOUR DAY—GRAB A SPOT AT THE BRIGHT SPOT, THE RIGHT SPOT. Just a hole in the wall—one counter, no tables, no booths. Ten stools—WE SEAT A THOUSAND CUSTOMERS, TEN AT A TIME. Hamburgers, hot dogs, foot longs, fries, hashbrowns, eggs, toast, bacon, sausage, chili, pie. That's it. Coffee, soft drinks, no wine, no beer. Bright lights so you have to see what you're eating—what you're really doing.

I punch his bill up on the machine—ring the drawer open and make his change. Enjoy your death, buddy. See you in the Meat Wagon. I don't say anything to him. He just says, "Thanks," and hustles out the door. Three chili dogs, mustard, onion, no relish—pale wieners, almost gray—they need the chili and the mustard all right. The snow blows down the street, and he disappears into it—all bolstered up and filled with death. I got it at the Bright Spot, the Right Spot. Death on a bun. Hot death.

I go down to where he was sitting, sweep the crumbs and crumpled napkins off the counter into my box, look at the smears on the counter top. Grease, two blots of chili, a dab of mustard. I walk back up to the counter, grab the mop, walk back, and swab away. People, even if they're not slobs like this guy, are a mess. I could be cooking people on that griddle and they'd be just as greasy. Oily. Oozing. That's how the police get their man—finger-prints. We leak oil wherever we go. Every one of us is like a broken tanker, leaking oil—leaving oily prints on everything we touch. Ring around the collar. Oily eyebrow prints on our glasses—kill trees to make little purple pieces of paper for us to wipe the oil off our glasses—trees die that man may see again. Oil oozing out of your scalp—wash and scrub all you want, until your hair squeaks like a caught rat, and it's oily again in a day. I knew a guy once who had a brilliant plan. Set up hair parlors all over the country. Drain the oil out of people's greasy hair—keep it—bottle it—market it under some clever name. DINKUM OIL—nature's own natural oil for every natural purpose. People with dyed hair could pour it back in. He would have made a fortune if he'd actually done it. Little bottles with labels with a thumbs up sign on them—DINKUM OIL. I mop the leavings away, scrub the counter clean, turn away.

Leaking. Everything we do is connected with leaking something—or trying not to. We ooze oil, we sweat, we spit, we sneeze, our noses drool, we cough, we piss, we shit, we shed bitter salt tears. When we procreate, pass our kind on proudly into time, we seep and squirt. And to stop it all, we invent soaps and powders and syrups and condoms and pads. When you cut us, do we not bleed—and women, do they not bleed to the clock? And when we die, do not all the floodgates open, and every foul thing in us come pouring out? Close the eyes of the dead so they won't have to see what they're doing. Alms for the dead, pennies for their eyes—and into the laundromat with the sheets.

I walk up by the window and stare out into the snow. It is falling steadily. The day is white. I forget for a time what is going on behind me. I don't hear those bellies gurgling and throats convulsing. All I see is now, and all I hear is silence—a white pure world, no one eating, no one dying, no one even living—just snow, evenly filling up the cracks and crevices of this deadly world. I drift out of myself into the snow. I am a flake of snow, turning slowly down like a crystal carousel, turning to a silent tune that I can hear—freed for once of death, freed for once, freed. And the bell over the door rings, and they walk in—the Fat Family—and I feel death rise in me like molten magma boiling up from the earth's rotten rumbling core.

Ding, ding, and in walks first the Fat Father—bulging and holding the door for the Fat Mother and the two Fat Kids, Fat Boy and Fat Girl—all so nicely balanced—all grinning and licking their lips—tongues popping in and out like snake's heads from holes in the eighth circle of hell. The Fat Father opens his camel's hair coat—reveals an orange-red jump suit underneath—a mustard orange scarf dangling down loose inside the coat. It suddenly hits me—with his red face and all those colors, he looks just like a giant hot dog—one dog, mustard only. He smiles, showing his teeth, and doffs his coat—hangs it on a hook on the wall by the red plaid jacket. The rest of the Fat Family follows his lead—all in hot dog jump suits. Then they waddle over to the last four stools at the counter—maneuver themselves onto them—the stools all creak and wobble. "We'll start," the Fat Father allows, "with four bowls of piping hot chili."

"You'll have to wait a minute," I say. "I've got to add beans to the pot." And he accepts it—looks a little hurt, but accepts it.

I reach under the counter—my hand finds the can quickly—I don't even have to look—the top and bottom of the can bulging and buckled, swollen and solid. I shield it from view with my body—bang a pot with my elbow, making it clatter to the floor, as I punch the can opener into the can. It hisses like an angry snake, an air hose, but no one hears. No one hears but me. The beans are brown and bubbling. I dump them quickly into the pot with the steaming chili—I pitch the can into the waste and turn around.

Red jacket has finished his burger—has wiped his slick lips, crumpled his napkin, and tossed it into the grease and crumbs on his plate, and is standing by the counter wrestling with his coat and waiting to pay for the slaughter. I take my time with his change—listening all the while to the chili come back to a bubble and boil. He rings the door open and saunters out into the snow. I turn back to the pot.

The Fat Family is getting restless—mumbling on their creaking stools—so I line up four white china bowls and start to spoon the steamy chili into the bowls. I hear their lips start smacking. The Fat Father actually says, "Yum, yum." Enough poison in half of one of those dozens of hot beans to kill a thousand men—spoon it out, turn to the Fat Family, deliver the goods, two bowls at a time—add the oyster crackers, a speciality of the house—plank down the bottle of Texas Pete hot sauce—the key to my plan. The Fat Family likes to douse on the hot sauce—squirt, squirt, squirt—Fat Father first, then Fat Mother, Fat Boy, and Fat Girl—the Texas Peteing order well established. I hold my breath until the Fat Father unscrews the tiny cap with his fat fingers and starts the familiar process—lots of pepper follows, half a shaker of salt—tug at the cellophane, crumble up those crackers—stir it all together—hot sauce, hot pepper, steaming meat and beans, steaming botulin—not hot enough to kill the sporulating anaerobic bacilli—hot enough for the Fat Family to wolf it down, dog it down, swine it down—and they do—yum, yum.

I dream repeatedly about the Fat Family—dream how they squeeze through the door—the bell gongs like one of Quasimodo's—how they bulge across the room—fill the room with their coats or with their astonishingly stretched yellow summer T-shirts—open their mouths like anacondas—groan for food—I have to shovel it in—Fat Father and Fat Mother pull at their clothes as they chew and gape—pull their clothes off, their bulbous fat so enormous, so white, that there is no way to tell one from the other—all sex hidden or overgrown—and the Fat Kids peep and whistle like huge baby birds, fat cuckoos pushing at the tiny edges of the stolen nest. And I shovel dead things into them, corpses of dogs and cats, lumps of dead rat and fetid bird. Shovel and shovel until I vomit—vomit in the food—but I keep shoveling—and they keep smacking their horrible lips—and I wake myself screaming—and sometimes I am heaving yellow bile out onto myself, onto my sheets, burning onto the dark floor.

I hate them—and my hands are shaking as I watch them dip and gulp and smack away at death—their own deaths this time. They come in once a week—not always on the same day—but once a week faithfully—always the four of them, eating as much as six or seven hungry lumberjacks. The Fat Father and Fat Mother must be in their early forties—the Fat Kids must be in their early teens. Balls of fat that walk and talk—that eat and eat—that need death on death on death so they can walk and talk and eat and eat and eat. The counter top around their plates fills up with crumbs and salt and pepper, squirts of Texas Pete, blobs of mayonnaise and mustard, chili sauce, onion bits, dobs of relish, and balled greasy napkin paper—and the floor around their stools is awash with spill and splatter.

Today they spoon down all their chili and order a round of chili dogs, all the way, three each—and, for once, I comply without a groan or mutter—I steam the buns and pop the wieners in, spoon on the mustard and the relish and the onions and the red chili sauce—I deliver them up with a smile. I smile and smile.

They pop those hot dogs in, licking and slurping like a fat, pimply woman in a cheap porn movie—hardcore—XXX—very little difference that I can see—Fat Porn—bulging and biting—slurp, slurp. Then they order and eat hamburgers—smack them down—rub their bellies and belch and burp—and underneath all that, all that chewed meat mass, bubbling in their own inner death, are the beans—taking their acid bath, beginning to ease down into the intestines—and somewhere from four hours to eight days, the Fat Family will grow lazy—all that fat pep will dwindle and smother—tired and so lazy—lolling back in their chairs and sofas—Fat Kids nodding off at their weary desks in junior high—and then the visual disturbances will begin—double vision, seeing Fat Family upon Fat Family, all seeing themselves and each other doubled, record-breaking fat flesh all around the room—blurred vision, unfocused fat—loss of accommodation, enormous blurred doubled fat in one eye, tiny blurred doubled fat in the other—total loss of pupillary light reflex, their pupils as fat and swollen as their disgusting sick bodies—snap on the lights and see them go blind. Poor, poor Fat Family—so very tired and bleary of sight.

They probably won't vomit, no splutter and gag of bilious half-chewed death—won't shit buckets of blattering multihued spume—will just stumble weakly around—("Don't know why I'm so tired, Mother, just ate a fine dinner.")—looking for the door, looking for the phone—("Which one is the real one, the big one or the little one?")—and before help can come, whooping and winking from the Rescue Squad station through the snow, paralysis will strike—knocking their speech off balance, making their fat tongues and fat lips waggle uselessly, making them unable—and this will hurt the Fat Family the worst—unable to swallow. There they'll lie, weak and blubbering—and if they do swallow anything, it'll come back hot and slick through their fat hairy noses.

The Bright Spot is empty of other customers by the time they finish—the afternoon is getting on into evening. The night man will be coming in soon, and I have things to do—chili pots to empty and scrub and polish, chili bowls to wash and rub. But no problem—they finish and compliment each other and the food all around. They swing to the right in unison like a circus act and plop to the solid floor. They suit up, coating their red-orange expanses with coats of many colors. The Fat Father eases up to the counter by the register, tugging a fat wallet from one snug pocket—unfolding some bills. As I ring up the variety of the sale, Fat Mother and the Fat Kids have entered into a lively debate about dessert—whether they should bundle into a station wagon and drive to a Baskin Robbins for a round of Matterhorns—or walk up the block through the snow to settle dinner and share buckets of Munchkins at Dunkin Donuts. I reach a total and miss the result of the debate while making change. "Thank you very much," says Fat Father, a warm smile squeezing out through his fat cheeks. "We enjoy eating here so much, it's always a real pleasure." "Well, thank you, sir," I say, "I always try to give good customers like you what you really deserve, the best." He smiles again, pocketing the fat wallet. The whole Fat Family smiles at me, bobbing their hooded heads like tethered balloons in a breeze.

I certainly owe the Fat Family something for all this good will—all of those cherubic smiles. Perhaps a warning—a suggestion. Why don't you drop in at the emergency room at your favorite hospital for a round of stomach pumps? Or, wouldn't you like to go home now for a session of finger-down-the-throat waggling? Or just possibly: Be quick, you've been poisoned by a homicidal maniac who hates you, who hates everybody and everything that's at home in this nightmare of a dying self-devouring world. Run while you still can, Fat Family. Run before the world splits in two and slows down. Run. Run. RUN!

Instead of any of these alternatives, I step around the end of the counter and open the door—ding, ding—and usher the Fat Family out into the snowy eve and on their way. "Thank you." "Thank you again." "Good-bye." "See you." "Good-bye." I listen to them squeak and crunch away through the falling snow. I breathe the clean air. I fill my lungs with the snowy evening air, damp and coldly, sweetly clean. Good-bye, Fat Family, I say to myself. Good-bye.

I turn back to the Bright Spot—some cleaning up to do before the regular dinner crowd—not so hungry or early as the Fat Family—lonely eaters, not shy of doing the deed on a solitary stool, too shy to deal with a restaurant or even a cafeteria line—hungry for cheap fast food—lowering their eyes and gobbling it down—and tonight the cleaning up must be a little special. The door dings shut behind me.

I begin with the chili pot, the bowls, the spoons—even before I sweep and mop and swab up the disgusting mess around the Fat Family's stools. I turn on the tap and start up the disposal unit in the sink. It grinds and growls like a starved eater, and I spoon it gobs of deadly chili. It swallows them manfully down and yowls for more. I feed it all the pot—watch out, sewer rats. I scrub the pot, the bowls, the spoons, first with the counter swab and its disinfectant, then under the hot water, soap and brush, scrub and scrub. I dry them with a towel, toss the towel into the dirty towel bin, put the bowls back in the racks, the spoons back in the plastic spoon bin. I zip open new cans of beans, spoon gritty meat out of the refrigerator, mix up a new batch of clean chili, and set it to boil. Then I turn to the mess.

I sweep the crumpled napkins, three or four at each place, the crumbs and fragments, orts and shards of the Fat Family's dinner off into my garbage box. I pull out the silly mop and slap and circle and sop at the mess that remains, orange and yellow and red and green, goo and gush. I mop it clean—rinse out the mop's red sponges—pop it back into its pot. I drag out the floor mop in its rolling bucket, and the broom. I sweep the floor all around where they sat, sweep the mess around the counter, into the back room, finally out the back door into the back alley. I am gagging and retching. I slam the door, the mess splattered out into the new snow. I go back and mop the floor, the long trail from counter to door—and then I am through. I lean against the wall, the mop propped beside me. My stomach is still heaving—my pulse is racing—my legs are watery and wet. But I fight it all down and back. I have swept and mopped it all away. I have cleaned the Fat Family out of my life. The nausea fades—and the bell over the front door dings.

It is the night man. We don't have much to say to each other—have nothing in common except our pointless jobs at the Bright Spot. "Shit of a trip over," he says. I tell him it's been a busy day. I check and count the money in the counter, fill out the sheet, and turn to leave. He has put on his apron and is scrubbing at the grill with the spatula. I usually tell him when the Fat Family has been in—today I don't. I put on my coat, pull my cap down low on my head, bending out my ears. I tell him good night—he mumbles some reply. I bell myself out the door and into the snow-filled advancing dusk.

The snow is falling more thickly now than it has all day—large floating flakes, turning slowly as they fall. I catch one with my eye high above a streetlamp which has just blinked on—follow its swirling descent, down and slowly down, pausing and rising again for a second as a car rolls by, drifts slowly on down until I lose it in the deepening snow on the street. Even the cars are muffled and almost silent. I hear a distant whir of engine and spun tire—but mainly there is silence. Images float through my mind like snowflakes—a horse galloping in snow, its tail flung out behind in full expression of the day's joy—an angelfish hovering in lit water, its long fins flowing around it. I scarcely notice what I am doing (walking), where I am going (home). The snow fills the air and my eyes. I am filled with the living world and content.

I will walk home through this snowfall—spend a quiet evening, go to bed. I shall not eat. I never eat dead things. The only thing I eat is death itself, and I have just finished a fat feast—and I am full.

Omniphobia

for Darby Crash
1958–1980
... walking on shallow water ...

1.01 *I am locked up* within myself, and I have swallowed the key. The days are long but filled with fitful sleep; the nights are longer and tossed in insomnia like a willful child in a wrinkled bedsheet. This is my story, the story I am afraid to tell, the story I fear to keep within myself.

1.02 *I take a certain pleasure* in being alone. I have no fear of being alone; rather I see it as antidote to anthropophobic panic, ochlophobic crushes, xenophobic cringing, tightening in and in, except at times like this when I realize so fully whence cometh my fears. A famous phobiphobe, no need to be coy about it, Franklin Delano Roosevelt, said, "The only thing we have to fear is fear itself." The omniphobe would say, "Another thing we have to fear is fear itself." But is *fear itself* not personified in *me myself*? Where then does my pleasure lie? I catch sight of myself in an unmasked mirror down the hall, cringing against the wall, safe in this sturdy house where only the wind, the dust, the rain leak in imperceptibly, safe but still afraid. Afraid of what? Afraid that at any moment fear may shove my heart up in my chest, that my network of nerves may choose to be suddenly airborne, that I may look wildly around and not be able to see even these familiar sights. I close my eyes. I kneel and squat upon this familiar floor. I hug myself with a mother's care. I am in no way afraid of being alone; I fear only being alone with myself.

2.01 *Trichophobia:* You are in the tight bathroom, windowless, a dull fan sucking at the damp air, half-blind, water in the eye, soap in the eye, glare of the fluorescent light in the eye, towel in the eye, and then you see, coiled like a nest of vipers, dangerous, live wires, black wires, hairs, single and evenly spaced, no, random, hairs, two here, one there, around the rim of the toilet, clustered and clustering, you stagger back, towel smacking at the limp air, bang into the wall behind, start, heart pumps, pumps, step toward the door, tremble in the knee, tremble in the throat, tremble in the bone, hair on the toilet rim, snap with the towel, one desperate lunge and the lid bangs down, bounces in the echoing tile, and the hair is gone, gone for now, you can handle the door handle, pull the door in, break into the narrow hallway, dripping a crooked path down the dusty carpet and—SAFE—into the bedroom, into the bed.

3.01 *The blade* of the tiny knife in his pocket nail-care kit snapped just as he was pivoting his hand around, twisting at the last screw in the wooden wall panel one last turn. His knuckle banged into the screw, knocking it loose as it scraped a groove of flesh away. His instinct to curse was stifled by his fear of being heard. He stuffed the blade back into the leather holster and shoved the kit with its small bundle of keys and the four screws into his right pants pocket. He sucked his hurt knuckle, then tugged with his fingertips at the wooden panel, prying it slowly out from the wooden frame in which it was set. His fingers tightened, bones braced, tendon and muscle taut, tug and countertug, moved the panel slowly forward, slowly, carefully out. Shifting his grip as the panel wrenched free, he managed to set it silently by the wall close to his side, propped it carefully with the base of the panel braced against the porcelain curve of the toilet.

1.03 *I am far madder* than anyone supposes. The people with whom I have commerce day by day may think me often strange, may label me eccentric, but never truly mad, never as truly mad as I am. My daily competence shields my continuous incompetence. Left in the lurch by family and friends, a "writer" who has not written in over ten years, I have no recourse but madness. Mumbling to myself I stoke the fire that needs not a prod to do better, I pace out the patterns on the rug, I contemplate the ceiling, dust dangling in the strand of some spider's hurried leaving. I snatch at food and thrust it into my mouth, I chew dryly without swallowing, I force in a glass of wine to rush my madness down, but it remains in place after the food has gone down, half-chewed and chewing on me by the minute. When the phone rings, I step quickly into the closet and shut the door behind me. I crouch as I am crouching now in the darkness of a mind all alone.

2.02 *Dementophobia:* You write long letters to acquaintances, rational and clear, making your points, sharpening them, wits on parade, clear, succinct, able, and alert, and wait for the replies, hoping they will prove what you wish proven, by their rational response offer evidence of the rationality of the letter, fear that no response will come or a note saying only: don't bother me again. Does everyone feel this way? The need to explicate: watch the commercials on television, engage in semiotic analysis, bubble and bottle, damp smile, shirt collar turned up tidily at the nape of the neck, nod your head and understand. Follow the squirrels across the trim lawn (you mow it twice a week), know that they are leading you, and that if you disobey or ignore, it would be proof that you are mad, to walk away, ignore the signs, scofflaw. Waking at 3 A.M. and the fear is like cold electricity, fear that you are mad, insane, demented, dotty, daft, gaga, gone, and a goner. Get up and count the cups in the cabinet, lose count and you start again, count them twice, make sure the numbers match, while the moon makes efforts to part the blinds, look in, and drive you mad, you lunatic, no, only the fear of madness, not the fact, only the fear, and the cups rattle and bounce on the shelf, and you knot up on the floor like a design in the linoleum and listen to the squirrels chatter on the roof.

4.01 *Deaf*, not hindered, he watches the drummer's hands, knows the beat in his blood, Alyx and Turner leaning into each other, laying down chord on chord, and he is whirling with the microphone, ready to growl, ready to let it all out. Forty or fifty guys are slamming not two feet away. They take a swing, a lunge at him, but he knows when to duck, when to fall, and he knows he can do more damage to himself in fifteen seconds than they could do all night.

He has drawn messages all over his arms and the loose flesh of his chest, an unknown tongue. The only thing he has to fear is himself. "Autophobia," he is screaming, letting his voice run counter to the beat, the notes, letting it grind down through them, bottom out on the B . . . "autophoBia." Goes on. "Scared of myself, scared of myself, cut my heart out watch it dry, cut my tongue out watch it try to make you understand, I'm dangerous, I'm dangerous, cut my eye out watch it cry, got to die, autophoBia, always alone in the dark." He wants to do what he did once at the Bang Club, smash a beer bottle, cut his throat, great ending, drench those fuckers swinging at his head right now, but Alyx made him promise not; he touches the scar like a snake around his throat, but Alyx sees him, knows him and what he's thinking, signals Jaybang, she and Turner making the static flow, feedback, crash on the drums so loud it makes even him notice that the song is over, so he falls down on his back, and bellows into the mike, into the end of the song.

1.04 *Waking at three in the morning* I am drenched with sweat, extend a bare leg, an exploratory foot, out from under the sheets. I discover that the room is cold, and I jerk the covers back, jump up like jack from the box, waver like terrified jack, my feet numb to the floor, grab for the floorlamp before I fall down to the ground far below, hang on and begin to shake, shake like shook jack in angry owner's hands. I shake the light on—nyctophobia dispelled by photonic display—and I realize that I am still covered with icy sweat, that my feet are firm and bare on the yellow Persian rug, that the room's walls are in place, that I have no sleep in me, none at all. I fear that my heart has stopped in some dark dream, an acrophobic fall perhaps, that I have leapt up, wet with the bay's wet waters as much as my own nightsweat, risen out of death's damp grasp (thanatophobia) just before going under for the third motionless paralyzed time. I am, then, afraid to go back to sleep, as afraid as I am to face my thoughts and doubts in this silent house. I could replace my own sour dreams with those bright, repetitive nightmares on MTV ("Twenty-four hours a day, like life"), but I'm afraid to face the hollow sound of the television set at this odd hour. I begin to shiver, and I climb back in bed, pull the cover tight over my wet head. But do not sleep, although perchance to dream.

3.02 *A musty smell* seeped into the room from the new opening in the wall. He cautiously leaned into the opening and tried to peer down into the darkness from which the smell came. He could see nothing, but the smell spoke of enclosure and dampness and earth. The only way out was clearly up, for to climb down meant moving only from one civilized trap into another more primitive but possibly even more secure. He pulled back from the opening, stared at it for a moment, memorizing it, before he stood, crossed the room silently on bare feet, and snapped the overhead light off. He felt his way back across the room and crouched by the opening in the wall. Without actually counting, he waited for the minutes to pass, waited for his night vision to develop, for his pupils to open and darken like that invisible hole in that invisible wall. But even after what seemed at least ten minutes, possibly longer, he could still see nothing, only the featureless dark itself. He traced the outline of the opening with his fingers, leaned his head carefully in again, but all was dark, above and below, the mustiness sliding through him nose to lung to blood, filling him with a heavy despair.

4.02 *He tries to bite* the nipple of Alyx' left breast off, tears it badly, so badly they have to go to the hospital emergency room, where there is nothing but trouble: Alyx naked with just a houserobe over her like a tent, and he is just wearing a pair of pants, no belt, nothing else, the ragged scar around his neck like a necklace, lights popping in his eyes so hot and bright he thinks he's on stage, starts to sing, "You think you're so full of shit, well, you're not it, no, you're not it." Alyx, pushing the stained bath towel into her hurt breast with one hand, holding the robe together with the other, managing to get him quiet before the nervous nurse decides to call the cop in the corridor into this small room, dim and cool, where she is taking down all the names and numbers Alyx can manage to remember: her folks' insurance number, her social security number, his street address, phone number. She watches him, knows he's seeing things, hearing things; God knows what he took, she can't remember much past the pain, the drive across the freeway, down one-ways backwards, up on the curb, can't really remember where he's parked the car, but here they are. He's jiggling on the plastic contour chair, he's making most of the moves for "Anger Is the Source." She is worried he will try to pull off his pants, wag that poor scarred thing at this nurse thinking he's at God knows what venue. Then he decides it's time to take a nap, and he does.

2.03 *Numerophobia:* You know they are even in your wallet, on the buttons of the phone, brassy on the front stoop, pages and pages of them in the drawer in the table under the phone, won't count, no, as long as the cover's closed, they don't count—SAFE—first time, last time, but nothing in between, countdown, COMING READY OR NOT, mushrooming all around, put them down, bit, bits, bits, a dollar, can't catch you that way, no way, how do I love thee, no way, just more than enough, okay, just more than enough.

4.03 *Listening to the Stooges* was the only way he got through high school, that and cutting classes, that and cutting his hair in different ways, shaving words across the bumpy ridge of his skull: IG, HELL, MOG, POP, DO IT. Kept him interested, thinking of new ways he could hurt himself, eating any unclean thing he could find, playing *Never Mind the Bollocks* over and over, louder and louder, until his balls hurt, kissing Alyx so hard he cut the membrane tugging his tongue down on her teeth, blood leading him to rake his tongue back and forth over those small, uneven, sharp teeth, until she choked on the blood and spit and pushed him away. He passed enough subjects to get out, to get away, but by then they had met Jaybang at a party they had crashed, and after that everything had changed.

3.03 *He extended* his right hand up into the darkness, feeling carefully up beyond where the pipes that he had first felt bent into the opposite wall, and on up, testing the surface of the wall for handholds, toeholds, exploring with his fingers what his eyes yearned to see: wood and lathes and the rough interior of a plastered wall. Below he could sense a void, an open emptiness, a potential fall, a drop down into the earth, bone shattering and closed. The space before him was a yard across, possibly only two feet. He could drag himself into this narrow space, trusting that somewhere above him there was another panel or some sort of opening to which and through which he could make his way. After thinking for a moment, he drew himself back out of the opening, slid himself around until his back was to the hole, and eased himself again into the opening and up into the space above. Grasping the arch of a pipe, he began to pull himself up and in when his foot twisted around, bashing into the propped panel by the toilet and kicking it with a bang and echoing crash over onto the tiled floor. The noise caused his hands to open reflexively, and he bashed back into the wall, his head and shoulders scraping down, a pipe joint banging his left ear and ringing his whole head. He caught the pipe and hung on, pressed back over nothing, hearing in his mind's ear the crash and bang, crash and skid repeated clearly and loudly over and over again. He hung for a moment, afloat in his blood's water, then, taking a deep calming breath, he began pulling himself up the pipe and on until finally he was erect in the narrow darkness, his toes pressed against the panel's frame. In a shaft, between the walls, he was stalled in darkness, ready to step out into darkness, hanging by his fingers and toes over darkness, moving upward into darkness, heading toward a darkness high above.

4.04 *He is humming* and tapping his fingers on the formica countertop, then talking eagerly, his eyes bright without drugs, clean as a whistle, he whistles, and Turner repeats the tune on his portable keyboard—pocket piano, Turner calls it—pooling their resources. He knows the tunes, they come to him whole, but he doesn't know the notes, never got past song flute in fifth grade, but Turner knows them all and plays them all. Jaybang gives them the beat, punk beat, fast and hard and steady—too fast, according to Turner, but you can't slamdance, he adds, to the Pachelbel Canon, nice bass line though. He was getting nowhere faster than usual when he and Alyx met Jaybang, just looking for a band. He had been strung-out and down, but Jaybang knew the goods even when it was on the floor. So they made a deal, and Jaybang knew Turner, so they had two people who could actually play instruments, and Alyx was learning fast: one lead guitar, one bass, one set of drums, and he could sing, growl, groan, mutter, utter the very truth, and the music would go bang, just the way it ought to. He hums the line again, and again Turner beeps it out, adds a mechanical beat, plays it fast. He nods his head, tries a few words, knows this is it. He is happy, and he glows like an angel in the slanting afternoon sun beating across the room. Alyx' kitten takes a run at his bare foot, and he stoops, quicker than the kitten is used to from him, swings it up to his nose, and croons; Turner runs it through again, the riff that does it, the kitten purrs, he has been straight for two weeks, and everything is looking good.

4.05 *He is working* his way through *Leaves of Grass,* skipping all the parts they made him read in school, imperturbe, nude, his pale loose skin grainy and mottled in the light falling down from the single bare bulb in the ceiling, his brow creased with effort, creased with thought. "You poor koboo whom the meanest of the rest," he says aloud, "look down upon for all of your glimmering language and spirituality!" He is nervous now, knees jumping, and he pitches the paperback onto the empty tabletop. This poor koboo needs some space, needs some time, needs a day in the shade, needs a day in the sun, needs to be left alone just for a fucking minute, needs to invite his soul. Come on in, koboo soul, got soul, uh huh, got soul, I gots soul, koboo soul. He pulls his jeans out from under the couch where he wadded them earlier in the evening, pulls them on, and a T-shirt, not a hole in it except the ones for the head and arms, the torso, walks around the small room eighteen times, goes out in the hall, yells, no echo, no answer, nobody home, just him, the last of the koboos, just him and one kitten asleep in some dark corner, and nowhere to go but up. "If I could get one night's sleep from start to finish," he shouts, pounds his fist into the wall, falls down in pain, poor koboo. "I could eat cat litter," he says, "if it would give me surcease from pain." So he gets up, walks out on the porch, walks out on the sidewalk, walks out into the street, stands there for a dark minute, and then decides to go see what's doing in the parking lot of the A&P, ten dollars, maybe twenty in a little ball in his hip pocket. Koboo, looking for koboo land, just over the rainbow, just down the road, open and empty like it always is for the glimmering koboo soul.

1.05 *It is necessary* just to stay alive (if staying alive is necessary) that I venture out, holding my breath in and easing it out, the muscles in the backs of my legs wet and weak, but stepping on. The

MOG Gala is this week, Chinese Puccini when my dark heart would prefer Berg or Schoenberg, dissonance and the ripper's cold steel. The silver of my dinner knives as I remove them from the washer is cold in my dry hands, colder than steel, silver that kills the beast. I need something sharper and colder than steel to cut the fear that tosses me whenever I think of attending that affair. In the dark, in my seat, the three ministers speaking of riddles on the bright stage, there I will be safe, will be alone. The roof will not come crashing down (for I will have entered the auditorium on the left side, will have tapped the left arm of my seat three times when I sat down). I do my rituals like Kafka's dog and snap at the air for the treat that might appear. There I will be safe, but outside on the sidewalk, in the foyer, mingling with masses of strangers, ochlophobic, xenophobic, the necessity of speaking to her (for it is necessary that I speak to her), of standing by her, her icy slim figure, slick and sleek, her hands, her hair. It is not just that I am attracted by her beauty (though beautiful she is) and am struck dumb by the fear of that which I desire like a lonely teen. That kind of fear I could understand and deal with. It is another, darker, less rational, more desperate fear. The necessity of speech, trying to hold her eye as her eye holds mine. Command performance, the future of my career hangs in that shared glance. I shall go, for I must. I place the knives away one by one; their handles hold no lingering warmth from my hands. These dull blades gleam. The ax on stage will fall. The Ripper's knife will slit the ligaments that hold me still, and I will wobble, stumble, shamble, teeter, tumble, sink, and fall.

3.04 *He found he was unable* to use his legs because there was not enough room between the walls to bend them sufficiently at the knee; it was hand and arm work, and toe and foot work: the hands and fingers testing the lathes and occasional two-by-fours, testing them, tugging at them, then pulling him up, his toes pressed into the rough plaster, tipped on lathe or beam, feet arching up as hands and arms pulled, held as the toes scrabbled in the dark for a new hold. The close space allowed him to press back and brace himself, stop to breathe, to gasp, to gulp the stale powdery air, the damp mustiness lingering only as an implied threat, the deadly below to which he could fall at any second, a banging, scraping descent, ripping at clothes and skin, the head battering back and forth, ear and nose tearing, teeth shattered and split. He pressed back hard, felt his head spin and then settle, a cold sweat congeal on his hands and face. He paused and breathed, he did not think or tried not to think beyond the simple muscular commands, press and probe, tug and countertug, pull and strain, press on. He paused, and then he started again, stretching his right hand up, fingers brailling the rough wall, and then he almost gasped with surprise. There was no more wall, or rather a top of the wall, a flat wooden beam, extending back farther than he could reach. He twisted up on his braced toes, pulled with his hands, pushed and pulled, braced and repeated, until he hung by his elbows, stretching his hands out before him, feeling only emptiness, the beam he hung on, perhaps another similar beam just beyond his fingers' reach.

4.06 *At his mother's house* he is as usual speechless, dressed neatly, shoes even shined, and she is vacuuming, works all day, sweeps all night, the small house already spotless, except for her untidy desk, stacks of freshman papers to grade, her red pencils bristling from the orange Moxie can: "The only legacy of my marriage," she often says to him, "Moxie, three crowned teeth, and you." He watches her work, does not volunteer to help, no use, useless to her mind anyway, sits in a wing-backed chair, watches her sweep, lifts his feet over the probing wand—"No worry about you ever getting married," she says—and wishes he had something to say. She keeps his room for him, baseball pennants, two stuffed animals, cat and kangaroo, red desk and chair, single bed tightly made, all intact, preserved, waiting for the prodigal's return. The window shade he painted so carefully is rolled up, Ezekiel poking his head through the stars, crawling along, the tree, the tilting sun and moon, sun watching closely, moon could care less, and Ezekiel raising his hand with wondrous surprise, wheels within wheels, clouds and fire and dazzling displays of all kinds. He had copied it onto the shade, no color, just red on white, copied it from the cover of his high school science book. No need to pull it down to see, it's all there, the whole room is there, in his mind's eye, his feet stuck up in the air, the vacuum sucking beneath him, the white room around him, no way out except the way he came in. His head spins, and he wants to ask the way in, but he knows his mother would mark it up to Oedipal *angst*. Her diplomas are on the wall over her desk, two degrees that doom her to teaching composition forever, diplomas on the yellow wall in her yellow room. But he is in the white room, all alone now, the vacuum roaring down the hall, so he lowers his feet to the dustless floor, and is no more.

4.07 *Jaybang is so pumped up* that he is setting the beat faster than ever. The crowd is wild, can't even slam, just pogoing all over the dark floor, up and down, not even then keeping up with the beat. It is so wild that Alyx is getting lost, starts playing chords quartertime, then halftime, letting Turner do all the work, and he does, challenges Jaybang to go even faster. The front rows of the crowd, sweating, their breath pumping in and out, are hanging on the chickenwire the club manager put up between the band and the crowd. "Saw it in a movie somewhere," he said. "Chickenshit," Turner said, but where else is there these days? Punk is dead, so many club managers say, we got a rockabilly band that'll pack them in and no rough stuff, no tables and chairs broken, no fights we can't handle, no cops. "So we play in a chicken coop," Alyx says, and then explains it to him when he finally shows up. It makes him mad, but even he knows that what is left is what they'll have to take. Turner and Jaybang set up the equipment, and he draws big elementary school scars all over his face and chest with a purple magic marker, long purple gashes with big purple stitches all along the lines. He is mad and takes it out on himself as usual. And now Jaybang is tearing the songs apart, Jaybang and Turner ripping at each other, staring at each other, tempo wars, and he is still singing, screaming, knows the tune despite the beat, follows Alyx' chords, watches all those fingers curved through the chickenwire, and when he gets to "Take it from me" the last time, howling it, repeating it, repeating it while Turner and Jaybang keep taunting each other with riff codas, "Take it from me," he suddenly kicks at those snarled fingers along the chickenwire, making the kids yank their hands back, but the nervy ones grab the wire and hold on, shaking it, daring him, until one last time he growls, "Take it from me," and throws the mike toward Jaybang, spins to the wire, hurls himself up on it, his fingers caught now, his toes clinging, shoving up, pulling up, up the wire, all the hands grabbing below him, and the wire rips out of the wood frame along the ceiling, and he sways out, swings out over the crowd, everybody backing and shoving away, Turner hitting crazy chord after chord, Jaybang hammering down, Alyx trying to hang on to her guitar and get to him as he falls. The whole chickenwire tears loose and drops him over the falling scrambling crowd. He is yelling like Tarzan but who can hear? The screaming is louder than the chords, and all Alyx can do is watch the boys caught under the wire, watch him as he jumps up and down on them, his feet are cut and bleeding, she knows the police are coming, and the show is over for tonight.

2.04 *Gephyrophobia:* Troubled water, high curving bridge, no way across, whitecaps, wind like a saw, swinging, buckling, standing tall, what goes up must, like a witch you cannot cross over, wide water, side water, stand on the bank and—SAFE—don't look up.

3.05 *Above his elbows,* by which he hung on the beam at the top of the shaft, he could see and feel nothing. Surely there must be some sort of flooring or more rough wooden beams, but he could not reach them if they were there. He shoved his toes deep into the wall, took a deep breath and heaved with his shoulders and arms, pulling himself up, scratching and scraping, until his arms came erect and fully extended, still nothing above him in the darkness around his head. He swung his hips up and onto the beam, and there he sat, his feet dangling into the dark shaft, perched on a wooden beam, unsure of what was around him or above him, catching his breath, and breathing a sigh of relief. He tentatively stretched his hand out in front of him, then swung it in a long slow arc as far as it would go; he then repeated the motion and completed the circle with his other arm. Nothing. Only the beam he was on, and another one like it on the other side of the shaft, two crossbeams only two or so feet long and nothing else. It was as though the shaft were a chimney extending up into this darkness and he were sitting on its cap, his feet hanging down inside and his arms reaching into a void. Were these beams ceiling joists? They were his only hope, the only evidence that he was not on some chimney top in a pitch-black night, poised to step off into a long fatal fall. He leaned out onto the beam to his right, thinking to pull himself astraddle it and to inch along it until he reached a wall. But then he wavered and almost fell over, dizzy and sweat-drenched. He lay down on the beam; it was perhaps two inches wide, or four; he could no longer judge or measure even the simplest things. He slowly pulled his legs up and out and lay flat on the beam, his left hand holding on to the parallel beam across the way. He could not move any farther in any way, so he lay there, trying to think, trying to figure out what to do next, what he could do next, whether he could do anything next.

4.08 *The Dead Guys* was what he had first wanted to call the band, but Alyx and Jaybang hooted him down, talked him out of it, gave him this list of other bands on a black wooden coffin lid they bought or made or stole, painted the list in red paint, propped it up in the bathroom at the house by the railway switching yards where it stood for a long time, may still stand:

DEAD AT THE CONTROLS
DEAD BEATS
DEAD BOYS
DEAD CERT
DEAD DUCK
DEAD EYE
DEAD FINGERS TALK
DEAD HEAT
DEAD IN THE WATER
DEAD JOHN LENNONS
DEAD KENNEDYS
DEAD MAN'S SHADOW
DEAD ON ARRIVAL
DEAD OR ALIVE
DEAD SOULS
DEAD STUDENTS
DEAD TRAVEL FAST
DEAD TROUT
DEADLOCK

They accused him when he pouted and wouldn't read the list out loud of not being properly grateful, and this made him mad, and he

OMNIPHOBIA 157

sulked around for a couple of days until they made him laugh by saying they maybe now ought to call the band DEAD STILL or DEAD STOP. "DEAD END," he said, then snapping his fingers, putting one finger on his nose, "Ah ha, " he said, "CUL DE SAC, that'll do, " and of that one he claimed to be dead sure.

4.09 *Agitolalia:* Thingsinthisplacearesowrongsofuckingbad Icantevenbegintothinktosaythethingsthatbugmeslamitout bangupagainstthewallonthefloorpushthroughthecrowdssaybad thingsdontlookbackDONTLOOKBACKbrainheavingthebeatlike headachescomingonallthetimeneverstopbangbangletsgo somewhereelseweveheardthesecreepssomanytimeswhatcan theydotheyhaventdonebeforewhatcantheysaytheyhaventsaid beforewhatcantheysayWEhaventsaidbeforebetterbiggobsofspiton thestagetheyretoooldanywaywhatdotheyknowtheydontknow whatitsallaboutjustactingjustactingLIKEEVERYBODYELSEIN THEWHOLEFUCKINGWORLDhuhImaskingyouhuhsowhatdo wewanttostayaroundhereforslamminglotsofpeoplerecognizeusI knowtrytopatmeonthebacktrytostartafighttrytopushmeto thefloortrytopushmeoutthedoorfightonthestreetgrabmyarm saygreatmangreateverybodystaringatthebandclapping theirhandsovertheirheadsgreatmangreatwhatssofuckinggreathuh bangbangbangJaybangissomuchbetterandwhatsthathesgot stuffedinthebassdrumhuhwhatdoeshethinkthisisanyway kidsstufflistentoallofthisnoisemyheadisswellingormyheadis shrinkingandmybrainisswellingIneedsomestuffrealbadmaybewe cangetsomestuffIamtoomuchheremostofmeisherefuckingallofme ishereandIDONTNEEDITANYMOREyougetthepictureyouget thesoundsomebodyonmywavelengthbreakingrightinFBIonthe shortwaveCIAontheweatherbandneveryouknowwhichwaytogoI knowIknowIRSonthelongwaveDOAatthedoorIwantmoreIwant moreIwantmorethanTHISlookatmelookatmelookatmeLOOKAT MEguessIbettergohuhguessIbettergowhywonttheassholesletus playherewhatdowedothatssofuckingbadhuhthoseguysinspitcity whatdowedojusttellthetruthsowhyhowcomejusttellmewhyhuh HOWCANYOUMAKEARTIFTHEYWONTLETYOUINTHE FUCKINGDOORletsgetoutofhereletsgohuhImsotiredmyfeetdont touchtheground.

2.05 *Phonophobia:* In the closet, crouched in the comforting corner, the pants legs and shirt-sleeves shielding you—SAFE—you make not a sound, even breathing, yes, scratch of finger on itching nose, yes, but not even a whisper, won't say a word, no phoneme, no morpheme, wigwag with your fingers a message to the dark, but will not, no, will not speak a word aloud, the phone still dangling from its twisting cord on the kitchen wall, the voice saying, "Who's there? Say, who's there? Who is this?" long since gone, tone gone, shrill siren whirring on and on and on and on.

4.1 *MTV is on*, and Carla is nervously letting the band look around her place, thick rugs, clean walls, framed paintings, prints, piano, baby grand, white, Turner is already at the keyboard, making it answer the MTV, some idiot kissing himself in black and white, piano in another key, fish in the foreground, big round eyes. He is quiet and polite, says thanks and no thanks, then goes for a leak and sees Carla's bedroom, four poster, the entire room pink and white, ruffles all over the bed, top and bottom, pillow sham and coverlet; he feels dizzy, this is all too much, backs right up and into an aquarium. No, no water in it, just shells and pink and white gravel, but one shell's walking, has got legs, spindly little crab legs, one big pink claw. He feels like the room's trying to swallow him, one big tongue, pink cheeks, hard gums, screams, grabs the crab in the shell, bolts into the front room, Turner jumps up, Alyx backs off, Carla like a statue by the MTV, and he's got his fly open, shoves the crab in, feels it hang on for dear life as he falls over a footstool, comes down with a smash right at Carla's feet, his hands waving, screaming—"Your goddam crab's chewing my cock off!"—writhing, Jaybang is laughing fit to kill, Alyx is mad to death, Turner is staring again at the MTV and Martha Quinn with a fatal gaze, while Carla is enraged, death in her eye, digs her hand in his fly, yanking and squeezing, pulls her hermit crab out, waves it in her hand as she gets up, looks at Alyx and finally says, "This is some gratitude," but Turner's laughing as loud as Jaybang now at some heavy metal band dressed up to the teeth, and he's screwed up on the floor in a ball, listening to everything and seeing nothing, knowing then for the first time that the next show is the last show, feels the ice on his brow, smells the death of the mastodons on the frigid air, and the noise is like light all over the world, hard white light, and he feels it to the balls of his feet.

1.06 *In the foyer,* a complex texture of black and white amid a variegation of all dazzling colors, I am at home in my anonymity, yet I still seek sanctuary by a wall. Firmly planted in my gleaming pumps, bib and tucker tightly in place, cummerbund binding me firm and flat, I feel myself tremble like a moored balloon, tug at these elegant moorings, feel myself a hollow shell that requires only the gentlest inquiring touch to split and shatter and scatter on this bright carpet, while the emptiness inside the husk . . . while that emptiness inside . . . I cannot see beyond this terrifying moment. Are these colors, this wave of conversation, this held motion, are these the agoraphobic source of my insubstantiality, the lighter-than-air vacuum that wants to lift me out of my substantial self? MOG moves around me, masked in eager converse, banter and persiflage, Gogic, Magogic, suit and gown, gem and gossamer glance. The performance has been striking, ax edge and deadly night, dawn that will not come: this intermission in a nocturaphobic nightmare is striking as well. I breathe deeply, air heavier than vacuum, I look around. I see her hand raised, her eye meeting mine, her finger curling, bone pivoting on bone, muscle and tendon, tug and countertug, the room suddenly still as a ghost, an ice thawing in my bones' subarctic marrow, and I begin to melt away, to drain away, to drift away, to fade away; she can surely see the patterned wallpaper right through me. I am giddy and gone.

4.11 *This is their last chance,* and he knows it, at least in this town, and where else is there to him? They have persuaded Carla to act as their agent, really just to talk to club managers, look straight, dress well, give them a little class. And she has class, drives a BMW, has an eastern accent, is clean to a fault. She enjoys it, talking to these angry men, men who remember the last time this band played their place, everything in shambles, blood on the dining room floor, and the next night there is no one there at all. He is standing, meek and mild, behind Alyx, resisting the urge to give her a good goose, make her land on this bald guy's face like a wet cat; just the two of them, Alyx wearing a painter's cap to hide her hair, face clean, smiling, just a little nervous, and he is in a suit, the one he graduated from high school in, cut all wrong for today but dark blue nonetheless. Carla does all the talking, Alyx nods, tries not to nod too much.

"What is this," he wants to say, "the fucking Last Chance Saloon?" Why beg? Who needs it? Kiss this guy's ass, that's the way AIDS is spread, brainAIDS, who needs it? And then he stops paying attention altogether, goes off somewhere inside where he works. Thinking it through: brainAIDS in a little tin box, stick them on and the thinking stops; got brainAIDS, immune to not one thought, every crazy thought a head can have, they're all polluting the blood supply, makes you really want to die. He is still able to see Carla's mouth moving, the manager's round mouth like he's mooing, Alyx nodding, nodding; he smiles like an angel, the words moving around easy, needs to talk to Turner, work it out: brainAIDS in the White House, spreading on the airwaves, gonna get some brainAIDS, nothing hurts anymore. He is smiling, smile so sweet the man thinks he's at church during boys' choir, Alyx nodding, Carla already giving up when the guy, can't keep his eyes off that smile, says, "Well, maybe one more chance; maybe it wasn't your fault last time," Carla's mouth open in surprise, Alyx nodding and biting her lower lip, and he's thinking, why did I ever come along, I don't do anybody any good, 'cause I got brainAIDS, and I'm gonna give 'em right to you. They are out on the street, trucks rolling by, sun like an orange off to the west, Alyx hugging Carla, calling her a genius, "right to you, right to you," he's moving now, moving out, doesn't say a word, who needs him, but he needs Turner now, "brainAIDS make you so happy there's nothing to do but die."

2.06 *Anthophobia:* Winter is such a relief, the ground hard and dry, and even after a long winter rain, the vegetation lies low, stays brown. But the earth turns on, and the solstice comes as it must to every man; you can almost feel the earth crumbling underfoot, stirring and probing, bulging and yearning, the first pale tendrils scouting the day, and one morning all along the neighbors' drive, hanging out, petal and pistil, pollen and probing bee, they appear, a host, dawdling and beckoning, ants already crawling up the pulpy stems, and the others following, reds and pinks, lavenders, a lace of white, brushy yellow heads close to the greening grass, tongues loose and wagging, the nerve in your loins loose and wet, and they creep up on you, ambush you in the optometrist's in a vase on the counter, they loll by the vegetables in the grocery, looking at you, beckoning and bobbing, on the prim aunt's hat, pressed in a dusty anthology, repeated on the wallpaper until your head whirls, flowering trees, budding girls, blooming idiots; you are never alone, yearn for the fall, the clean aseptic arctic blast, and you are—SAFE—under layers of clothes, mittens and mufflers, hats and boots, and not a tawdry tepal, swollen pollen sac, ovary, style, or stigma in sight, no lurid whorl of sepals, all covered up, buried and bound, and you are free to walk your way without a doubt.

3.06 *Afraid, alone, stretched out* on the narrow beam, he decided not to crawl along the beam. He could not exactly say why he made that decision, but somehow it seemed too splintery, and somehow it seemed incapable of holding his weight once he moved away from the crossbeams. These were practical reasons not to go on, but something else moved him, made him want to stand up, straight up, reach his hands up, stretch as far as he could on tiptoes into the darkness above. He pushed himself back along the rough beam until his knees were braced into the shaft again, and he turned himself around again and sat up on the shaft lip. Then he pressed his feet against the beams defining the shaft, pressed his palms against the beams behind him, arched his back, thrust forward with his arms and swung himself forward and up onto his knees, teetering on the edge of the shaft, and then he was kneeling on the other side of it, and then he wobbled up into a crouch, and then he stood carefully erect, wavering and waving his arms until he gained a kind of balance. He stood there for some time before he dared stretch one arm up high above his head, reaching for he knew not what.

4.12 *He has been in love with Alyx* since the sixth grade when she came to class in her girl scout uniform, she and four other girls, making the whole room in the hot slanting afternoon sun seem cool and green as all outdoors. He was shy, too shy to actually know her, but, of course, he knew her enough to say hello or good-bye. He knew a lot of things, but it still made him nervous. It was like when Roy and he were sent into the hall for making noise, and Roy showed him some kind of paperbound biology textbook he had found, full of cutaway flowers and skulls and skeletons, a cutaway of a tongue sticking out, bone and gristle and muscle and gland. "Poison ivy,"

Roy was saying, pointing at another cutaway of a pregnant woman with the baby curled up inside her half-belly like a kitten, "poison ivy." Roy was five years older than he was, had been kept back year by year until this year when he would be old enough to quit school for good. "You know Madeline," Roy said. "She's got one so big you could get lost in it, big as a train tunnel." He didn't know what to say, but Roy liked him, took care of him when the other boys pushed him around, so he said, "No kidding?" And it made Roy nod with pride. He tried to connect poison ivy with Alyx and Sue and Ruth and Judy, but it didn't seem to apply. They were different, and that day when they wore their girl scout uniforms to class he forgot all about poison ivy, and he tried to write a poem about it, but he didn't know how, and Alyx caught him looking at her and tossed her blond hair as she looked quickly away, so he moved back by the classroom door, put a sharp pencil in the pencil sharpener, turned the crank slowly until he saw the teacher turn her head toward the window and the bright afternoon, and he bent over and went right out the door, down the hall, moving fast, down the steps, and out the big double door onto the hot gravel of the school yard, not looking back, just moving on.

4.13 *He was so convinced* that he was so ugly that no girl would ever be able to look at him seriously for more than a few seconds that he would flinch and duck his head whenever he caught sight of himself in a mirror. He shaved his head for the first time in seventh grade, and stood up to the stares because he knew now just what they were staring at. He had ripped the sleeves out of his jean jacket, jean genie, and was kept nervously in the principal's office for an hour after school. He could not believe he was alive much less awake when he found Alyx waiting for him on the steps in front of the school. "Do you like Iggy and the Stooges?" she asked him. "I've got *Raw Power* at home. Do you want to go listen to it?"

3.07 *A prayer crossed* his mind, not a prayer asking for anything in particular, just fragments of a prayer he had learned as a child. His fingers touched nothing as he eased up on tiptoe, nothing. The shaft had been so comforting compared to this, so secure and so directed. He had been going somewhere in the shaft, but now he was, except for the transverse arches of his feet, without sensation, untouched and touching nothing. A vertiginous lightness swept through him, and he almost lifted up into a little hop, but instead came down hard on his heels, and turned almost without volition, feeling his way with a cautious foot, stepping, inching his way back onto the beam, this time in the opposite direction. He stepped a few steps and stopped, trapped now by this single beam since he was unsure on which side its parallel twin lay. He stretched up again, again felt nothing, and again stepped on along the beam. His legs were beginning to ache, and he pounded at his thighs with his fists, stepped on, stretched, reached up, and stepped on. There was no turning back. He must move along this invisible balance beam until he found something over his head to hang on to, or until the beam ran out.

2.07 *Nulliphobia:* Punching out clusters of random numbers on the pocket calculator you found on the table by the leather chair in the dark study, in a dark study factoring in squares and square roots randomly, the green numbers dancing in the dark, the decimal point flowing back and forth across the narrow screen, punching in your birthday, adding seventy, a chill at the bone, adding seventy more, adding, multiplying, dividing, subtracting, the width of numbers spreading and reducing, abstract accordion, when it appears, zero, square, square root, multiply, add, subtract, divide, quickly, quickly, zero set and unyielding, nothing, nothing to do, punch and punch, feel yourself lifting off the chair, whole body light as air, light as light, aloft, punch and punch, hit 1, hit 2, hit and hit, + and +, + and +, then the friendly flow—SAFE—begins again, afraid to turn it off, let the light wink out, black out, blank out, [99999999.

4.14 *Turner is questioning Alyx,* and he asks her whether she plans to stay in the business if the band breaks up or if (he doesn't actually say it, but he makes it clear) he should go off the deep end and leave them all high and dry. "I'm not in the business," she says. They have been practicing on the guitar all afternoon, Turner patiently teaching her tricks and shortcuts, ways to hold her own on an instrument she hasn't been playing very long, and he asks her just what it is they have been doing then. "Not business," she says.

"Maybe what's good for business, but not business." She strikes a ragged tough path up the neck of the guitar with edges her voice doesn't have. "I'm just with him," she says, "and if that means the business, then it's the business." He is the most intelligent as well as the stupidest person she has ever known, she wants to tell Turner. Do you think, she wants to tell Turner, that I would put up with what I do for the business? Do you think, she doesn't say, that I would mop his blood off the floor and watch him jerking on his back all the way to the hospital and hold his poor hand that doesn't feel a thing, that I would do that for the business? She plays some more rough notes, discord and keen clean line. You think I would take the abuse I do, bear my wounds, be strung out and wrung out at my age, just for the business? He has taught me more for good and for bad than I could ever have learned in school. "You maybe going to college?" Turner says, tuned in without hearing a word. "If he goes," she says. "You're not real liberated," Turner says. I'm free to be, she plays the familiar lines, what I want to be, but I want to be nothing you could understand. "Okay, okay," Turner groans, gets back to work, "I guess you're just a love slave," and adds wearily, "love, love, love." Love, she says to herself, love, yeah, maybe that's just it.

4.15 *He likes to dance* around the room with "Lust for Life" turned up high, his favorite song, although he thinks the highly disregarded version of "Nightclubbing" on *TV Eye* is not only the best Iggy Pop piece he has ever heard, but the best thing ever recorded by anybody. He wants to sound like that when he talks about the weather or cuts his mother's grass and always, always when he's on stage. He makes Turner and Jaybang listen to it over and over until they claim to see his point. "I don't have time to keep up with my contemporaries," he says when Alyx brings an X record in, or Black Flag, the Cramps, or Screamin' Sirens, "I have got to know the classics inside out." He does listen to her records when nobody's around; he likes them, he learns from them, but he won't say a word. And then he plays Metallic K.O. to hear the bottles smash on stage and hear the insults and the rage and the deep bloodlust of the crowd, ready to kill the boy singer, ready to turn the hate and hurt of his art to real hate and real hurt. He feels a chill, pulls on a long-sleeved shirt, says to no one since no one's there, "Goose stepped on my grave again." He wants a record, too, wants them to record, but when the time comes he backs off. "Anybody can make a record," he says, and Alyx groans, hits his arm. "We'll sing it to the air, those soundwaves go on forever, let the Arcturians listen if they want to." Only Alyx knows he is afraid to record, no, afraid to hear coming through a speaker what he hears now only in his head. No, he does hear it through speakers, not that, it's that he's afraid to hear it when he's not singing it, afraid someone else will be hearing him sing when he's in the grave with dead ears, dead brain, dead soul (he's afraid). Turner gets furious at him when he backs off, but then Turner's not planning to be around here forever. He's already recorded as has Jaybang with other groups, so they throw up their hands and leave him to his own explanations. "It's the goose," he says to himself, "I don't want the goose to hear the words."

1.07 *The black snake,* headless and cold, twisted half belly up, black back and pale belly both on view, Möbius stripe on the suburban sidewalk; ophidiophobia; and the head, gaped mouth, slit eyes, wavering tongue, gone, only the cold bloody stump, kill the brain, snake stump, when the body is stripped of mind it must snarl like this long trunk, light pools around it, black snack for the ants and beetles making their careful way in this direction, scaled ridge and stone, dirt and dust, leaf mound, snake mulch; gleaming like a beaded bag on her arm, at the Gala, she raises her delicate hand, the tendons, muscles, flex, tug and countertug, finger bends, beckons, eye caught in these complex signs, sememe and lexeme, moves like a caught bird from shining fingertip to hand to wrist across the open space to eye, light pools around it, the pupil widening in this slow tide of light, and the snake snaps in the dust like a windowshade whipping away from the closing fingertips, finger and finger, bone, tendon, muscle, move and countermove, the sudden burst of light, burst of headless motion on the ground, burst of electric passion eye to eye, starburst, collapsing star, black eye that folds the world within, snake in the road coiling like a neon sign, coil and recoil, shade flapping around the roller, rattle and flap, nerves like water, bare wires, burst of light, dark snake's spread, eye that opens and opens and opens and opens.

3.08 *His feet faltered* on the dark beam, so, his leg muscles shaking and jerking, his arms waving for balance in the darkness, he dove his hands down onto the beam, held on in a crouch, and then lowered himself into a sitting position, coiled like the Little Mermaid of the statue in Copenhagen, welded scar around her neck, or a black snake in a dusty road on a pitch black night. My thoughts are wandering, he thought, saying the words over again in his mind, hoping by stating his condition to alleviate it. The fear expressed, he has often told himself, is the fear lessened, or at least the fear made rational, subsumed into the rational process that makes us human and perhaps more than human. My thoughts are still wandering, he thought then, I must concentrate on this beam and this beam alone. But his mind wandered even as he spoke, out into the darkness around him. He had no idea what shape or size the building was, whether he was at its top or in some innerwall cul-de-sac leading nowhere from nowhere. He held on to the beam with both hands and waited for the muscular jerks and cramps of his legs to subside. He dared not shout for fear of who might hear. He had no way at all to assess the extent of the darkness around him through which he had been moving. Even the way back down the shaft seemed blank and hopeless to him; descent itself, the very idea of descent, seemed noxious and deadly. No, no more thinking, no more assessing of positions or locations, only action was open to him now, eyes open and staring, or eyes sealed tightly shut. He must move on down the beam, come what may or may not. He rose to a shaky runner's starting crouch on the beam and then suddenly boosted himself on into a stand. He eased slowly forward, toe out testing, then swinging the other foot forward, toe out to test, then the other forward, and on and on. And then his left foot felt nothing below it. He swayed perilously, teetered, steadied himself, arms wild, and found with a ginger foot that he had reached the end of the beam, and that the beam reached nothing at all.

4.16 *One time he handed* Turner a piece of paper, lined notebook paper with three holes for the rings, with lyrics scrawled and marked over and marked out in messy ballpoint blue ink. "I want to make something of this," he said, "something I can really sing." And they did, all that afternoon:

I just heard it
on the telephone,
the idiot's in a room
all alone,
they've hung him up
to dry,
it makes you
want to cry:
Detox, detox,
DETOXIFICATION.

They scrub you out
with a Brillo pad,
they wrap you up
in plastic Glad
you're alive, yes, glad
you're alive,
unwired, so tired,
so uninspired:
Detox, detox,
DETOXIFICATION.

Poison in the air,
poison in the trees,
poison in the food
you do not need,
you're all hung up,
don't know up
from down,
it makes you
want to drown:
Detox, detox,
DETOXIFICATION.

Drown in your tears,
fly in the sky,
the poisoned sunset

burns your eye
like a call on the phone
when you're all alone
with news from abroad
with news that makes you
want to cry:
Detox, detox,
DETOXIFICATION.

4.17 *He is at Alyx'* house, sitting in the television room, watching a performance of *Turandot,* a live gala, with Alyx' parents on their 26-inch monitor set with the stereo sound turned up high. They have given up on trying to keep him away or keep Mary, as they still call Alyx, away from him, and besides he is very neat and very polite, sitting up straight with all of his clothes ironed sharp. It is act 1, and he watches the verbal crawl across the bottom of the screen spell out: BUT TAKE AWAY HER FINE CLOTHES AND SHE IS FLESH, RAW FLESH. "Cold woman," he thinks to himself, his face poised in pleasant attention, "take away the glitter and she's just live meat." Alyx' dad mixes cocktails during the first intermission, but he politely refuses. He wants to be alert for the cold woman. In the second act he reads: THE RIDDLES ARE THREE, DEATH IS ONE. "Cold woman with her riddles three, the chopperman behind the tree, three blind mice put their heads together, just takes one blow to set them free, one for my master, one for my maid, and one for Mister Three, dead men see Mister Three, dead men see Mister Three." He is happy and laughing during the next intermission; Alyx' parents have a mild buzz on; Alyx is stoned and into the music, her fingers flutter as she hums a theme. *Nessun dorma:* NO ONE SHALL SLEEP. "No one shall sleep when the cold woman opens the door, and after the point where the maestro died, the chopperman's slice at the end of his life, he goes with me to see Mister Three, he goes with me to see Mister Three, no one shall sleep with Mister Three." He skips the end, goes out to the telephone table, and writes it all down on the telephone pad, uses four pages, the pencil going blunt in his fist, getting it all down, Cold Woman, Mister Three, life, love, and death. They are all applauding on the screen and throwing flowers when he reenters the loud room. Alyx' father is yawning, Alyx' mother is dabbing at her eyes with a tiny handkerchief, and Alyx is somewhere else where every moment of light and dark is a miracle. He is very happy (grinning like a possum, Alyx' father says), and he is ready to go.

2.08 *Pedophobia:* You keep your feet off the ground, walk on air, buy air-cushioned shoes, or sit sole up, sole feeling fear, keeping the feet covered and out of sight, no barefoot boy, you, earth calling you, hand poised, finger curled, beckoning, bones bent, tendons and muscles calling, earth's suck, suck you up, suck you down, feet yearning for earth, these feet are meant for walking, barefoot, barefoot and pregnant, bare earth, far from barren ground, worms, ticks, amoebae, eager to enter, crawl in like fey children, staring at you on the bus or in the shopping mall, spreading their limber legs, winking, rape in their wide eyes, barefoot in the grassy park, you shrink like a salted slug, you shrivel, fill the tub hot and wet, pour in the bubbling salts, climb in, feet drowned in suds, body clean, dirt dissolved in salty waves, alone—SAFE—in your own house, your own bath, your own floating self, far from earth, footless and fancy free.

3.09 *He did not cry out,* but he felt a terrible cry rush through his whole body. He swayed in the darkness on the narrow beam; he felt the blackness that surrounded him, the nothing that enclosed him now on three sides. The thought of going back squeezed his chest, made sweat spring out on his forehead. No going back, and no way forward. He could leap out into the void and fall, however far that might be. He might survive, for the beam might be only a few feet above a solid platform, a floor of sorts, one that might lead him onward. Or he might die, broken-necked or merely crippled, like a rat in the wall, his stink eventually spilling into one of their rooms, making them gag and seek him out. Or perhaps never scented at all, lost forever or until the building is razed, in any case, lost for now. Unable to think straight, unable to decide, he stood straight, trusted to his body's demands, or whatever part of his mind that might be now in charge. He bounced once, twice, on the balls of his feet, crouched down, and sprang upward, jumped with all the force of his shaking muscles, toes pointed behind him, up into the darkness and out, stretching his arms above his head, his hands curved to catch whatever they might find.

4.18 *It's not the slammers* that Alyx worries about, ragged hair, sleeves missing, desperate faces, rushing at each other in endless repetition, reaching out to grab him, swinging at him, wanting to mark him, count coup, claim turf. They don't want to hurt him, not really; he is too important to them. They want to touch him, to be him, but not hurt him; he amplifies their thoughts so loud the whole room aches; he is their mind and voice, their pain's live reprieve. He has nothing to fear from the punks who hold out their alienation to him as he meets and beats it eye to red eye. He is one of them; he does to himself what they want to do to the world. It's the others she worries about, self-centered, self-concerned, back in the corners, standing along the walls, staring at each other, trading tidy little envelopes and raw cash, tiptoeing to catch sight of some MTV celebrity who just might be slumming, laughing behind their hands, speaking critically of the band as though they knew anything at all. These are the ones she fears and worries about, the ones with too much money, too much time, empty hands, raw noses, the ones who are always inviting the band to parties, telling who will be there that they know, where no one that they know will ever go. She tries to say yes and mean no, get them out of the way with no fuss; he always has something stupid and very apt to say to them, makes them mad, makes them feel like they don't belong. She usually doesn't hear what he says, just watches them recoil, or yell an obscenity, or sometimes take a swing at him, hit him, knock him down, or most often walk away vibrating, shaking, anger eating them alive. These are the ones she fears with their loafers with no socks, their US Male shirts and pants, little rock locks of hair at the backs of their necks. If they ever get it together, coked up or choked up, tremble their way to the edge of the stage, challenge him in midsong, that she fears will be the end.

4.19 *Carla is furious* at him for balking at all of her promotional plans. She has been driving him across town, the windows rolled down in her BMW sedan; she pounds the side of the car with her hand and yells "Hey baby" when she sees macho guys or pretty boys on the sidewalks, then guns away, laughing, laughing, but now she is angry and drives silently and fiercely. He holds on tight and doesn't say a word. He has tried to tell her that even if she does raise enough money from among her friends for the band to make a video, there's no chance in this world or the next that it could get anywhere on MTV's *Basement Tapes.* "Why don't you do a love song?" she asks. "Would that hurt you so much, a little lost love, a broken heart?" He tries to think up an answer she might understand. "You do have a heart?" she asks. "All my songs are love songs," he says, and she takes a corner flat out. He holds on and ducks his head. "Look," she says, "Turner has played with a lot of session bands; he's backed up top people; we just make sure the MTV people know who he's played with; they like celebrity names; they'll get real excited." He can't explain that it's not even integrity he's concerned about, and he certainly can't tell Carla about the goose, and he can't even bring himself to promise her that after the next engagement, the performance he feels and fears may be his last, he'll start planning for a video. He just holds on tight, watches her small hands clenched on the steering wheel, watches her feet stretching and digging at the pedals, and hopes they'll make it, make it home, make it to Alyx, who can handle her, make it around the next corner, make it at all.

2.09 *Amaxophobia:* Nero Wolfe, for one.

4.2 *Alyx has saved* the only copy of the poem he made into their song "Anger Is the Source." He balled the poem up and threw it into the wastebasket the day he and Jaybang had worked out the song. It's not that she thought anyone would ever want to publish it. Rock singers have a hard time getting their poems published, and she knew that this one was too rough anyway. He had pointed out to her with pride that it had the word in it (and more than once) which his dictionary of slang called "perhaps the most notable of all vulgarisms." He threw it away, and when she protested he said, "It's too rough and too honest for anyone to want." But she wanted it, and later that day she retrieved it, smoothed it out, and put it in the brown envelope where she keeps all his poems, most of them to her, the ones he used to write before he got so deadly rough and honest:

Anger Is The Source of Revolution But I'm Too Fucking Beat To Get Mad

Precision lies in distance,
Cold heart, cold hands,
Lie like a small corpse on the tongue,
The repeated statement: it does not matter,
To me, it doesn't matter, doesn't matter,
Take it from me.

They can put their hands in a chest
After the first quick cut, spread it
Like cold cunt in a cave, but what
Do they find but bone, meat, gristle,
Soul hunched in the corner with a nasty
Grin, and a stale rich smell.

That's it, babe, the inside out of it,
Lies in the distance, cold heart, old hands,
The corpse begins to stiffen on the tongue,
What does it matter after all is said
And never done, just like rubber gloves,
Take it from me.

To put it another way: precision lies
In distance, up close, bunched, here,
Hair on the chest, tree in the eye, might
Note: soldiers on the beach, bomb in basement,
President on the nightly news, his tongue
Like a cold corpse in a cunt, old heart,
Cold hands, eyes like rubber loves.

To paraphrase: precision lies in,
Distance lets the world go by, smoke
Out the gas pipe, stale mixed smells,
Cunt caved in like a rubber glove,
Present on the nightly news, lie in the eye

Like canned heart, old, cold, presence
Lies in decision, a failed bitch spell,
Take it from me.

Baby heart, baby hands, distance
Like a cold fart, corpse's ass on the tongue,
It can't be done, it does not matter,
It does not matter, it does not matter,
Take it from me, new gristle, cold tongue,
Bold hand, the repeated statement:
Decision lies in presence, precision
Dies, incision, a pale stitched hell,
Tomorrow like today, tomorrow lies today,
Precision, indecision,
Take it from me.

1.08 *She beckons*, and I respond, walk toward her through this labyrinth of well-dressed figures. They are scarcely real to me, my knees liquid, the backs of my legs electrically light and weak, my head afloat. I manage a greeting; take her small cool right hand (muscle and tendon, ligament and bone, artery, capillary, and vein, smooth layer of cool delicate skin) in my unnerved left hand, nod when she breathes introductions to faces I do not see with names I do not hear. My heart flutters near my throat but does not break into a trembling rush. I speak and am spoken to. I smile and blink and nod. In short, I survive, and when we are called back to our seats in view of distant China, I have agreed to join her party after the last curtain call to extend the evening in their elegant company. I found agreement simple, and going a mere matter of walking to an exit and being whisked away. The advantages are enormous, I remind myself, as the applause settles and dies, and the great curtain trembles and lifts.

2.1 *Arachnophobia:* Pet cat in the corner, busy and occupied, you do not notice what she is doing until, pumping like a faulty pump, plop, plop, she heaves and plunges out a puddle of bile and dust and wound slime, then you see that she has been eating a spiderweb woven low by the baseboard in a corner where you never look, and near her, scattered and scurrying, small spot quicker than your eye, spider, you flinch and run, you run and flinch, to crush with your shoe sole invites rain, flood, disaster, trees crashing over, cars caught and smashed, but you roll up the news and swing it hard, not looking where it lands, swing and swing until—SAFE—you are alone, cat scared and long gone, small stain you hope on the paper you throw away unread, cooling puddle by the door.

4.21 *A bunch of guys* who looked like or at least were trying to look like Billy Idol had come into the club the last time they had played here, the bad time, the worst time. They hadn't really come to listen to the music or to dance or even to make trouble; they had just come to strut and preen, bleached hair, black leather, little studs. "One of them probably *is* Billy Idol," Jaybang had whispered to Alyx. "Who could tell?" Alyx certainly couldn't, and she knew he couldn't care less. He was pleased with his singing tonight; she could tell that. He had his shirt all the way off, and he was snaking along on his back halfway through "Autophobia," and the slammers were shoving in close, grabbing his arms, sliding him along on his sweaty back. He was pretty strung out, and he was forgetting the words pretty badly, but he was in full voice, growling his way through whole lines so that no one could make out a syllable. The place was full and full of smoke and heat when they finished a set and scuttled in the small room just off the small stage with a rock writer with hair the color of a flamingo and an earnest way of looking him right in the eye. She wasn't having much luck getting him to talk to her even though she knew Turner well and he had told him to trust her. She was forced to do most of the talking just to keep things going at all. She was telling him about T-Bone Burnett's "Trap Door" as though it were the answer to a key question he had not yet been asked, when the door bashed open, and the manager came in shouting, grabbing his arm, and trying to pull him back onstage. The whole band went along, leaving the writer looking after them, and they found the room tossing like a rough sea, a tempest of screams and fights, Billy Idols and cool boys punching at each other's faces, punks and slammers wrestling and smashing anything they could reach. Jaybang made a dive for his drums, shoving them toward the corner and out of the way. Alyx tried to hold him back, but he found the live mike and started yelling into it, "I'm dangerous, I'm dangerous," waving his other arm, kicking at anyone who came in reach. Alyx was still holding on to him when he was pulled off the stage and into the crowd. The speakers rolled his raucous screams and her amplified cries out into the general outcry. The police were at the door and the place emptying when she finally managed to get them both under a broken table and out of sight. He was laughing and spitting blood into the microphone (dead, its long cord long since snapped away), saying over and over, "Cut my heart out, cut my heart out watch it cry, cut my heart out watch it cry, cut my heart out," and his eyes were so dry and blank she was sure he could not see her at all.

3.1 *His fingers found* a metal bar and wrapped convulsively around it even as his face smashed into something hard and his feet banged into another bar and gripped it, pressed it. He hung there as he fought unconsciousness, pain radiating from his smashed nose throughout his body, hung there until he realized he was on a ladder of rungs bent and lodged in a flat featureless wall. He hung and held on, and then he really felt the pain, the pain of his barked knuckles, his bare splintery feet, the pain of his overstressed and overtensed muscles, legs and back and arms, and the hot brutal pain of his nose, crushed and bleeding. He hung on, and then he began to climb, hand and hand, foot and foot, tug and countertug, rung by rung, up into darkness, not even a thought of climbing down. His legs and arms were aching with the strain when his right hand hit what seemed a smooth metal ceiling. Holding on tightly, feeling something akin to genuine vertigo for the first time, electric scrotum and whirling head, he felt carefully with his free hand up and back and around on the smooth surface. It seemed to be a trapdoor or some kind of door, raised slightly from the surface surrounding it. He tested it with his fingers but could not feel it give. He pushed himself on up to the next rung and the next, bracing his back against the metal and then heaving suddenly with all the force he could muster. The door grated and gave, pushed up, and he followed it, shoving with his feet, opening it up and back, and, with a final burst to desperate strength, pulling himself up beyond the trapdoor into more darkness onto what felt to be a flat graveled roof.

2.11 *Postophobia:* You open the flap of the mailbox, your knees go wet and weak, you dip in your fingers, pluck out the mail, you cannot stand to look, the catalogs you can bear although you do fear to throw them out without at least a glance, but it is the letters you fear the most, the bills with angry threats, the pleas for help from starving babies, indigent institutions, politicians of left and right, Live Aid, the Cancer Society, Nameless College, Featureless Fund, the Metropolitan Opera Guild, Jews for Jesus, Smalley Gospel Institute, you open them all and stare and stash them in a box where they can possibly be found again, but even more than these, the hand-addressed letters with no return address or one that you do not recognize, the threat of a visit, threat of a call, the threat of legal action, the letter that threatens your very life like that of the Filipino general who dared to break the chain, the letter full of good news, good news and bad, bad news, professions of friendship, professions of love, professions of lust, requests for help, words you cannot avoid, you tear the flap open, glance inside, see it is a letter and put it where you are unlikely to find it again, letters from your closest friends, from former friends, from enemies sick with rage, you pound the mailbox like a punching bag, your fist bulges with scars and inflated ganglia that sting for days, for weeks, for years, you cannot stop the mail, rain, sleet, nor hail can stop the mail, the box bulges and you take it in, the letters you cannot open, cannot read, cannot ignore, you hold them in your hands, the lurid stamps, blurred cancellations, printed labels, misspelled names, scrawled names, your name again and again, the mail that demands you take it in, the mail that will not cease, the mail that will stack up for years after you are dead and gone, mail without end.

4.22 *Alyx is happy* to see that the usual crowd is here, the fans, the ones they know, punks and slam dancers, the others who really care for the music but avoid the melee, the older ones who look out of place but aren't. She had been afraid that after the violence and bad press of the last performance they would stay away. But they are here in their denim and leather, clashing colors, rock buttons all over their jackets like the decorations of Latin American generals, greeting each other, circulating, excited to be hearing the band again so soon when it seemed like never. There is another crowd here tonight, too, the one that has always worried her, more than enough of them, hanging around the door and the bar, neat and tidy in chinos, girls in bright new designer jeans and Wham T-shirts, watching each other like lazy cats, waving long-neck beer bottles in greeting or recognition, keeping cool, a little tense, jump if they're touched unawares. "Must be a Young Republican convention in town," Jaybang says to Alyx, and she laughs and nods, but they do not make her happy, not at all. He is happy, has been walking around the floor wearing the jacket with his buttons, Germs, X, Blasters, Richard Hell, of course two Iggy Pops, big rattly ones, and the ones he calls his movie star buttons: the Runaways and Fear. He looks fifteen again, cherubic, the light in the room making his skin glow, "almost like an angel," Alyx thinks, "almost like he was halfway healthy," Jaybang thinks. He has been working on a poem all day; Alyx has no idea whether he is straight tonight or not. The drugs and the poems both make him smile and drift, except when they make him mean. He drifts around the floor, mingles for a time with the Young Republicans, doesn't say anything to them, just drifts through, and if they speak to him, he doesn't hear a word they say. He drifts back to the stage and backstage in plenty of time for the four of them to run through the program, start moving around, get nervous, get pumped up, feel the beat before the beat begins. He hangs his jacket carefully on a coat hook, takes off his shirt, his shoes and socks. He decides not to make a mark on his skin, says, "I'm clean, and I'm ready." They grip hands in a careless stack. "We have returned," Turner says. "We shall return," Alyx adds. "There is no return," he says, quietly, to Alyx alone, "save in the dreams of others." And Alyx knows he's saying his poem to her. But he doesn't continue, smiles like a baby, turns to the stage still holding her hand, pulling her along. Return from where, she thinks, where does he think he is going? And goose bumps ripple all along her bare arms.

2.12 *Apocalyptophobia:* You count chapter and verse, count words in each line, letters in each word, watch for the sign of the Beast, last days, in long books you tremble and squint and read page 666 with care, scan the news for mentions of the Middle East, the valley of Megiddo, plain of Jezreel, look always to the north for the thunder of armies, Gog and Magog, mystery, Babylon, you count the letters in prominent names (Ronald Wilson Reagan—6 6 6), find the flash and blast of the bomb in scripture page by page, find scripture's warnings in everything you see and touch, every word you hear, find yourself in scripture ("My heart panted, fearfulness affrighted me: the night of my pleasure hath he turned into fear unto me."—Isaiah 21:4), the beast and bitch, the whore in every woman's face, the beast in every man's, you punch through channels on your television set and see last signs, the preacher's plea for cash (Mammon), the rock singer's wrinkled face and fading hair ("Our bones are dried, and our hope is lost."—Ezekiel 37:11), the diva's horrid riddles three, Beast, Bitch, Gog, Magog, Megiddo, Mystery, MOG, the drummer's terrible rattling beat, car bomb, pipe bomb, the unexploded bomb that blows your face away, the bomb that prints your shadow in concrete, levels tall buildings with a single bound, the actor's withering face, the wrestler's bleeding brow, Babylon, Babylon, Babylon, the armies trampling from the north, the sudden spurt and flat dark when you push the remote button off—SAFE—and sink into your chair in the dark room, safe in a dark corner, safe in a dark house, safe in a dark night where no thief can come.

3.11 *He could see the flat roof* stretching away from him, the dim shapes of various pipes and vents, and above him, so bright they caused him to squint his eyelids, more stars than he had ever seen, stars and planets and (he supposed) moons, although there was no earthly moon in view. He lay on his back under the still river of light, seemingly so near that he had only to stretch out a hand in order to dip his fingers in the heavens and stir stars until they spewed arcing tails like rings of comets. He was dizzy with fresh air and freedom and delight. The night air was still and silent around him, and he lay low, holding to the graveled roof as though he were looking down and the stars were reflections in wrinkling water waiting to receive him. The damp smell of the open shaft beside him drew him back to himself, and he sat up abruptly, caught the metal door which stood erect, and lowered it quietly and carefully back into place. That done, he began to look around the wide roof, afraid to try to get up until the strained muscles stopped jumping under his skin, until his mind became as clear as his eyes and stopped wandering off into the night sky. He could see surprisingly well, and he knew his pupils must be swollen huge like black tunnels into his skull. He shuddered at the thought, crawled to his knees, and stood up. He could see what seemed to be the edge of the building to his left, and he moved cautiously across the graveled surface of the roof toward it. The galaxy lit his way, and he moved steadily without fear of falling. He skirted two ventilation ducts, one swilling out a rotten smell into the clean still air, and then he reached the low concrete parapet toward which he had been heading. The top of a large tree swayed in the starlight far below, no movement of bird or squirrel, and he could make out a wide flat surface humped with familiar shapes stretched out beyond it. He could not really tell how high he was, but a sudden vertiginous tingle ran through his legs and into his scrotum. He went to his knees beside the parapet, and, pressing his hands tightly against its harsh surface, he peered again into the still dark. He braced himself on hands and knees on the roof and tried for a moment not to think at all. The stars defined a dim horizon before him, but he could not tell how far away it was. The next step could be easy or hopelessly hard; he dared not think, but must only rest and regain some clarity of thought. His ears filled with his own blood's rush as he scanned the sky for signs of a possible dawn which must not come. Alone on a rooftop under the stars, shoeless, scraped, and broken, breathing in harsh gasps, with only the tiny knife blade and four ragged wood screws for a weapon, he could not decide what to do. The night sky hung still and starred as he tried to make up his mind to begin again. "Up or down," he asked himself, "Up or down?" Then, "Up or down, at least I'm out."

4.23 *They are all rocking,* moving on, moving out, Jaybang building the beat under them all around them like a solid floor, solid walls. And he knows the words, sings them deeper in his voice than Alyx has ever heard, but she is not sure that he knows just where he is. He looks right into her eyes when the moves draw them together, but his eyes are whirling, wheels within wheels, flashing and popping like the lights of the room. In the bright light and the sweat that stings her eyes, she can't see beyond the edge of the stage, the rough chop of the slammers, and she flinches every time one of them climbs up where he is twirling and singing, bending double or bouncing high, keeps playing but holds her breath until it turns out to be just another stage diver plunging back into the sea of fists. Between songs he taunts the boys in the back, proves he did see them on his beatific tour around the floor. "Faggy boys," he yells at them, "dry bones with your fingers stuck in your flies. Well, I'm Lord of the Flies, you want to try this bone for size?" And he tugs at his pants as though he is going to pull it out, but he never does. Just having a good time. They start "Cold Woman" then, and he is making dervish tracks all across the stage. "Snake without a head," he sings, "right there in your bed, oh, everybody's got one, why don't you use yours?" The beat protects him, Alyx thinks, just like a wall, nothing can hurt him as long as the beat goes on. "Mister Three," he sings, "Mister Three, come with me to see Mister Three." She looks at Jaybang, turns her back on the crowd and stares him eye to eye. He sees her and winks, the sweat on his torso making him shine like a star, his arms pumping and steady, holding the beat tighter, harder and faster than any metronome could follow. Turner is making his guitar scream when she spins back around, Jaybang is like a rock, she is driving the bass line through, and he is strutting to the edge of the stage, strutting and leaning out. There is no return, Alyx thinks, and the sweat is like ice on her arms, her electric hands. The crowd has changed, is too still down front when the song should be stirring them to froth. She takes quick steps, runs to the edge of the stage alongside him, sees rows of tidy boys, not dancing, holding their broken longneck beer bottles up at him, jeering at him, begging him to dive onto them, waving their jagged glass, beckoning to him, looking at each other and laughing, screaming, daring him to come down to them.

1.09 *The events of the terrible predawn* proceed on stage. The orchestra soars, the figures move and sway and sing. Liù approaches her end (and Puccini, his) as the frozen princess dominates the stage (her finger curling, bone pivoting on bone, muscle and tendon, tug and countertug). Liù can face the torture no more, can keep her secret safe no more, cannot face the break of day. I am half a part of that dreadful scene, and half apart in my dreadful thoughts. The vast room squeezes me tightly, every breath held, every eye stretched wide, as Liù seizes the blade, knives in a drawer row on row, and kills herself before the coming of the dawn. I am poised on the edge of my seat, my feet in their black pumps shift and press down at the floor. *"Alzati, Vecchio!"* Ping cries down from the stage. Get up, old man, and I find myself standing, find myself ducking, moving, quickly and invisibly, light and fast, up and away. I cannot stay for the end; this is the honest end. Puccini knew that this is the end, and it killed him. I am running across the foyer while the icy figure of the princess remains frozen and still. No thaw. And yet the air is mild outside. With long safe hours before the dawn, I am running hard, and I am gone.

2.13 *Omniphobia:* Try to say this does not afflict you living as you do in Babylon, this is the one that haunts us all, blast of the atom bomb that will sear your window white and blast you through the wall, flash of the bomb that will smear your eyes like jelly down your face, the power plant that vents its radioactive steam into the air you breathe, the airplane that will stagger out of the sky and smash you flat, the tire that bursts and skews your car into the rail, electric rail, bridge that falls, hair on the walls, bomber, submarine, missile's high arc, cancer's bite in your spleen, sunny day that plants cancer in your skin, food you eat that spreads cancer in your intestine walls, healing pill that leaves you with aplastic anemia, disease that eats your bones from the inside out, lover's kiss that slips herpes into your blood, blood donor's gift with AIDS mixed in, you waste away in the presence of strangers' scorn and fear, door to the public toilet that awaits your touch, stranger on the street who needs a fix, knife in the gut, bullet in the brain, madman at the wheel, car that reels across the curb and tosses you away, undertow that sucks you deep into the sea, firing squad, electric chair, mob with their torches at the door, snake in the grass, snake in the bed, rats in the wall, flea with plague in its bite, tick's feverish suck, smoke that fills you, fire that burns your flesh down to dry bone, spider in the bookcase, bad mushroom, poison fish, the surgeon's smile, anesthesiologist's needle in your spine, scarred heart, snapped neck, the stranger's grin, splinter in your toe, the gas main's blast, electric wire's descent, tree's fall, dog's bite, cat's scratch, numbers on the wall, letters on the wall, silence in the night, dawn's early light, rocket's red glare, bombs bursting in air, madness, dementia; emptiness, hand on your hand, footstep in the hall, no way up or down, alone, alive, and, *worst of all*, your own face in the mirror, graying hair, wrinkled skin, cracked teeth, brittle joints, dim eye, deaf ear, body that will not stay the same, and, *worst of all*, betrayal, abandonment, the life of lies, and, *worst of all*, the mind that lies, the mind that betrays, the mind that abandons, and, *worst of all*, the hand on the knife, the finger on the trigger is your own.

3.12 *The yellow sodium light* slammed into him like a physical blow as the night sky snapped out. It seemed as though he could feel the rush of infinite photons into the dark tunnels of his eyes, the pressure causing him to stagger back blindly, to duck and cower, to tuck his head into his shielding arms and fall back onto the grinding surface of the roof. He stifled a whimper in his throat and rolled into a trembling ball. The yellow glare penetrated his hands and glared in his eyes. Fear washed through him, and his legs writhed out blindly, his heels biting into the grit. He sat up abruptly, still holding his hands to his eyes, his breath ragged and uneven, his heart heaving up and pattering out of control in his chest. This runaway of his nervous system frightened him worse than the sudden light, and he managed to sit up very stiffly and pull in a long slow breath, holding it tightly in as his heart stopped still, hung silent for as long as he could hold the breath, and then kicked violently back into its normal rhythm as he burst the air out. The desperate maneuver stilled the fear as well. He was drenched with sweat, his bladder felt suddenly swollen and full, his hands fluttered on his face like caught birds, but the fear was gone. He edged his fingers apart and found that, by blinking and squinting, he could see again. The yellow glare spilled over the parapet and blotted out the sky. He eased himself up onto his knees, noticing for the first time the sharp gravel pushing into them, and looked cautiously over the edge of the parapet. The lights were mounted on tall poles well below him, illuminating a flat expanse of asphalt with the painted lines of a parking lot, although there were no vehicles in it. He could not understand why the lights had come on so suddenly with not a figure in sight. Beyond the lot, he could see an expanse of grass and distant trees, and what appeared to be a high chain link fence. Had there been a power failure helping him in his escape? Or were these lights the first step in the process of his recapture? He touched the small bundle of keys and the broken knife blade in his pocket, that blade the most important key to his ultimate escape, one way or the other. Had the whole thing, he thought, his being kept alone in that particular room with the easily opened wall panel, his being left the key chain with the nail-care kit, his being allowed to climb and leap and climb in the dark, had it all been planned, been designed from the start to lead him to this end? He could not decide, but in any case his time was short and his escape would soon be noted. Or his location discovered. He stood by the parapet without fear, leaned over, and looked for a way down. He could see only a featureless descent of brick wall stretching far below him. He was still trying to decide whether to walk directly to the other side of the roof or make his way all the way around the roof's perimeter when the first searchlight sliced its blade of light along the distant fence. The next one lit the sky behind him on the other side of the building where he had been thinking of going. He stood in gaping disbelief as the next one burst out from somewhere before him and swung directly into his eyes, splintering into pinwheels of color and glare as he simply stood there, poised on the balls of his feet, his hands stretched out in futile defense, still as a statue or the ventilation pipes around him, silent, his mouth and eyes wide open, his hands open, his heart leaping evenly in his chest, its pump the only sound in the dazed panorama of this silent night.

4.24 *Alyx tries to push* him back with her guitar, facing away from the raging glass breakers below her. "What are you doing?" she screams into his ear. "Leave them alone. We can't have a fight. Not tonight." She keeps playing, but she is afraid to signal Turner or Jaybang to end it, afraid to move away from directly in front of him, so that all they can see is that he is working the crowd, and they play hard, play well, on and on. He stares straight into her eyes this time, really sees her, sees the fear in her face, the desperate fear. He shouts to her, "I've got to give these guys some moxie," mouths the words large so she can read his lips even if she can't hear him. "I've got to bring those guys to life," he says, "even if it kills me." No, she thinks, no, still blocking him from the edge and the glass, he's still in that poem. Or, she thinks, he thinks it's 1970 and he's a Stooge in Detroit. God knows what he thinks, she thinks. He follows the beat, whirls right around her, right by her, right over her as she stumbles and falls backwards, her hands abandoning the guitar as it howls with static and dissonance, her hands reaching for his legs, for his ankles, for his bare feet as he dives up and out, arms spread back, toes pointed, just out of her straining hands' reach. Jaybang and Turner don't know what is happening, keep trying to play as Alyx shrieks through the noise and sees his blood rise up from the tangled floor in a terrible spray, and she knows that it is all over and that wherever he was going, he has gone.

1.1 *I am shivering* although it is not cold. I am in bed. My formal clothes spill off a chair and onto the floor. My gleaming pumps are kicked off by the closed, locked door. The room is dim, the dawn's light kept out by windowshade and thick drawn drapes. My night has been chewed up by fitful dreams and waking thoughts. I cannot stay in bed. I fear the snarled sheets and twisted covers. I manage to sit up, lower my bare feet to the yellow rug. I manage to stand up, stand staring at the knife-thin lines of light around the thick dark drapes. I manage to walk across the room, find the draw cords with my nerveless hand, and pull the drapes apart. Light burns through the windowshade, the thick yellow paper, the sketch in stark black lines of Ezekiel knocked to his hands and knees by the weight of sun and stars in the sky at once, his staff under one hand like a snake with a severed head, crawling through the ragged crack at the horizon's rim to see the wheels and fire that lie beyond. The day has come and found me in. I reach out to the bottom of the shade, dry hand, dry bones, tug and countertug, tug at its string. It snaps away, rattles up into the roller with a bang that snaps me erect. The light cuts in and blinds. I blink and tear. I squint and stare. I cannot see what I know is there.

4.25 *Alyx is so angry*, so enraged, so mad, despite the drug her mother's doctor is keeping her on, that she cannot speak his name, much less look into the envelope of his poems that she has brought with her to her parents' house. But finally she takes it out of her sweater drawer where she has hidden it and holds it to her breast as she rocks and cries. "This is all I have left," she says over and over, her face red and twisted and streaked white with tears. "Why didn't you stay to the end? I just want to hold you and be warm again, and this is all I have fucking left." She pulls the sheets of paper, different kinds and sizes, yellow and white, wrinkled and smoothed out, handwritten and typed, holds them to her blind eyes, and then suddenly flings them at the closed door, her voice a wordless moan. After a time she goes down on her knees and gathers them up, the tattoo on her left hand of an old-fashioned keyhole, their secret sign (only he had the key) looking so stupid and sad to her now. She finds the one she is looking for, the one she has never seen, the one she knows will be there, slipped into the envelope for her to find the way he always liked to do. She reads it, and the tears start again. She even hears his voice stumble on the words he knew only from reading but had never heard. Just like in the fucking movies, she thinks. She reads it to herself, she hears his voice, she cries until her chest aches, and she says as loud as she can, screams it so loud she hopes he hears, "Was it worth it, you damn dumb bastard, was it worth it?" And then, exhausted and still sobbing, she stacks the pages, tidies them, slumps her head over onto the floor, lies down, her mind whirling and battered, drifts off to sleep, the pages stacked beside her with the last one on top.

Saving the Dreams of Others

The opportunity to avail oneself,
The opportunity an old memory, a fact
Remembered and forgotten, recalled, remembered,
There is no return save in the dreams of others,
Standing on a bridge, in the shadows of a corner,
Discussing my coming departure as though,
As though . . . the opportunity
Had not arisen. Here, take my hand,
I'll help you across the hard parts, the parts
Made difficult by time, like a footnote or parenthetical remark,
Or forgotten appendix, that is my job,
To help you make the leap into understanding,
There is no time remaining, no time, none at all,
Even less than you supposed: NOTE THIS:
Note and remember, file in a dream, keep it close at hand,

Stepping through the veil as though it were not there
Is no harder than staying behind: **There is no
Return save in the dreams
Of others.** There is no return.
Saving the dreams of others, follow the line like a wandering
Stream, one word sliding into another,
No return save in the dreams of others, no return,
Save the dreams of others, save the dreams, save the dreams.
Is this at all helpful? Have I taught you enough?
Taut and tough lines like stale meat. There, I've
Said it: there is no return save in the meat of others.
So, farewell then, farewell; we raise our hands
In pained salute: farewell: salute: there is no return
Save in the dreams of others. Dream on.